Dressing the part

The next day I dressed carefully, as I always do for an investigation. I had what they call an "office-ready" gray pinstriped suit with a pencil-slim skirt that hit just above the knee and a no-nonsense jacket that hugged my curves, which I'd bought on sale at Ann Taylor. Most of my clothes come straight from Dolce's, but not all of them. She understands that sometimes I shop at the mall. With the suit I wore a pair of black, medium Sam Edelman stacked heels I picked up at Neiman Marcus. I'd have to change when I got to work in case the customers thought I was in mourning, which I wasn't. Even though I was an admirer of the chef, we really weren't close enough for me to mourn his demise.

Although I would certainly go to his funeral. I have found that a funeral brings out the best and the worst in people. People cry or they laugh or they say something inappropriate that they shouldn't, which is helpful when you're looking for a murderer. I knew I wasn't supposed to be looking for a murderer, but how could I help it?

Murder After a Fashion

GRACE CARROLL

BERKLEY PRIME CRIME, NEW YORK

THE BERKLEY PUBLISHING GROUP
Published by the Penguin Group
Penguin Group (USA) Inc.
375 Hudson Street, New York, New York 10014, USA

USA | Canada | UK | Ireland | Australia | New Zealand | India | South Africa | China

Penguin Books Ltd., Registered Offices: 80 Strand, London WC2R 0RL, England
For more information about the Penguin Group, visit penguin.com.

MURDER AFTER A FASHION

A Berkley Prime Crime Book / published by arrangement with the author

Berkley Prime Crime Books are published by The Berkley Publishing Group.
BERKLEY® PRIME CRIME and the PRIME CRIME logo are trademarks of
Penguin Group (USA) Inc.

For information, address: The Berkley Publishing Group,
a division of Penguin Group (USA) Inc.,
375 Hudson Street, New York, New York 10014.

ISBN: 978-0-425-25219-2

PUBLISHING HISTORY
Berkley Prime Crime mass-market edition / June 2013

PRINTED IN THE UNITED STATES OF AMERICA

10 9 8 7 6 5 4 3 2 1

Cover illustration by Jennifer Taylor / Paperdog Studio.
Cover design by Rita Frangie.
Interior text design by Tiffany Estreicher.

ALWAYS LEARNING   PEARSON

One

::::::::::::::::::::::::::::::

I'm not a native, but I do know one thing about San Francisco. The weather is as unpredictable as the people. Take that warm cloudless September day when I was on my way to work wearing a pair of Bruno Magli Italian leather sandals. They were all the rage that spring and summer, and I still loved them because they worked with either a pair of jeans or a skirt. No matter what else you're wearing, those shoes make you look like you made an effort. And believe me, I always made an effort. Not just because my job was selling clothes and accessories in a boutique, but also because that's the way I was. I still am.

I was on the Thirty Stockton bus in a bright jade blue flowy dress by Cladiana that could go from work to cocktails and a cream-colored linen Nicole Farhi blazer that gave the outfit a daywear look, and was reading a depressing article in the *San Francisco Chronicle*, "Changing Weather Patterns Spell Doom for Humanity." Suddenly the sky clouded over and just as I got off the bus, it started to rain, dampening my clothes and the chic fedora perched jauntily on my head. Talk about doom. Rain in September in everyone's favorite city? Not going to happen. But there it was.

When my boss Dolce saw me come through the door of the historic Victorian house she'd converted to a stylish shop, she said, "Rita, get out of those wet clothes. You'll catch your death. What were you thinking?" She shook her head. It wasn't really a lecture, not from Dolce. She was simply showing her concern and sympathy for me, the daughter she never had.

"Isn't it true," I asked, "that September, October and November are the best months in San Francisco weather-wise? 'Fall days are warm and sunny, nights are cool and clear.' That's what I heard before I moved here. What happened?" I shivered as I tossed my damp hat toward a rack on the wall. "Can't be global warming."

Dolce shook her head again but said nothing about the weather changes indicating the end for humanity. Maybe she hadn't read the paper (which I wished I hadn't), or perhaps she was in denial, which wasn't a bad place to be.

"Go put on something warm. You'll feel better." She waved an arm at the racks of fall clothes in earth tones and basic black hanging on racks in the large showroom that used to be the salon of the grand old Victorian residence. Once upon a time in the mid-1800s, this Hayes Valley neighborhood was filled with even more of these beautiful homes, along with smaller houses for the craftsmen hired to build the mansions. Thankfully the area was spared the fire that burned much of the city after the 1906 earthquake. But old houses are not always taken care of the way this one had been. Dolce's aunt who'd willed her this house had saved it from demolition, and Dolce had restored it to a bit of its former grandeur. Her small, well-appointed apartment above the shop might have once been the servants' quarters.

I wondered if those old-timers had worn black and earth tones too? Or had they tired of the same-old, same-old and longed for some warm fall days to break out the satin slippers and their bright, flirty Victorian dresses, if there'd been such a thing. I sighed and went to pick out something that said fall in the strict sense of the word, but the only word I could think of was "dull."

Pawing through a shelf full of cashmere sweaters in shades of eggshell, eggplant and ochre, I just couldn't get excited about wearing such blah colors. I refused to let the rain dampen my spirits the way it had my clothes. I had to deal with the unpredictable nature of the weather and the populace. Wearing a bright dress lifted my mood, but was I pushing my luck by pushing my fashion sense to the brink?

"Remember to mix it up," Dolce called from the jewelry section where she was arranging a display of chains, huge chunky rings, cuffs and leather bracelets. "Add some mohair with brocade or popcorn knits. And tweeds with flat wool. Instead of linen, why not try a tailored wool blazer with padded shoulders."

Why not? Because my shoulders didn't need any padding, but Dolce was my boss and she was usually right when it came to fashion. That's what made things interesting, I told myself. Different styles, different people, different seasons and different weather.

It was so typically Dolce to offer me anything in the shop even though I couldn't really afford the haute couture she sold. Either she gave me a huge employee discount, or she just gave me things that were left over from the last season.

Dolce must have seen me dawdling indecisively because she said, "If you want to, you can just add leggings or a straight-leg pant under the Alexander Wang botanical print dress on the rack. It offsets the graphic element, don't you think? And add a belt. Belts are in and very figure flattering."

I guess everyone needs some figure flattering, so I didn't take her suggestion personally. I chose a sand leather belt from Yves Saint Laurent that went with the dress, a pair of dark leggings and Hunter Champery wedge boots and went to the dressing room to change my look from spring to fall. I hated to ditch my sandals, but I gave in and added the wool blazer too.

Dolce gave me an approving thumbs-up when I came out. "That's better," she said. "I think we'll have a big crowd in today. Especially with this rain. It reminds everyone that they need to update their wardrobe for fall."

Which was just what she'd done for me. Updated my wardrobe with a new dress and a few special additions. I was warm and dry and even more stylish than when I'd arrived. Someday maybe I'd be the saleswoman Dolce was. Until then I'd work at it with her as my example and enjoy the ambience in the shop.

It was not only the ambience but also the gossip I enjoyed. Usually. But today the conversation seemed a little less than stimulating. It went like this.

"Guess who was with Brianna LaRue at the Edwardian Ball? I'll give you a hint. It wasn't her husband," Tracy Livingston said to a small group of her BFFs who were gathered at the accessory counter looking through a stack of our latest shipment of scarves in silk, chiffon and wool.

"They're done, over, kaput," Angela Boursin said, rubbing her hands together. "Everyone knows that."

"Does everyone know why?" Maxine Anderson asked eagerly.

The others stared at the Missoni sweater set she wore with pearls as if she had come from a different era. It was partly her dated outfit from last year's collection and partly her naïveté that earned her pitying looks and made her stand out from the in-crowd. And made me feel sorry for her. But what could I do to help her fit in except what I'd always done, make tactful suggestions. After that, customers had to make up their own minds. Not that I'm an advocate of "the customer is always right." Far from it. But all I can do is give advice and fashion tips.

As a rule, our customers don't have jobs. Most of them spend their days doing charity work and having lunch and shopping, which is good for business. But Dolce wouldn't be the success she is if she didn't have a philosophy of treating everyone with respect, whether they're super rich or only extremely well-off. Whether their taste is impeccable or downright terrible, Dolce never misses a beat.

"Of course we know why they're breaking up," the ladies chorused.

Maxine was afraid to ask why, I could tell. She didn't have to. They told her anyway.

"She's having an affair with her Pilates coach."

I tried to look shocked, but I felt like I'd heard it all before. Socialites having affairs with their yoga guru or the swimming pool guy. And frankly I didn't care what they did after they left our shop.

For a moment I was afraid I was going crazy. Here I was folding sweaters, some chunky, some bulky and some belted, while I shamelessly listened to empty gossip. Was this really what I should be doing with my life?

What was wrong with me? I had the world's greatest job and the world's greatest boss. I was wearing a dynamite outfit that everyone had noticed but . . . something was wrong. All I'd ever wanted was a dream job and some cutting-edge clothes to wear, but all of a sudden I wanted more. I wanted somewhere to go after work. And someone to go there with. In other words, I wanted a life.

I needed a place to wear the clothes besides to work and I needed purpose and I needed a man in my life. I was spoiled. Since I'd come to San Francisco over a year ago, I'd met three eligible men who'd taken me to all kinds of fun events. But I hadn't heard from any of them for months. That didn't help my outlook.

Instead of brooding about my sudden onset of angst, I took Maxine aside and asked her if I could help her find anything. I hoped she'd take my interest as it was intended and not as a knock on her personal lack of style. I was trying to make up for the others being so snarky.

She gave me a grateful little smile and said she was looking for a pair of wide-leg pants. It was a good sign that she was trying something new and trendy, and I pulled out a few for her to try on.

"Do you like your job here?" she asked after she'd chosen a pair of Max Mara palazzo pants in a herringbone tweed that had a relaxed kind of cool and gave off a super-casual vibe that I told her was new and different. I folded and wrapped them in tissue paper at the front desk.

"Oh, yes," I said. "We've got the latest in clothes, jewelry, hats and stockings all under one roof. What's not to like? I love fashion. But I also love to eat. I'm not much of a cook, so tonight after work I'm going to sign up for another class at Tante Marie's Cooking School." I didn't usually confide in new customers about my other life, such as it was, but I wanted to say something to Maxine besides the usual. I sensed she didn't have many friends here. Not that I would ever be her friend. None of the customers were my friends. We came from different worlds. They were all older and richer and married and better connected than I was.

"I've heard of it," she said. "Someone recommended it to me. I've been meaning to go sign up for lessons from the celebrity chef, Guido Torcelli. He's only doing one class as a favor to the owner. As you probably know, he's Diana Van Sloat's personal chef. When she's in town, that is, and not filming commercials in Hollywood. She buys her clothes here, doesn't she?"

"Yes, she does," I said. "She's been Dolce's best client since forever. Guido's usually too busy to do the classes. Diana has him on retainer," I explained. I'd never met the rich and gorgeous Diana Van Sloat, but I'd heard plenty about her during my time as Dolce's salesgirl.

"Well, have fun," she said.

At the end of the day, before I left, I spoke to Dolce about my lack of social life. I hadn't planned on it, it just slipped out. I didn't complain, I didn't whine. I just mentioned my single status with what I hoped was a rueful smile. But being the sensitive person she is, she picked up on my anxiety. She frowned, carefully knotted a Ballantyne print scarf around her neck and waved me into her office, once a former closet. I sat down opposite her, and she rested her elbows on her desk and looked at me.

"The last I heard you were seeing three different men. One was a doctor," she said. "What happened?"

"Good question," I said. "Dr. Jonathan works nights in the ER and when he's not working, he's surfing, which doesn't leave much time for dates. Unless he's seeing one of those attractive nurses at the hospital. Which I couldn't blame him for. They have so much in common, and there's the proximity of course." I tried to sound like I was understanding of his professional responsibilities and okay with them, but it hurt to think of him out on the town without me. Naturally I wanted the best for him—a fulfilling and rewarding job healing the sick and wounded, and a lively social life as well. But why couldn't his social life include me? Wasn't I lively enough? Compared to a kind, caring and selfless nurse, maybe a clerk in a boutique didn't measure up.

"Isn't there a way you could run into him the way you first did when you fell off that ladder and had to be taken to the hospital?"

"You mean like have another accident or come down with some rare disease? It's possible, but it would have to be something severe and sudden because that's the kind of cases he sees in the ER. I just can't count on that happening again." I gnawed on a fingernail while I tried to think of some plausible reason to drop in at the hospital. "When I had the accident with the ladder, I was only unconscious for a short time, and when I came to in the hospital, there was Jonathan. Talk about luck."

Dolce nodded and moved on to candidate number two. "What about Nick the Romanian gymnast you met on the plane, the one with the crazy aunt?"

"The last I heard, he was recovering from a sprain he incurred at work. He's probably training some students on the uneven bars for the Olympics. As for his aunt Meera, she scares me. I know she's not really a vampire as she claims, but she's definitely weird."

"And that very attractive cop who you helped solve the murder of our dear Vienna?"

"You mean Detective Wall. I don't think he'd appreciate your framing our relationship that way."

"However he frames it, he can't deny you risked your life on the high seas to trap that murderer into confessing."

"I only did what anyone would have done," I said modestly. Though it was possible that no one else but me would have plunged into the cold waters of the Bay just to solve a murder.

"It's a shame Bobbi couldn't have been brought to justice before she drowned out there," Dolce said.

"On the other hand, it saved the city the cost of a big, expensive murder trial," I said. "I have to say that Detective Wall finally reluctantly agreed that I'd tried to help him, but not that I'd succeeded. He got assigned to the Central Station, so he doesn't hang out in our neighborhood anymore except when there's a major crime. I certainly wouldn't mind running into him, but he disapproves when I butt into his cases. It seems the only time he wants to see me is when I'm involved in a murder as a suspect. That's when he calls and comes by and tries to get me to confess, especially if he thinks I'm guilty. What are the chances of that happening again? I mean really." I laughed lightly, although I'm aware that murder is no laughing matter, especially when the victim is someone you know.

"So that's what we need to do, stir up some excitement, shake things up a little," Dolce said, her eyes gleaming with anticipation. "Think up a reason to see the doctor and/or the gymnast, and then we have to encourage our friend the detective to come around too."

I wasn't sure if she meant we should try to arrange another murder on the premises or just commit a minor infraction like parking illegally so I could get another chance to romance an officer of the law. Surely she didn't mean either. I couldn't believe she'd suggest I do anything even the slightest bit illegal. Maybe I shouldn't have confided in her about my ridiculously small problems. Now she felt she had to do something about them. Something I might not want to be a part of. Like getting sick or breaking the law. On the other hand, if I got desperate . . .

Not long ago she'd had to cope with the death of Vienna, her treasured employee. Dolce seemed to have finally bounced back to normal, while I was moping around complaining about a trivial matter like no men in my life. Of course, I said nothing about being bored at work or irritated by the shallow nature of the customers.

I wondered if, of the three men who passed in and out of my life, Dolce preferred the doctor, since he was the first one she'd asked about. If she did prefer him, she wouldn't say so outright. Just in case I ended up with one of the others. At the moment it looked like I'd end up alone. But enough of gloom and doom.

"Any plans for tonight?" Dolce asked hopefully.

I couldn't bear to say no, so I told her I was going back to my former cooking school.

"I plan to sign up for another class from Guido if he's still teaching. He's the celebrity chef at the school and a dynamite teacher. The thing is, I really need to learn my way around the kitchen." Even though my kitchen was so tiny I could stand in the center and reach the stove and the fridge as well as the sink. Just telling Dolce my plan made it more likely I'd follow through with it. Because the next day she was sure to ask how it went. I couldn't say I'd flaked out and hadn't gone. She'd be disappointed in me, and I needed to have a little pressure on me or I'd slip back into my old lazy ways.

I could have said I was going swimming at my health club or shopping at the Marina Safeway, where the produce department was a well-known hook-up spot, or attending a speed-dating party, but I'd save those activities for another night.

"I'm looking forward to another delicious dinner at your house," she said.

"As soon as I get a few more lessons under my belt, I'll have you and William over to dinner again," I promised. I was good at promising things and then panicking when it came down to the wire. But how do you try something new if you don't step out of your comfort zone? Easy for me to say, but harder to do.

I didn't know if Dolce was still seeing William Hemlock, a dashing retired airline pilot she'd met at a society benefit. I sincerely hoped she still was, though she hadn't mentioned him lately. We had a few unwritten rules, my boss and I. One was that we didn't criticize the men in the other person's life, and two, that we never said "I told you so" when things went wrong. Even though Dolce felt comfortable asking about my social life, I didn't want to ask her about William in case the news was bad or there just wasn't any news at all.

Before I left, Dolce took a look out the bay windows of the great room and said I should keep the clothes I was wearing, since the weather appeared to be cool and gusty, but no rain. Then she hugged me and told me to have a good time at cooking school.

"You too," I said, "have a nice evening." I waited for her to say something like, "I'm going to William's house for a cozy cheese fondue dinner," or "I'm going to meet his overly possessive grown children at last to see if they approve of me," but she didn't say anything about herself. Instead, she focused on me.

"I'm worried about you, Rita," she said, holding me by the shoulders and looking at me with a concerned frown.

"Who, me?" I said, raising my eyebrows. As if that were a crazy idea. I was fine. Really I was.

"You didn't seem yourself today. Even Frieda Young noticed it when you showed her a bow blouse when she wanted a sweater. She thought you seemed distracted."

I almost said "Who, me?" again, but I bit my tongue. "I'm sorry about that. I got off to a bad start today, you know with the rain and all, and I never got readjusted. I'll be fine tomorrow." I tried to smile, but my mouth just wouldn't cooperate.

"It's clear to me what's wrong with you," she said.

"Oh?" I said. Dolce is very perceptive, and I was afraid she had cottoned to how I was feeling disillusioned about my job, the customers and life in general.

"No murders, no mysteries for you to solve. No police cars outside, no yellow tape around the place. No investigations and no handsome detective hanging around either. This is what you've gotten hooked on. Without the excitement of a puzzle to solve, you're bored, Rita. I knew there was something wrong. I could tell."

"Me, bored? Not at all," I insisted. I shook my head to indicate what an absurd idea that was. As if I wanted someone else I knew to be murdered here at the shop or at their home. As if I enjoyed being hauled down to the police station to answer questions no matter how sexy the detective was. I always thought that Dolce was always right. But not this time. If I secretly longed for another murder on our doorstep, I'd know it, wouldn't I?

"Those cases were ages ago," I said, referring to the murder of one of our customers and Vienna's homicide. "I'm relieved everything's back to normal." But she had me worried. Was it possible I was a thrill-seeker junkie? That I really liked being in the middle of a murder investigation? Did I like waking up in the middle of the night worried that either she or I would be accused of a horrible crime? Did I like having nightmares about being locked up on Alcatraz Island in the old crumbling prison on false charges of a white-collar crime like embezzlement or maybe even crimes I'd actually committed, like jaywalking, littering, gambling by buying lottery tickets, speeding or . . .

There I'd be in my cold dank cell while tourists came by to look at me through the bars. They'd be listening on their earphones to the audio recording of "Doing Time, the Alcatraz Cell-house Tour." They'd hear, "In cell five fifty-four is Rita Jewel, arrested for interfering in official police business. She waived her right to a court-appointed attorney, preferring to handle her own defense. That was a mistake, since a jury of her peers convicted her of meddling. On the plus side, she's writing her memoirs on the back of old envelopes and she will be eligible for parole in ten to fifteen years."

I'd been on a tour of the Alcatraz prison, and that made my nightmares all the more realistic and frightening.

I really didn't want to be involved in any more crimes. I

didn't want to invite a violent crime into my life just so I could help solve it. But if someone asked me for my help? What if Detective Wall begged me? I smiled at the thought of him pleading to join him in an investigation. Of course I'd have to say yes. Anyone with a conscience would do the same. Even though I'd be risking being locked up for my trouble.

After our little conversation, Dolce and I both pretended everything was back to normal. I said good night and I'd see her tomorrow. I finally left the shop and my sandals behind. I was glad that day was over.

I stood on the sidewalk for a moment in the blazer and dress Dolce had given me that could surely go from work to cocktails, but they didn't mean cocktails *by myself.* I had no intention of going into the bar across the street, but I thought I heard someone call my name. When I turned to look, there was just the usual crowd of swinging singles clustered around the entrance to the bar, and not one of them even looked my way. Yet, I felt a pull toward the place as if from a giant magnet. It was downright eerie.

I gave in and headed across the street. I'd just stay for a moment, look around to see if there was anyone I knew, then I'd leave. The doors were open; the crowd spilled out onto the sidewalk. I walked in and threaded my way past a group of hip young twenty-somethings dressed just as you'd expect: the women in skirts above the knee, boots and fitted jackets, the men in dark slacks and button-down shirts. Everyone on their way home from work, just like me. But no one in a dress like mine. I wanted to think I stood out in a good way. But so far no one had given me a second glance.

The noise level was high with the clinking of glasses, the laughter and the loud conversations. While I was debating whether to stay long enough to order a pineapple martini, listed on the blackboard as tonight's house special, or a glass of Pinot Noir, I heard someone across the room call my name.

Unfortunately it was *not* one of the so-called men in my life appearing out of nowhere to buy me a drink. It was Meera, Nick's crazy Romanian aunt, waving to me. There was no way to miss her, since she always dressed in Victorian clothes. Tonight she was wearing a long satin ruby red dress with a full skirt and a bustle. And I thought my outfit was eye-catching.

I wasn't the only one staring at the vision of a self-proclaimed one-hundred-twenty-plus-year-old on her feet in her high button shoes, gesturing frantically from the corner while calling my name. Heads turned to observe the woman who waved at me, the fringe of her bodice shaking and shimmering with her every movement.

"Rita," she called, "Rita Jewel."

Now everyone was staring at me and at her. No doubt wondering how I was connected to this caricature. If they knew she not only claimed to be older than everyone in the bar put together but also insisted she had night vision and immortality, they would roll their eyes or maybe run outside screaming. Which I was sorely tempted to do. But it was not possible for me to run anywhere. I was stuck. Wedged between two groups of twenty-somethings holding glasses in their hands. Meera knew I was there, so I reluctantly made my way to her table, where she already had a drink waiting for me. As if she'd known I would be joining her.

"I'm glad I caught you," she said and clasped my arm in an iron grip. "I hope you like old-fashioneds. They're made with bitters, sugar, water and spirits, a twist of lemon and a maraschino cherry, as you see. It's the original recipe and quite authentic."

When she let go of my arm, we sat down and I took a sip from the glass. It wasn't bad, I had to admit. "I'm surprised the bartender knew how to make something so passé."

"He didn't. I had to instruct him. He was very grateful to me for adding to his repertoire."

"How did you know I'd be here?" I asked. "Or were you expecting someone else?"

She shrugged as if of course she knew I'd be there, since as a vampire she had extrasensory powers and could see into the future.

"I understand you work across the street. I thought you might drop in," she said. "I haven't seen you lately."

"Actually I'm on my way someplace," I said nervously. God only knew what she'd do next. Follow me home? Throw me to her nephew once again? Force him to get in touch with me even though he didn't want to? I certainly didn't want anyone to see me hanging out with this woman in her Victorian costume. Getting stuck with Meera was not what I needed after a tiring day of helping rich women find the perfect outfit for parties, balls, concerts or just hanging out in their mansions. Usually I loved doing just that, but Dolce was right, something was wrong with me today. Maybe it was the weather. Maybe I was tired of life in general. Sitting in this crowded bar hadn't changed my mind about my job being even more trivial and unimportant than ever.

"I'm going to sign up for a cooking class," I blurted.

"I'll go with you," she said, holding her drink in her jeweled fingers.

"You wouldn't want to go with me. You don't need cooking classes." It was true. I knew that she made interesting and authentic traditional Romanian dishes. I had sampled them. "Didn't you tell me your grandmother had taught you everything she knew about cooking back in the Dark Ages?" She'd claimed she was from a long line of excellent cooks.

"Where is the class?" she demanded, ignoring my question and looking up into my face with her big dark eyes.

"A small culinary school on Potrero Hill." I had no idea if they were still there, but I intended to find out by going there and knocking on the door. I could have called, but I needed a reason to get out and do something.

"And who is the chef, if I may be so bold as to ask?"

If she could be so bold? Bold was Meera's middle name.

"I'm hoping to get into a class taught by a certain Italian chef named Guido."

"Guido Torcelli?" she said so loudly the people at the next table turned to stare at us. I wanted to hide under the table, but as usual Meera was undeterred. "You would pay money to take classes from that famous imposter?"

I blinked rapidly. Now what? She was going to tell me he too was an ageless vampire but a terrible cook? Had he upstaged her at the Cordon Bleu in Paris in another life?

"I know him. And I know he knows nothing," she said, curling her lower lip and shaking her head. "Worse than nothing. He steals recipes and says they are his. He wrote a cookbook, you know. More than one. All full of stolen recipes. Including my *toba* and *pittie*."

I must have looked puzzled because she translated. "Dishes using pigs' feet in aspic."

I took a drink of my old-fashioned to calm the queasy feeling in my stomach. "I don't think it's the same person. He's Italian. He doesn't teach Romanian cooking or write about it. No pigs' feet," I assured her. But I could tell by her expression she was not assured. "He does write cookbooks, but they're completely Italian. Why would he use Romanian recipes if he's Italian?"

"I don't know. How should I know? Perhaps because Romanian cuisine is different he wants to set himself apart from all those other boring Italian cooks. But our cooking requires more effort, more native intelligence. Anyone can make pasta fagioli and chicken tetrazzini." The sneer on her face was unmistakable. "But try making *ciorba de burta.* Which only I can teach you. You don't want to even go near that charlatan. You are much better taking classes from someone like me," she said. "Of course, there is no one *like* me."

I choked on my drink. I couldn't have said it better myself. Then I said, "I didn't know you taught cooking." I could have said, "I would not take any classes from you if you were the last cook standing. Not in this lifetime," but I was trying to be polite, and with Meera it wasn't easy. She was very strong willed. But so was I. She didn't take no for an answer. I'd tried in the past and failed. Most of all, I didn't want her bad-mouthing me to her nephew, the very attractive Nick Petrescu, whom I was looking forward to seeing again. "I've already had a class from him and I found him to be an excellent teacher," I said resolutely.

"Compared to what?" she asked. "How many professional chefs do you know?"

"Well," I said, "only that one, but he's the real deal. I mean, he's Italian and maybe part French, and he has a TV cooking show. He even gives classes in his chateau in the summer."

"Does he?" she said, her eyes narrowed. "I don't believe anyone could learn to cook on the television. As for the summer, I could give classes in my country too. At the family home near Sibiu in Transylvania. It's not a measly chateau;

it's a castle in the beautiful unspoiled countryside with horse-drawn carts for transportation. Very charming. Very authentic. Which is more than I can say for Guido, that phony. Yes, that's a good idea you've given me. If you come to the castle, I will lower my usual fee."

"You're too kind," I said, "but I couldn't accept."

"Very well," she said. "Pay whatever you like. I will tell my poor nephew to join too, then there will be two young people in the class. Nick needs a distraction."

"Oh?" I said, not wanting to appear too interested. Because the minute I did, Meera would have us betrothed with a wedding planned at the family castle. Though I was neither rich nor titled, she might want Nick to find an American wife so he could get a green card. I wondered why he hadn't contacted me for several months. I didn't have to ask. Meera was happy to give me an update.

"He has just returned from a trip to our country where he almost was engaged to a fortune-hunting woman, but luckily her family didn't approve of him," she explained, shaking her head. "Not rich enough, I suppose." She sniffed disapprovingly. "Some people don't appreciate family history and titles."

So I was right. Titles were important to some people; others followed the money.

"Don't worry," she said, "I don't believe he was heartbroken, since this was an arranged affair. You will be good for him. Cheer him up."

Like I was in a position to cheer anyone up.

....

As we left the bar, Meera asked, "This is where you work, no?" pointing to Dolce's shop across the street.

I nodded.

"I must come by to refresh my wardrobe."

I was almost speechless picturing Meera leafing through the racks looking for vintage clothes at Dolce's. She'd be disappointed to find we stick to the basics—Proenza Schouler, Miu Miu, Narciso Rodriguez, Armani, Marc Jacobs . . . No one she'd ever heard of.

"I'm not sure we have anything you'd like," I said when I found my voice. As if she'd come across anything at Dolce's even remotely to her taste or from her era.

"New clothes or not, I would like to see the place from the inside again," she said.

"So you've been there before?" I asked. Why hadn't I seen her?

"I believe I went to a meeting there once of the Ladies' Protection and Relief Society."

"I've never heard of it," I said.

"This was some years ago. Before your time. San Francisco was a small town, about twenty thousand or so. We women were in the minority, especially the respectable ones. Females were quite a civilizing force on society in those days. What was it someone said? 'The sight of a woman on the streets of San Francisco is more rare than the sight of a giraffe or an elephant.' " She had a faraway look in her eyes and a wistful smile on her ageless face. It was almost as if she believed it herself. Maybe she did. "You do remember my vampire tour of the city, don't you?" she asked, leaning toward me until her forehead almost touched mine.

I stepped backward. "Yes, of course." Now I'd done it. Started her down the path to the good old days, and I do mean "old." From experience I knew it was best not to contradict her but merely treat her like it wasn't unusual to hear about the past from someone who claimed to have lived it. That's what her tour was all about, the sights and sounds of the San Francisco underground world past and present. I admit it had been interesting. The woman loved performing for a crowd; that was obvious. And the crowd had eaten it up the night I took the tour.

What was also obvious was that she knew her history. She'd gone out and bought some old clothes and told anyone who'd listen that she was a vampire. And voilà, she was no longer just a woman of a certain age who liked to wear old dresses, she was an icon, a link to the past who made her living giving city tours and now, apparently, cooking classes too. She was still in vintage clothes. What next?

"Do you sell jewelry at your store?"

"Yes, of course. Are you interested in acquiring something new?"

"I'm interested in selling a few choice pieces left to me by my mother. An antique brooch with a cameo figure of an angel set in gold, an eighteen-carat snake ring that was my grandmother's and a few other items you won't see anywhere else."

"I'm sure my boss would be glad to have a look at them," I said. If they weren't saleable, Dolce would know how to turn Meera down gently. And if they were really outstanding, she might take them on consignment.

"Very well."

Then I wished I hadn't said anything. I could just see her walking into the shop one day in her bustle skirt and feather-trimmed hat with her odd jewelry and suddenly starting to examine the fixtures and the woodwork. She might peel back the wallpaper to test for authenticity. Perhaps reminisce about the meetings held there and the balls and the parties.

Then she'd open her reticule and spread her jewelry collection on the counter. What would our customers think?

"I must be going," she said, taking an antique windup watch from her pocket to check the time. "I'm late for work at the restaurant."

I assumed she meant the pizza place called Azerbyjohnnie's where she was a hostess the last I'd heard. She was certainly a jack-of-all-trades. And tireless to boot. I had to give her credit for that. Besides the upcoming cooking classes and her guided historic tours of the city, she was still working at the restaurant. And all while wearing long skirts and lace-up ankle boots. The thought of one of Azerbyjohnnie's designer pizzas made my mouth water. Lunch had been a Caesar salad delivered from the restaurant around the corner because we were too busy to go out. No wonder I was hungry. Some women can live on lettuce and a few croutons, but not me.

"Thanks for the drink," I said. "I'll see you soon." I tried to sound vague, but of course she was having none of it.

She handed me a calling card bordered in pale flowers with her name and address (of what I guessed was the bed-and-breakfast she was house-sitting) written in calligraphy.

"Forget about Torcelli," she said, waving her finger at me. "He may be famous, but he's worthless as a chef, and furthermore, he won't be around much longer, I can tell you that."

Now how did she know that? Was he going to retire and move back to Italy when he was doing so well here in the U.S.? He was on a level with Mario Batali, Lidia Bastianich and Giada De Laurentiis. I watched while Meera briskly crossed the street, the hem of her dress brushing the pavement. I wasn't surprised to see how many people turned to stare at her. Yes, this was San Francisco where the people were unpredictable, but even so, there weren't that many women in Victorian dresses, at least not in this neighborhood. Not too surprising, I don't think she minded being stared at. In fact, she seemed to enjoy the attention.

It wasn't late, so after I was sure Meera was out of sight, I walked to the corner and hopped on the Twenty-Two Fillmore bus, which went within two blocks of Tante Marie's Cooking School. Not that I was afraid of Meera trying to stop me, but I didn't want to make a scene right on the street where I worked. If I was lucky, it was possible that the renowned Chef Guido was giving a class that night and I could join in on the spot. At least I'd be able to register for something in the future.

A half hour later I was at the door of the cooking school. I peered inside the window but didn't see anyone. Not Tante Yvette or Guido or any students. I had yet to meet Tante Marie; perhaps she didn't even exist. But Guido did. I knocked on the door.

I was in luck. The handsome chef, wearing a striped collarless shirt and a chef's toque, came to the door and opened it just about six inches.

"It is Ms. Jewel, I believe. Are you alone?" he asked, peering out at the street. As if I might be traveling with a posse.

I nodded yes to both questions. I was flattered he remembered my name. He was now a huge star in the world of celebrity chefs, and I was hardly the star of the class I'd taken with him. Maybe that's why he remembered me, because I'd had a few problems following directions. After all, at the time I hadn't known the difference between chopping, slicing, mincing and dicing. I wondered who he thought I'd be with. Maybe he'd asked because I was alone the last time I'd been here and he was worried that I didn't have any friends. I was worried too.

"This is not a good time," he said, his foot wedged against the door so I couldn't have squeezed in if I'd wanted to. "We just finished a class. And I'm about to call it a day. Shouldn't you be on your way?"

Maybe he was right. After a tiring day and drinks with Meera, I ought to go home. But not before I'd at least tried to enroll in one of his future classes. Even in the dusk I could see the chef looked tired. His face was creased and his voice sounded hoarse. It must be grueling teaching cooking to the socialites who were attracted to him and his classes. Almost as tiring as selling accessories to the same rich women.

"I'm sorry," I said, glancing behind him to the rear of the room and the spotless kitchen where I remembered watching the chef in action and then eating a delicious dinner with him and the other students. "I just wanted to sign up for another class."

"You can register online. In fact, I recommend it. That way you can be sure of getting the class you want. Beginning Italian cuisine, sauces, antipasto, pasta and more."

"I'll do that. I just wanted to tell you—"

"Not now," he said. "For the moment I am fully booked."

"Let me give you my phone number and you can let me know when you have an opening," I said.

He didn't say yes or no, so I reached into my bag and scrawled my number on a take-out menu from Meera's restaurant, Azerbyjohnnie's. I handed it to him.

"I'd really love to take the class because I—" He then closed the door, and I heard him turn the lock with a definite click. I stood there wondering if I'd said something to offend him. Had I been so inept at that last class he wanted to get rid of me? I wasn't used to being shut out like that. That was when I realized I might have come all this way for nothing. Would he really contact me, or had he forgotten about me already? Or did he have no intention of letting me in another class but didn't want to go into the reasons? I hadn't even had a chance to tell him how much I'd enjoyed his last class. Maybe that would have made a difference.

I don't know what I'd thought, that Guido would throw his arms around me in true Italian style, kiss me on both cheeks and invite me in for some leftover antipasto? Since I'd taken his class, he'd become even more famous than before, publishing a cookbook of family favorites called *Rustico—Regional Italian Country Cooking.* I'd fooled myself into thinking that I'd made as much of an impression on him as he had on me. If I had, it was probably a bad impression because I was such a klutz in the kitchen. Now I realized I was just one of many students who'd fallen under the spell of Italian cuisine and the dramatic chef who made it look so easy.

I walked slowly down the street thinking maybe a cooking class wasn't what I needed after all. When I thought about it, I realized the reason he'd even remembered my name was because I stood out and not in a good way. He must have been extremely tired after a day of nonstop classes, and then I had to show up just as he was ready to call it a day and remind him of how hard it was to teach cooking to novices. Even well-connected novices with lots of money. I tried not to let myself take this brush-off personally. But what else could I think?

No matter how hard I tried to cheer myself up, I still felt low. It had started before I left work, and now I was really in the dumps. I knew what was wrong. I was hungry. I stopped on the corner and leaned against a fence. First, I called a cab to pick me up on the corner, and second, I phoned Azerby-johnnie's to order a pizza.

"Meera?" I said.

"Meera isn't in tonight. Not yet. Can I help you?" said an unfamiliar voice.

I ordered their Tuesday special vegetarian pie with mushrooms, olives, red onions, red peppers, artichoke hearts and arugula, to be delivered to my house. It was a relief not to have to deal with Meera on the phone. She always tried to talk me into a different pizza than the one I wanted. Or she insisted on having a conversation with me when all I wanted was to place my order. But I wondered where she was. She'd definitely said she was on her way to work.

When the pizza came to my house a half hour after the cab dropped me off, I asked the delivery man where Meera was tonight. He said she'd called in sick.

"You know her? She's a character," he said.

I had to agree. But was she really sick? And if so, was it contagious? She'd breathed on me more than once at the bar. I went to my tiny little bathroom, barely big enough for my claw foot tub, which I absolutely could not live without. With a job like mine, after a day like I'd had, I needed a long, hot, relaxing soak. I stared into the oval mirror and stuck out my tongue. It looked smudged and bumpy to me, but what did I know? Maybe it was always that way and I'd never noticed. My face was flushed. I could be coming down with something. Maybe I should put in a call to Dr. Jonathan and ask what was going around, if anything. I could also ask the Admissions Department if any vampires had checked in tonight. They'd get a kick out of that.

I could also call Nick, Meera's nephew, to see if he knew anything about her. Just to make sure she was all right. However wacky Meera was, she was always dependable as far as I knew. So why hadn't she gone to work?

But before I called anyone, I had to eat my pizza while it was hot. If I was coming down with something, I needed some to keep my strength up and fortify my immune system. Fortunately my appetite was good. In fact, I was ravenous and soon polished off the entire pizza along with a glass of two-buck-Chuck Merlot.

Feeling so much better, I changed out of my new work clothes and filled the tub with hot water and some all natural Pacific sea salts and sank into the water until I was so relaxed I felt like a jellyfish. Then I put on my Barefoot Dreams cozy bathrobe over the subtle blue and white striped pajama set Rachel Roy made famous by wearing it on the red carpet of a movie premiere. No movie premiere tonight for me, but I like to look my best at all times. With my phone in hand I went into my bedroom. Propped up against the distressed oak headboard, I called the ER at the hospital and asked to speak to Dr. Rhodes. The snippy clerk asked if it was an emergency. I hesitated a minute, then confessed it wasn't. I did leave my name and number and my symptoms, but from the way she acted, I took it that having a flushed face and bumpy tongue was no big deal, so I wondered if she'd even give the message to him.

I'd just hung up when my phone rang. It wasn't Jonathan.

"Rita," Dolce said. "Have you heard the news tonight?"

Before I could say no, she said, "Isn't your culinary school on Potrero Hill?"

"Yes," I said. "Why?"

"Didn't you say you were going there tonight?"

"Yes," I said. "Why?"

"Because the celebrity chef Guido was shot to death at his cooking school."

I gasped.

"But I just saw him," I protested.

"Was he alive?" she asked.

"Of course," I said. "At least I think so."

Two

....

It's hard to even think about getting a good night's sleep when the person you saw alive a few hours ago is later reportedly dead and the cause was not natural. At least that's what they said on the ten o'clock news. The police were investigating the incident as a homicide. They showed Guido's photograph, a photo of him grinning at the camera with some of his Hollywood buddies who'd hired him or hung out with him, and then gave a brief history of his stellar career as a chef. There was also a mention of Tante Marie, who was actually a one-time resident of Potrero Hill. The news included a tour of the school and a video of the sheet-covered body being carried into the ambulance. That's what did it, convinced me he really was dead. Even another extra hot bath with herbal Dead Sea salts couldn't stop me from shivering and shaking.

I kept thinking of how Guido wouldn't let me into the

school tonight. Was that because his murderer was already on the premises? Was Guido protecting me? What if I had been able to prevent this heinous crime by forcing my way into the school and disarming the killer, but instead I'd allowed the chef in a heroic gesture to send me out of harm's way?

Or was Guido expecting his killer, only he didn't know it was a killer. He thought it was a friend or a relative or a student of his. If only I had access to his cooking school, I was sure I'd find something written on his calendar or his bulletin board. Right now the police were probably combing the place for clues like the menu I'd scrawled my number on. So once again I'd be on the list of suspects when they realized whose number that was.

I kept expecting the phone to ring. Either from the police or from Meera, because she along with Dolce knew where I was going tonight. But my little apartment under the sloped roof of an old house on Russian Hill was quiet except for the voice of the newsman going over the gory details of the murder. The suspicion that it was an inside job. No evidence of a break-in. Interviews with neighbors who reported seeing a woman in an off-white Juicy Couture blazer at the door earlier in the evening. Me, wearing Juicy Couture? Never. Must have been someone else.

There was an interview with the detective assigned to the case, my sometime friend Jack Wall, who looked tough and suave at the same time in his tailored off-the-rack Alfani suit and a solid black skinny tie. He said he would find the perpetrator and bring him or her to justice. What else could he say? How long would it take him to figure out I'd been there at the scene?

Turned out it didn't take him that long. I had a half hour

to figure out what to say. Of course I'd tell the truth, but the truth isn't always so easy to figure out.

I just had to tell him I didn't kill Guido. Of course not. What possible motive would I have? I adored Guido. Everyone adored Guido. He was an inspiring teacher, a TV star, a man whose memory would live on through his books and his TV classes. Not the Guido I'd seen tonight; that Guido was not himself. The Guido I knew, the Guido who taught our class and countless others, was urbane, suave, gregarious and fun. By the time Jack called, I had calmed down and jotted down a few questions for him. I knew he'd have a few for me too.

"Tell me you weren't on the scene of another murder tonight," he said, his voice stern and official. We were off to a bad start. But he had to sound that way. It was his job. I pictured him in his office, not in his suit, but instead he'd have changed into something casual but pricy, like boot-cut jeans that fit as if they'd been made for him and a designer pin-striped shirt with the sleeves rolled up. And on his feet, propped up on his desk, he'd be wearing Gucci black leather sneakers. He might have had them on when he was on the news.

"Are you referring to Guido Torcelli?" I asked calmly.

"I am," he said. "May I ask where you were this evening?"

"Of course. I have nothing to hide. And a good alibi. Are we doing this over the phone?" I asked.

"At this hour I assume you don't want to come down to the station."

"Not in my jammies and bunny slippers, no," I said. Though I had no intention of hustling downtown at this hour, I wanted to see how far I could push the envelope. Surely he wouldn't make me come down there tonight, would he? "But if you want to come here . . ."

"That won't be necessary. I'll see you at the station tomorrow morning, if that's convenient," he said. There may have been a trace of sarcasm in his voice. I wasn't sure.

"Aren't you going to tell me not to leave the country?"

"Do I have to?"

"I hope we can work together on this, Jack."

There was a long silence during which he was probably trying to decide how to tell me politely to mind my own business. That he didn't need my help. That he was the cop and I was a suspect.

"I'm counting on your help," he said at last. "I feel sure you want this case solved as soon as possible so we can all get back to our jobs."

"But this is your job, isn't it? To solve murders. If you have any others on your desk, I'd be glad to—"

"Rita, let's not go overboard, shall we?" he asked. I could tell I was pushing his buttons, but somehow I couldn't help it. I wanted to remind him of the past murders in which I had helped him whether he'd wanted my help or not. Of course, he was trying hard to stay calm and not alarm me. That must be what they learn at the police academy.

"Sorry," I said, trying to sound contrite. "I just want you to know that—"

"I know. You want to help. Good. Let's leave it at that. Before I let you go, tell me if you're still at the same address."

"The same place where you came to dinner with Dolce and Nick and his aunt, yes." It wouldn't hurt to remind him that he owed me a dinner.

"And your work address is the same?"

Thinking of Dolce's reminded me of bumping into

Meera. Where had she been tonight? She wasn't at work. She didn't want me to take classes from Guido. She wasn't fond of him, to put it mildly. She didn't do it, did she?

"Rita?" he said. "Are you still there?"

"Of course I'm here. And I still work at Dolce's. I'm just thinking. This murder is very upsetting."

"They usually are," he said dryly.

"I mean to me personally. I knew the chef."

"How well?"

"I took one class from him, and tonight I went there to sign up with him for another."

"Is that the reason you were at the scene of the murder?"

"Yes, it was. If you like, I'll make you a timeline of my whereabouts tonight. How would that be?" I asked sweetly.

"I look forward to it. Just for the record. Tell me, how did Mr. Torcelli seem tonight?"

"Distracted. Definitely not himself. I had the feeling he was trying to get rid of me."

"And this upset you, am I right? Made you angry?"

"No, not at all," I protested. "Well, maybe a little. But not enough to shoot him."

"How do you know he was shot?"

"I heard it on the news." There, Jack. I had an answer for all his questions. So far. "I was thinking that maybe he was expecting someone else or the someone else was in the shop already . . . Are you taking this down?"

"Not now, but I will tomorrow."

"Are you going to make me take a lie-detector test again?" I asked.

"Do you have any objection?"

"Of course not. Only a criminal would object. By the way, how did you know I was there?" As if I didn't know.

"Your phone number was written on a menu and lying on the table at the cooking school. Care to explain that?"

"Yes, I care very much. I gave it to him so he could notify me when the next class came up. Is that a crime?"

"Let it go for now. We'll talk further tomorrow when you can fill me in on your activities before and after your visit to the cooking school. Is nine o'clock in my office convenient for you?"

"I'll have to check with Dolce, but I'll plan on it."

He hung up, then I called Dolce to fill her in and tell her I was going to be late the next day.

"All you have to do is tell the truth," she said.

Oh, if only it was that simple.

After I talked to her, I tried calling Meera but got a recorded message advertising her walking tours of San Francisco. She was probably asleep, so I left her a message to give me a call. When she did tomorrow, I'd wait to see if she'd tell me anything, and if she didn't, I'd tell her I wanted to take her up on the cooking class offer. Now that Guido was dead, it was time to find a new class. But I wouldn't say a word to her about Guido. Let her bring him up if she wanted to. I sure didn't. Then I called her nephew Nick Petrescu and left him a message that went like this:

"Hi, Nick. Rita here. Long time no see, as we say in America. How are you? If you are in town, give me a call. I understand we'll be taking cooking classes together from Meera. I hope your Olympic hopefuls are doing well."

....

The next day I dressed carefully as I always do for an investigation. I had what they call an "office-ready" gray pin-striped suit with a slim pencil skirt that hit just above the knee and a no-nonsense jacket that hugged my curves; I'd bought it on sale at Ann Taylor. Most of my clothes come straight from Dolce's, but not all of them. She understands that sometimes I shop at the mall. With the suit I wore a pair of black Sam Edelman medium stacked heels I'd picked up at Neiman Marcus. I'd have to change when I got to work so the customers wouldn't think I was in mourning, which I wasn't; even though I was an admirer of the chef, we really hadn't been close enough for me to mourn his demise.

Although I would certainly go to his funeral. I have found that a funeral brings out the best and the worst in people. People cry or they laugh or they say something inappropriate that they shouldn't, which is helpful when you're looking for a murderer. I knew I wasn't supposed to be looking for a murderer, but how could I help it?

I could only hope that no one at Dolce's would have any reason to bring up the subject of Chef Guido's murder. At least when I got to work I could escape from the cloud of suspicion that Jack would try to hang over my head. After a grilling by the police, it would be a relief to concentrate on clothes and accessories. Just yesterday I'd been sick of them. Not today.

But first I had to get through my meeting at the police station. I'd made notes and I was as prepared as I could be. Jack would be civil, but I didn't expect him to talk about anything other than Guido's murder. Would I have to take an oath? Would I have to tell him what Meera said? Did he really think I'd kill anyone no matter what they did to me, like turning me away from the cooking school? Or had Jack called me down there to get me to finger someone else? He should know better after what we'd been through together when he'd wanted me to turn in my boss Dolce.

Satisfied with my clothing choice, which I thought made me look serious and sincere and most of all honest, I pulled my hair back into a chignon to complete the businesswoman look and took a taxi to the Central Police Station. I couldn't face another bus, not today in my totally tailored designer suit.

When I told the clerk who I was, she made a call and in a few minutes Jack came out to meet me. He looked me up and down, and I couldn't tell if he was pleased, shocked, amused or puzzled by my appearance. I knew I looked and felt different from the style-setting fashionista he knew who wore cutting-edge clothes everywhere, including at home. Except when being questioned by a homicide detective.

I knew I didn't look like most of the suspects who came down to the station. Just a glance around the waiting room and I saw poorly dressed vagrants, slick drug dealers in shiny suits and a woman in a tight metallic skirt who looked like she might be a prostitute. On the other hand, if she had a tweed or leather jacket to pair it with, she could even go to lunch at the Garden Court. Jack escorted me through the bulletproof glass doors leading to his office.

Today he was wearing a three-button charcoal Burberry blazer with a striped button-down Moschino shirt open at the collar and a pocket square that matched perfectly. He always managed to look like he was comfortable in his clothes, which were top of the line and more expensive than anyone in public service had a right to wear. The story was he'd made a fortune before he became a cop. How else could he afford to live the way he did, with a sailboat and a pied-à-terre with a bay view and a closet full of designer rags?

And why had he decided to devote himself to catching criminals instead of lying on the beach in Barbados sipping

piña coladas surrounded by lonely bikini-clad women on
the prowl? I'd heard stories, but who knew what was true?
Maybe even Jack had forgotten how he'd gotten where he
was. Where he was today was in a windowless office with
a wall full of pictures of himself receiving various awards.
I didn't doubt for a minute that he deserved them. He was a
hard worker. But even hard workers need help. I like to think
that was why I was there.

"Sit down," he said, waving toward a straight-back chair
that faced his desk.

I looked around. "No lie-detector test?"

A faint smile played across his face. His iron jaw was as
firm as ever, his gaze steady. "Not today." He took out a
small voice recorder from his desk drawer. "Do you mind?"

I shrugged as if I didn't have a care in the world. Tape
me, film me, depose me, I have nothing to hide. That was
the vibe I hoped I was transmitting.

"Let's start with your relationship with the chef."

"I didn't have one," I protested. "I took a class from him.
One class. I thought he was charming. A fine teacher. So
did everyone else in the world, obviously, or he wouldn't
have risen in the ranks of celebrity chefs."

"Everyone else in the world," he repeated. "Who do you
mean exactly?"

"Specifically I mean the other people in the class and in
general, everywhere. Don't ask me to name names, I have
no idea. My class was months ago."

Jack picked up his phone and told someone to get him a
list of all the cooking school students from the past year.

"Just last year?" I asked.

"The past *years*," he said to the person on the phone. His
assistant? His deputy? He hung up and turned to me.

"You said you took one class from him, but that wasn't the only time you'd seen the chef. Why did you choose to go to see Mr. Torcelli yesterday?"

"I'd only had one lesson from him, although I enjoyed it very much. That's why I went back last night to sign up for a refresher class. I realized cooking was probably something I needed to work on."

"You realized it last night? What time was that?"

"What time did I go there or what time did I realize it?"

He didn't roll his eyes, but I was sure he wanted to. He just waited, so I continued.

"It all happened after work. I went to have a drink across the street at the bar."

"By yourself?"

"Yes. I mean, I went in by myself but I met someone there."

He looked faintly disapproving, I thought. Did that mean he disapproved of singles' bars or my drinking or my picking up men at singles' bars? Or did it mean he was disappointed I wouldn't confess I'd shot Guido so he could wrap this up and get on with the rest of his workload?

"Name of the person you met?"

"Meera. I don't know her last name. I mean, I must have known it but I can't remember it. It's Romanian and it could be Petrescu because that's her nephew's name, but I'm not sure."

He looked at me as if waiting for me to continue. So I did. "We had a drink and then we left," I said.

"Together?"

"We walked out together, then I took the bus and she left on foot."

"You took the bus directly to the cooking school?"

"Yes." I was sorry Guido died, but I had nothing to add to the investigation besides what I'd already said. Nothing, zip, nada. Except for the part about his allegedly stealing other chef's recipes. But Meera was not a reliable source of information, so I felt fine about leaving out what she'd told me. I wracked my brain to try to change the subject before he could come up with another question.

"Tell me," I said, "are you policemen sponsoring that youth fishing program again this year?"

"What?" Startled, he looked up from his notes.

"The one that enables city children to enjoy the natural beauty of the ocean and the Bay outdoors. For some kids I understand it's their first trip to go under the Golden Gate Bridge."

"Where did you hear about that?" he asked with a puzzled frown on his face.

"I don't know. I read it somewhere. Why, is it a secret? Ever since I participated in solving that homicide—you know the one—I've been following the police news. Your department does lots of good work, which you should be proud of."

"Thank you, Rita," he said with only a touch of sarcasm dripping from his voice. "And now if you don't mind, I have a few more questions for you."

I crossed my legs, smoothed the lapels of my suit jacket and told him to fire away. Maybe not a good choice of words.

"Tell me again why you went to the cooking school last night without an appointment, without an invitation and without knowing if it was open. Why not call ahead?"

"Ah," I said, stalling for time. Why had I gone there like

that? In retrospect it was a dumb idea. "I was hoping I might join a class on the spot. Frankly, I was hungry. After class is over, we all sit down and eat the food we made. Or rather, what the chef made. It's part of the experience, to talk about the recipes, the techniques and how everything turned out."

"Last night it didn't turn out very well, did it?" he asked, staring at me.

"I don't know. Oh, you mean because of Guido's murder. I thought you meant the food. You'd have to ask the class about that. You do have a class list, I suppose?"

"Yes, we do. Thanks for the suggestion. We'll be talking to everyone who was there last night."

I nodded my approval.

"You said you were hungry," Jack said. "So you thought you'd take a cooking lesson instead of buying food."

"It may sound strange, but even though I often buy food, I don't know what to do with it unless it's already cooked. Then I eat it. Oh, I know, you're thinking of the dinner you crashed at my house, aren't you? And you wondered, as did everyone there, how did Rita pull this off when she doesn't know how to cook?"

He managed to look slightly contrite, which is unusual for Jack. Not just unusual but unheard of.

"Someone invited me to stay to eat that night. I appreciated it, and I assumed you knew how to cook. Everything was very good."

"It was Meera who invited you. She's the one I was in the bar with last night. She will verify my story."

But who would verify Meera's whereabouts after we parted? She hadn't gone to work, so where had she gone?

"And will you verify hers?" he asked as if he'd read my mind.

"Of course I will if you want me to." But I couldn't verify where she'd gone after I saw her. That's what worried me.

"Right now I need her full name and her contact number."

I told him what I knew, which wasn't much: that she worked at Azerbyjohnnie's but I didn't know her schedule. Also that she was house-sitting at a San Francisco B and B. I didn't say anything about her relationship with Chef Guido. Jack hadn't asked me, and I wasn't going to tell him how she hated the chef. He'd jump to the wrong conclusion. Or would he? Maybe he'd jump to the right conclusion, that she had something to do with this murder. "I have to warn you that she will say she's a vampire."

He nodded as if that was no big surprise. I guess that was why he was such a good detective, because of his calm demeanor. While others were falling apart and running around in circles, Jack never seemed rattled.

"That's all, Rita," he said, switching off his machine. "I hope you'll let me know if you hear anything pertaining to the case."

"Of course. I'm as eager to get this mystery solved as you are. Well, maybe not that eager, but you know how badly I want to put this behind us. For me, I will find another cooking class, but it won't be the same. Nobody else had Guido's charm and charisma."

"Nobody? You mean he had no rivals?"

"I . . . I don't know," I stammered. "I think all great chefs have rivals. Most of them are temperamental with huge egos. But don't ask me. He's the only chef I know personally, and I met the man only once. I was one of many in his class."

"Once? I thought you went there last night."

"Yes, but that was not a meeting, that was an encounter. It's different. We spoke for maybe two minutes. He said I was too late, he said he was closing. He didn't let me in. He looked nervous."

"Why was that?" Jack asked, twisting his pen in his fingers.

"How should I know?"

"Your best guess," he prompted.

"Maybe he wasn't alone. Or maybe he was expecting someone and he wanted to get rid of me. Maybe he was just tired. Or he had something in the oven and he heard the timer go off. Maybe sometimes a cigar is just a cigar." I sighed loudly, indicating my nearing the end of my patience.

Jack looked at me as if I'd lost a few brain cells. Why hadn't I kept my mouth shut? Why hadn't I just walked out when he turned off his machine? Because I'm a big blabbermouth, that's why. I love to talk, almost as much as I love wearing the season's hottest fashions.

"Wait a minute. You like to solve mysteries. Who in your opinion had reason to kill the chef?"

I couldn't say Meera. I didn't want to finger her any more than she would point at me. "No one, that's why I wonder, have you considered suicide?" I asked.

Jack's eyes opened wide. At my perception? Or at my audacity?

"Here's the thing," I said. "He seemed depressed last night when I saw him. Maybe something went wrong. His soufflé fell or his students cancelled or his chateau was foreclosed on or he got news that his Barbaresco sheep escaped from their pasture. So he took out his gun and shot himself."

"Then where is it?" Jack asked. "Did you see it?"

"The gun or the chateau?"

"The gun," he snapped.

"No, I didn't. Here's my theory. Maybe he didn't die right

away. Maybe he threw the gun in the garbage or out the window or he hid it in the Cuisinart before he expired."

"Why would he do that?" Jack asked.

I had the feeling he was humoring me, trying to get me to make a fool of myself, which wasn't that hard. "He was ashamed of committing suicide, or he wanted to blame someone else for his death."

"Who would that be?" Jack asked, coming out from behind his desk.

I shook my head and stood up to leave. "I have no idea," I said. I really didn't believe Meera was his rival even though she wanted to think so. She was a good cook, but she was not a professional as far as I knew. "Maybe some of the other students will know. I didn't do my homework. I just went to his class because someone recommended it, and I have to say it was wonderful. That's all I have to say. I don't think it's an exaggeration to say that he was well liked. Not just by me but by most or all of his students and all of his tele-viewers. At least that was my impression." I looked at my watch. "I'm late for work."

"If you think of anything else you've neglected to tell me . . ."

"Yes, yes," I said impatiently. "I'll give you a call."

"Do you need a ride to work?" he asked.

"That would help," I said frostily. Was I guilty of with-holding evidence by not telling him what Meera had said? Maybe he thought he could bribe me to tell him something incriminating if he offered transportation. Not me. He called someone on the phone, then he told me Officer O'Doul would meet me in front of the station in an official car.

It was the least he could do, I thought, after all I'd done for him. But I had no intention of calling him with additional helpful hints about this case. I'd done enough. When I'd helped him out the last time, what had it gotten me? Just a few warnings, no medals, no rewards, no key to the city.

Dolce was waiting for me at the door of the boutique. She stepped outside when she saw the cop car let me off, and she looked around before she spoke. "How did it go?" she said softly so the customers inside wouldn't hear her.

I shrugged.

"He doesn't think you killed the chef, does he?" she asked, wide-eyed.

"Who knows what Jack thinks. He holds his cards close to his vest, although he wasn't wearing a vest today. I just wish he'd solve the case soon so I can forget all about the chef and his murder."

Dolce took me by the arm and we went inside, straight to her office. We got a few curious looks from our usual customers, but apparently Dolce hadn't heard enough from me. Not yet.

"Sit down," she said, closing the office door. "Tell me everything. What he said. What you said."

"I said I didn't do it. Who knows if he believes me. He knows I was there at the school last night."

"He wouldn't call you down to the station unless he suspected you, would he? But why? Why would you kill a chef?"

"I wouldn't. I wouldn't kill anyone, especially not a chef."

I was so tired of questions without answers, I was relieved when someone knocked on the office door.

"Dolce, are you there? I have a question. Is it true when the days get short the hems get long?"

Dolce gave me a look and went to the door. Life goes on. No matter who gets shot at a cooking school, women still need clothes. I needed clothes for a funeral. Guido's funeral. Why did I want to go to the funeral? No, I didn't really know the man, but I'd been to funerals before and as depressing as they are, I'd always learned something important. Was it too much to hope for that Guido's interment would be just as enlightening? Like, for example, the murderer just might be there and give himself away. Not to everyone, of course, but a sensitive person like myself might have an "aha" moment. Fortunately I'd have no trouble finding something appropriate and chic to wear. Those were words we lived by at Dolce's.

Three

The story of Guido's murder was in the newspaper.

Hopefully lots of people would attend Guido's funeral, either rivals to celebrate his demise or admirers to mourn him. I prided myself on being a student of character, so I was looking forward to meeting Guido's friends and relatives, hoping to find who would stand to gain by his death. Of course, if they all flew in from Italy the day of the funeral, I'd have to cross them off the list and then where would I be? I'd be back to being suspect number one.

Since his death was public knowledge, I could no longer pretend I didn't know anything about it. I could still pretend I had nothing to do with it. But that wasn't pretending. I'd had nothing to do with it. Nothing. No matter if the police didn't believe me.

I tried to act normal by waiting on some of our regular customers, like Patti French, whose sister-in-law MarySue had been murdered last year. I showed her a classic crisp white shirt by Theory, a wide snakeskin belt by Lauren and a flirtatious above-the-knee fringed leather skirt by Ralph Lauren. She told me she'd heard hems were going down, but I assured her with her legs she needed to show them off.

She knew she looked terrific in the outfit and told me I was a genius. The kind of words I needed to hear after what I'd been through. After I rang up her purchases for a tidy sum, I went to the office and tried to call Meera again. I got her number from the restaurant and called her cell phone. Yes, even faux vampires have cell phones these days. I didn't expect her to answer, so when she did, I was struck almost speechless.

"Meera, where were you last night?" I blurted. "I called in a pizza order, but you weren't there."

"I took the night off. I was tired. When you're my age, you will see what I mean. Oh, to be one hundred again. I am working three jobs, you know. I deserve a night off. Why, did you get the wrong pizza?"

By "my age" she meant close to two hundred years old. Yes, I imagine at that age I might be tired too.

"No, no, it was delicious," I assured her. "Have you heard the news about Guido, the chef?"

"Yes, and I'm not surprised. The man was asking for it."

"Asking to be shot? You mean because he stole your recipes?"

"Not just mine. Not at all. I could give you a list."

"You might have to. The police are investigating his murder. I had to appear at the police station this morning."

"You? Why?"

"Because I went to see him after I left you last night."

"Was he alive?" she asked.

Why did everyone ask me that? "Yes," I said, irritated by the question. "But not for long."

"Then you didn't kill him."

"Of course I didn't. I liked him. I thought he was a great cook and a fine teacher."

"Hmmpf," she snorted. "That's where you're wrong."

"Did you kill him?" I asked. A crazy question, I knew. But Meera was a crazy lady. She was just crazy enough to do it and then confess because she was proud of it. And she didn't fear death because as a vampire she would live forever. So she claimed.

He won't be around much longer, I can tell you that, she'd said about the chef. How did she know unless she was in on his murder? Maybe she didn't do it herself. Maybe she had someone else do it. I had the feeling she knew more than she was letting on.

"I don't mind that he's dead," she said. "You know why, but I didn't kill him. I haven't seen him for years, and I had no wish to see him again. But I am going to his funeral."

"When is that?" I asked. When I wanted to ask, *why* is that? Why go to his funeral if you didn't like him and you didn't kill him?

"I heard from a friend it's Thursday, at the All Saints Funeral Home in Colma. The place will be full of chefs, and I know they all feel the way I do. There will be plenty of dry eyes in the house, you can count on it."

"I'll take your word for it," I said, "but if his students are there, it will be a different story. We all admired him. I would never have given that dinner party I invited you to if I hadn't had a cooking lesson from Guido to give me confidence. I know how you feel about him, but as a teacher he was excellent. Knowledgeable but modest, helpful and kind, which is rare for someone as well-known as he was and just what you look for in an instructor." I hoped she got the message I was sending. If she didn't shape up to be helpful and kind, knowledgeable and modest, she'd never succeed as a chef.

I didn't tell her how different Guido had seemed last night, preoccupied and nervous and definitely not charming. He wanted to get rid of me, that was for sure. But why? If I knew that, I'd have a handle on who did it.

I paused, wondering if what I'd said had caused Meera to do a little soul-searching. What kind of a teacher would she be? She might be talented, but she had the chef's typical ego. It remained to be seen if it would get in her way. Would she throw tantrums, dress down the incompetent students and hurl insults? I wouldn't be there to find out.

"After the funeral, there will be a lunch at the Tante Whatever-Her-Name-Is Cooking School," she told me.

"How do you know all this?" I asked. I was a little jealous that she who bad-mouthed Guido and probably many other professional chefs knew more about his funeral than I did.

"Word goes around," she said with a casual air.

....

My hope was I could find the murderer there at the funeral. I also hoped that Jack would not only absolve me of the crime, but that he would also never know how Meera felt about the chef. Though by now she was probably on his list. In any case, I loved a good funeral, full of drama and tension and usually followed by a buffet to feed the mourners. The last one I went to for our assistant clerk Vienna was followed by a spectacular spread at a gorgeous home. And the murderer was definitely there among the guests. If only I'd figured it out sooner, I could have avoided getting dunked in the cold waters of the Bay. This time I'd pay more attention. Not only was this event a chance for me and for the police to discover the perpetrator, it was also going to be beyond gastronomically satisfying. I was looking forward to it.

Before I went back to the showroom, I changed out of my suit into a sketch print dress from Robert Rodriguez in a leafy green that said spring. I knew it was fall, but spring is my favorite season. I wore a Lauren Jeans denim jacket with it for warmth and to de-fuss the dress and dial down the summer factor of the print. Then I added a tomboy touch with a pair of Puma sneakers. I could have worn a pair of the colorful new Gommino loafers with the rubber pebbles on the bottom, but Dolce had just gotten an order of the athletic shoes in and I wanted to try them out. Both Dolce and I agree that a good way to sell clothes is to wear them and show the customers how they look. So I try to wear boutique clothes as often as possible.

It was a little tricky being between seasons like that. Dressing for the in-between season required imagination and variety, combining unusual elements in a new way. That's what the customers expected me to do. I couldn't let them down.

Was it only yesterday I was in the dumps, finding my job to be superficial and tedious? Dolce was right: a new murder and some new clothes had done wonders for me. It had given me a challenge and new energy, both at work and elsewhere, like at the police station.

Back out with the customers, I immediately got a lot of attention for the shoes and the dress. Dolce noticed and gave me a thumbs-up for my original pairing of items. When I stopped by the accessories counter and slipped on a pendant necklace, I was ready for prime time.

"Sneakers with a dress?" Margot Black stopped trying on straw hats and stared at me.

"Loafers work too," I said, pointing to a pair of the new Gomminos. "These are the ones you see on every celebrity's feet these days. They're handmade by Italian craftsmen. The pebbles keep the leather from wearing out. Want to give them a try?"

Before she had a chance to say no, I'd grabbed an Alexander Wang print dress from a hanger and sent her into the dressing room. I fetched a pair of the loafers in purple and handed them to her to try on. By this time I had a small audience of Margot's friends and other customers waiting for her to emerge.

She was tall and slim with gorgeous voluminous long hair, and everyone agreed she looked fabulous. They even clapped. I beamed and took at least some of the credit for her appearance. Inspired, I handed her a set of seven Ross-Simons silver bracelets, which set off the whole outfit. I realized I needed more jewelry myself, though I couldn't afford a set like this.

"But where will I wear it?" she asked, gazing at herself in the full-length mirror from loafers to her tousled hair.

Everyone chimed in.

"To lunch."

"To tea."

"To meetings."

"To the zoo. The movies. The museum."

All this attention was more than she could take. She returned to the dressing room and changed back into the short skirt and leggings she'd come in with.

I didn't push or hustle. That was not the Dolce way. We suggested, we hinted, we demonstrated, we modeled, but we never insisted. I'd be surprised if Margot didn't buy the whole outfit.

I moved on to showing someone else some long skirts and dresses. I loved a certain long, silk crepe Lanvin dress worn with some Cynthia criss-cross platform sandals. "On cool days a long skirt can be layered under tunics or short jackets or chunky cardigans. A dress is almost easier to wear," I said. "You don't have to come up with something to wear with it unless you want to. You've got it all."

The customers were gathered around me listening to me expound in my print dress. How could I not love my job? What's better than a captive audience of rapt listeners? Nothing. So I continued.

"For evening your hem should hit the floor," I told them. "But for daytime you want a skirt that brushes the tops of your shoes." It just so happened we had a whole rack of long dresses for sale and all the bangles to wear with them.

When someone asked what to do about flyaway hemlines, I said, "When you walk down the street and your skirt billows out behind you, it adds a touch of glamour. And who doesn't want to look glamorous?"

No one said they didn't want to look glamorous. How could they? All of a sudden everyone was going through the racks looking for long dresses. From the rear of the store Dolce was signaling to me, making the motion of a telephone call.

I went back to see her. "Your doctor is on the phone," she said. "He couldn't reach you on your cell."

I nodded. I usually turn it off at work.

"He said he was worried about you, something about

your tongue?" she said, looking concerned but very smart in her vintage wool suit and sling-back heels.

I blushed. Was your doctor supposed to discuss your symptoms with your boss? Of course, Jonathan was not my personal physician. And he'd probably gotten worried when I didn't answer the phone. As for my tongue, I'd forgotten all about it.

"Oh, it's nothing," I assured her. Then I hurried to the office and picked up the phone.

"Jonathan?" I said.

"Rita, I just got your message. How are you?"

For a moment I forgot what I'd called him about.

"Better. Much better."

"Are you sure? You'd better come in for a complete checkup when you get a chance," he said. "Wouldn't want you to arrive on a stretcher like last time."

I sighed happily. Finally someone cared about my health and well-being.

"It may be nothing, and I didn't want to bother you," I said.

"That's what I'm here for," he said in his reassuring voice. "I'm working tonight, so how about having dinner with me in the hospital cafeteria? I owe you after that dinner you gave at your place. How are your cooking classes going?"

"Oh, that. They're on hold right now while I look for a new teacher."

"I thought you liked the one you had. You said he was some dramatic Italian guy."

"He was, but he isn't anymore. He was murdered last night."

"No kidding." Death didn't freak out Jonathan. Not in

his line of work. He accepted it as part of life. Which is what we all should do.

"This dead chef matter. Nothing to do with you, is it?" he said.

"Well, actually . . ."

"Rita, don't get involved if you can help it. You can't risk another concussion." He was referring to the time I fell off a ladder. Actually I was pushed by a woman who was later murdered, but that's another story. "I'll see you tonight then at six?"

I agreed and went back to the showroom. Dolce was dying to know what Jonathan wanted. I could tell by the way she was looking at me and sending signals by raising her eyebrows.

"Dinner tonight," I said in an undertone as I passed her in the hall. She beamed at me. Probably imagining a six-course meal at the Blue Fox, when it was just going to be macaroni and cheese with a glass of iced tea in the cafeteria where you could almost imagine the woman behind the counter asking if you wanted fries with your angioplasty. That wasn't a fair assessment. When you're in a hospital, you want comfort food. And they delivered it.

Dinner with Jonathan in his white lab coat with his spiky sun-bleached hair, his broad shoulders and his sea blue eyes was always a treat no matter where it was. Compared to the no-nonsense detective who thought I might be a serial killer, Jonathan was warm and caring with the world's greatest bedside manner. I was looking forward to seeing him again. I'd tell him I was actually fine. I'd say I knew nothing about Guido's death. Of course, if he had any opinion about the cause of his death, I'd be all ears.

And then we could talk about Jonathan surfing at Santa Cruz or whether he'd found a new apartment. My aunt Alyce always told me to ask questions of people in general and men in particular to get them to talk about themselves. That's what she did to land herself several husbands who never stopped talking until they expired or divorced my aunt.

Maybe I'd find out if Jonathan was dating anyone special. If not, I'd invite him to dinner again. That would give me the incentive I needed to learn to make something different. Something wonderful. Something easy. Maybe something Romanian. Just so it wasn't pigs' feet in aspic. Or maybe Jonathan would forget I owed him a dinner and he'd ask me out again.

On my way in to the cafeteria I stopped by the Admissions Department to see what I could find out about Guido's case. I knew it was a long shot. Those admissions clerks are a closemouthed bunch, as I'd learned on another occasion when I needed information. Anticipating their questions this time, I said I was the niece of Guido Torcelli and I wanted to know what time he'd been brought in last night. I assumed an ambulance had brought him.

The woman stared at me for a long moment as if she might remember me from the last time I harassed her with my questions. Then she told me that information was not available.

"Even to family members?" I asked incredulously while I blinked rapidly as if ready to burst into tears.

"That is correct," she said stiffly. "Unless you have a paper from the coroner giving you permission."

"I do have one," I said, "but I left it in the car. I wouldn't ask, but my mother is broken up over this. She can't let go.

She doesn't believe he's dead." The more I talked the more I threw myself into this fictional family drama. "It would help if she could see his body," I said. "Otherwise she won't be able to come to grips with it, you know?"

"That's out of the question. No visitors are allowed in the morgue."

I nodded as if I understood. I supposed that Jack could get into the morgue. He'd probably already been there, examined the body, reviewed the bullet hole and made an assumption about how, when and who shot him. After all that drama, I got nothing out of her. I guess I wasn't surprised, but I was disappointed. I shot her a cool look, then I went to the cafeteria to meet Jonathan.

I loved going to the hospital as long as I wasn't sick and I could eat in the cafeteria with the doctors and nurses. It made me feel like an insider, especially with Jonathan sitting across the table, his tray covered with enough food to sustain him throughout a long night of emergencies. I chose a meatball sandwich with provolone cheese and a dish of bright red Jell-O.

I was glad I'd worn the print dress and the Puma sneakers when Jonathan told me I was looking good, and I knew it was true. He said he wished I could come every night because of the way I brightened up the cafeteria scene. Having dinner with a gorgeous physician like Jonathan was better than any medication. He made me feel charming and beautiful. We talked about his summer, his new apartment, his father, who was a doctor too, and he asked me lots of questions about me and my life. Honestly, he could have been a therapist the way he pumped me up, and I assumed he did the same for all of his patients, when they were not sedated, of course.

Watching Jonathan eat his first course of chicken noodle soup reminded me of Guido. I don't know why but it did. "Speaking of my cooking teacher," I said, "I wonder how he got here from his culinary academy, and what time." I figured even though he probably couldn't tell me, it wouldn't hurt to ask. "I stopped by to see Mr. Torcelli around seven and he was alive then."

"I'll see if I can find out," Jonathan said.

See what a difference it makes to talk to someone who doesn't have an ax to grind? That exact opposite other kind of person would be Detective Wall.

Jonathan took his phone out of his pocket and punched in a few numbers. He mentioned Guido's name and asked for some information. When he hung up, he put his phone back and said, "Ten o'clock. Does that help?"

"I don't know. It doesn't tell me when he was murdered. It doesn't get me off the hook."

"Off the hook?" He put his fork down. "Don't tell me someone suspects you of killing him."

"Let's just say I was at the police station this morning answering questions. I was one of the last, maybe *the* last person to see the chef alive. So the more I can find out about his last hours, the better off I'll be. I have a strong motive for finding out who killed him. Which is why I'd like to know how he got here, who called the police, who brought him here or anything relating to his murder. Because I don't like being a suspect. Some people might say I was meddling." Like the woman at the front desk. Like Jack.

"It's not meddling if you're helping solve a crime, am I right?"

I was happy to finally talk to someone who understood me and my motives. I only wanted to help. That's all. Well, maybe not all. I also wanted some excitement in my life. But not too much.

"You say you're going to the funeral?" Jonathan asked.

"I think I should. Not that we were even friends, but still, I want to honor his memory. I feel terrible that I might have saved Guido. If only I'd insisted on coming into the school, but he closed the door in my face."

"And you let that stop you? I'm surprised to hear that, Rita." He gave me one of his trademark smiles that warmed me even more than chicken soup.

I blushed. Not sure if that was a compliment or not.

"Jonathan." A high voice interrupted our conversation. We both stopped eating and looked up at a very attractive blond nurse who was carrying a tray with a salad on it. "How are you?"

"Fine," he said. "Sally, this is Rita."

She didn't look at me, that's how unimportant I was.

"Are you on tonight?" she asked Jonathan.

"Seven to three," he said.

"Then we'll be working together," she said with a flirtatious smile.

I was afraid she was going to pull up a chair and join us, but Jonathan didn't invite her and neither did I, so she moved on across the room. I couldn't help but think that every nurse in the place must be hot for him. I would be if I were a nurse. I wasn't a nurse, but I was hot for him anyway.

We both had coffee because Jonathan had to be alert for the many hours to come as he treated domestic violence victims, and patients with drug overdoses, flu, chest pains, fevers and heart attacks.

"What's up with your friend the gymnast?" he asked.

I shrugged. "I heard he had an accident at work involving some uneven bars, but I haven't seen him in a while." I could only hope that Jonathan was wondering if I was interested in Nick romantically. I wanted to be sure my favorite doctor knew I was free and still single.

He glanced at his watch. "Give me a call if you want someone to try your new recipes out on. I can't exist on hospital food alone, you know."

I felt awful that I hadn't called Jonathan and kept in touch more often. He was really a great guy with a great job and an A-one beside manner. Jonathan gave me a big hug before I left the cafeteria, and said he'd be in touch.

I stood outside the main entrance of the hospital wondering what I should do next. It was too early to go home and too late to call anyone. When I checked my messages, I saw that Nick had called me. I phoned him, and we made a date to meet in Cow Hollow near his house.

He asked if I liked tea and I said, "Of course."

"What kind? Green tea, black tea, oolong, herbal?"

"I don't know," I confessed.

"We'll go for a tea tasting. They know me there. I often bring some friends from my country or not. Like you."

I met him at the Hong Kong Tea Emporium, which sounded large and impressive but was a small cozy teahouse on Chestnut Street.

He greeted me European style with a kiss on each cheek. There is something so different about being with a suave European man. His accent, his manners made me feel like I was in a foreign movie. I almost forgot to ask about his aunt, like did he know where she was last night. I told myself to hold off and asked him how he'd been.

"Very well," he said. "I have completely recovered from

my accident, and I am ready to plunge headfirst into the social life again."

"That's good news," I said. Because I too was only too ready for some social life. Then I asked him to explain the different teas to me.

First he introduced me to the hostess, who wore a long silk Oriental gown. I felt underdressed in my denim jacket. I didn't like the feeling.

"It is my pleasure to introduce you to Yum Yum, the tea hostess. I have learned from her everything I know about tea, so now I know more than many people. So very often-times I am the one who needs the explaining about your country, but not tonight."

I sat back on the bar stool and watched Yum Yum pour hot water over tea leaves.

"You will see," Nick said, "that tea tasting is not like wine tasting. No bitterness, no slurping and no spitting."

I was glad to hear it.

"And also," Nick continued, "the food that goes with the tea is much more strange than at a wine tasting."

That had me a little worried. I like to think of myself as an adventurous eater, but I draw the line at certain things, like pigs' feet. I didn't need to worry. Our hostess started by immersing white and green tea leaves in boiling water.

"Three minutes is enough," she said. "Anything longer and you will have bitterness."

With the tea she served nori rolls. She kept pouring different teas starting with green. With oolong tea we nibbled on tea eggs. I was glad I hadn't overeaten at the hospital cafeteria.

"What do you taste?" Nick asked me when we were

drinking the oolong tea. I swirled the tea around in my mouth, then I took a guess. "This one has hints of honey and gardenia," I said. It turns out I was almost right. But it wasn't gardenia, it was rose hips. Nick smiled proudly, and even the tea lady was impressed I'd come so close. She brought out two more for us to taste. A high-quality white tea and a long-leafed green tea on the sweet side. I loved them both.

"Your friend has good taste," the hostess told Nick.

I reveled in the compliment. After the day I'd been through, I didn't mind hearing even more good words than those I'd heard at the hospital tonight.

"High-quality tea at a high price," she told us. "But worth every penny. These are teas you will not find anywhere outside China except for here."

"Delicious," I said. "I have to have some to take home." I bought a couple of tins, which I'd save for special occasions or maybe gifts, although I thought I deserved those teas more than anyone I knew who might be just as happy with something off the shelf.

"Would you like to have your tea leaves read?" the hostess asked us.

"You mean to predict the future?" I asked. I didn't believe in that voodoo. It was the kind of thing Meera would do. I said, "No thanks." But out of nowhere a woman wearing a long gown and a veil appeared at our table.

"I am your seer," she said.

Uh-oh, a seer might tell me things I didn't want to know. But I was strong. I was good at acting. I would listen attentively but not take anything she said seriously. I had enough to worry about.

Four

::::::::::::::::::::::::::::::

I thought I said, "We don't want a seer," but I'm not sure because she pulled up a chair to our table and began peering into our teacups. She paid no attention to Nick but told me to swirl my tea around in the cup. Then she said I should concentrate on my future destiny. As if I didn't do that all day long.

"The cup is divided into three parts," she said. "The rim represents the present, the sides are the near future and the bottom the distant future."

I looked into my cup pretending to be interested, pretending that I believed whatever she said and wishing we'd left after we finished our tea. Nick was gazing into the leaves in his cup, and I wanted to say, "Tell his future if you want, but leave me out of this."

As if the woman sensed my lack of belief, she said,

"Don't worry, in this cup I see that good fortune outweighs the bad."

"That's a relief," I said. "I could use some good fortune."

"You will find love and happiness," she assured me, tilting the cup back and forth. "I see a marriage here. Possibly your own." She looked up at me to see how I took this news. I tried to assume a positive expression. But really. First a vampire and now a fortune-teller. Did I have "gullible" written on my forehead?

"But first," she continued, "you must spend time alone."

"Alone?" I asked. She didn't mean that small prison cell from my dream, did she?

"Not for long. You will have company in a few months or perhaps years, I am not sure."

"Thank you," I said. I'd heard enough. I'd have more nightmares tonight for sure. "And now I really must go. Thank you, Nick. It's getting late." I was not in the mood to be told I was going to prison for killing Guido or for anything for that matter. I loved the tea, but the last part of the tasting left a bitter taste in my mouth.

If Nick was surprised by my cool behavior toward the tea-leaf reader, he didn't let on. We left and he walked me to my bus stop because he said his car was in the garage. Saying nothing about the seer, he asked if all the caffeine from the tea would keep me up at night. I didn't tell him that I had plenty to keep me up at night, like worrying who killed my cooking teacher. But I did take the opportunity while we waited for my bus to casually ask how his aunt was.

"But you have recently seen her more often than myself," he said in his charming Romanian accent.

"Yes, I saw her last evening. She appeared unexpectedly

to surprise me at the bar across from the shop where I work. We had a discussion about my cooking class. She didn't approve of the teacher."

"I know," he said. "Because she is a chef herself and very proud."

"I'm worried," I confessed. "Meera spoke quite harshly about Guido Torcelli, and later that evening he was murdered."

"Yes, she told me. Quite a . . . how do you say?"

"A coincidence?" I prompted.

"Yes, I think so. So you approved of this chef?"

"He was very good, lots of energy, except for the last time I saw him."

"You yourself saw this man? And was he at that time alive?"

Not again. How many times did I have to say it?

"Yes, quite alive. Good night," I said as my bus came around the corner. "I'll see you soon. And thanks for the tea."

"I look forward to seeing you again soon," he called to me. But he didn't mention any date. That was my trouble. I had three men I was interested in, but I couldn't seem to close the deal on any one of them. My fault.

I slept well that night despite all the caffeine from the coffee with Jonathan and the tea with Nick and my men problem. And the disturbing fortune I'd been given. I like to think it was thanks to my strong belief that the woman knew nothing and that somehow soon the real killer would be found. I told myself before I went to bed that the answer would be clear at the funeral on Thursday. All l I had to do was keep my ears and eyes open.

....

On Wednesday Dolce hung an "Out to Lunch" sign on the door before the funeral and we went through the racks looking for our outfits. It wasn't like this was the first time we'd gone to a funeral together. It was the third. Each one was significant. One was for one of our customers, the other for one of our staff. Today it was someone Dolce didn't even know and I'd only met twice. What they all had in common was that Detective Jack Wall was convinced I'd had something to do with the murders. It seemed like by now he'd give me a break, wouldn't you think? I mean, as it turned out I'd had nothing to do with the other murders but something big to do with solving the cases.

I was determined to continue to do what I could to protect the innocent (me) and bring the guilty to justice. I had no idea who that might be; I just knew it wasn't me.

"I appreciate your going with me," I told Dolce while I stood in front of the mirror staring at myself dressed in a modestly priced black Joseph pantsuit with a frilly white Orvis shirt and a pair of Eric Rutberg Vallanta high-wedge sandals. I could see the expression on Dolce's face in the mirror. She didn't look pleased.

"Too boring?" I asked.

She nodded. "We both know the rules: dress up to show respect. Don't wear red. Don't call attention to yourself. Black is safe. But . . ." She didn't need to go on. I knew what she meant. How to make a fashion statement while not saying "Look at me."

"I don't want to call attention to myself," I said, "and yet I want to make an impression so people will talk to me, spill some dirt so to speak, if that's not disrespectful."

"You're trying to find Guido's murderer," she said. "How much more respectful can you be?"

"If only everyone saw it that way," I replied ruefully.

"Here's something," Dolce said, going to the rack of new fall dresses. It was a simple, long-sleeved black sheath from Tahari that hit me right below the knees. For a moment I was shocked. It fit perfectly, but it was almost ordinary. That's when Dolce pulled out a bold (there she went again) metallic faux-fur jacket from Kate Spade. I tried it on, and she clapped her hands in delight.

"I knew it," she said. "With black gloves and sunglasses to hide your puffy eyes from crying, you'll be sensational. I know, you're not going to cry, but no one has to know that.

"And after the funeral, another day perhaps," she said, "you can wear the jacket with skinny leather pants and a tank top. How cool!"

"You really think . . ."

"I do," she said. "I think it's sensational. Wait until our detective sees you. I think I know what the verdict will be— too gorgeous to be guilty."

"So he'll drop all previous charges?" I asked her as I walked around the shop in what I hoped was a runway strut just to see what it felt like.

"Only guilty of looking fabulous," she said.

"What about you?" I asked, feeling guilty for focusing on myself so much.

"I'll wear my old black suit. It's classic, and I'm not there to impress anyone. I just want to blend in and fade into the woodwork."

"And keep your ears open."

"Will do," she promised, and then we were off in a cab to the classic Italian church, with its twin spires and gleaming white stone exterior, in the heart of North Beach. It was so Italian it was once known only as La Chiesa de Italia de Ovest.

Standing at the entrance, Jack was dressed appropriately in a timeless, elegant black Italian suit, by Boggi if I wasn't mistaken, a Versace silk striped tie and polished Calvin Klein slip-on dress shoes.

"Good to see you, Rita," he said solemnly. "You look very nice. You too, Dolce."

I looked better than nice in my feathery faux-fur jacket and sunglasses. I knew it. He knew it too. I could tell from the way he was looking at me. It gave me a warm glow under the faux fur.

"I wouldn't miss it," I said. "Nothing like an Italian funeral for tradition, last rites, prayers, mass, remarks and all that. Last chance to see Guido. Or . . . I mean, is he, um, available for viewing?" I stammered.

"I believe so," he said. "It looks like an open coffin."

"Good," I said to myself. I wanted to see him, and most of all I wanted to see who else wanted to see him either to pay their respects or to be sure he was dead. Who would it be?

"I thought maybe you'd come for the reception and the food afterward," he suggested.

"Well, there is that. I was glad to hear they were holding it at my cooking school."

Dolce and I proceeded inside where we sat in the back so we could watch everyone come in. "Tell me if you see anyone who looks suspicious," I whispered to Dolce.

"What do you mean?" she asked, craning her neck to watch the mourners arriving.

"Someone who looks overly upset, like they're putting

on an act," I whispered. "Or someone who looks too happy, like they're really not sad at all. Or someone who looks nervous, like they're worried they'll be accused of murder."

Dolce nodded as if she understood. "Some people are going up to look at his body," she said to me.

My heart started to flutter. I thought I'd have no problem surveying the corpse, but now that I was within walking distance of the coffin, I wondered if I could handle it.

"What's wrong?" Dolce asked. "You look pale."

"Nothing. I'm fine. It's just . . ."

"Nervous?"

"A little. I mean, it's not like it's my first funeral, my first open casket. But . . ."

"Do you want me to come with you?" she asked.

"Do you want to?"

"Not really. But I will. I mean, I should. But I'll go up by myself and have a look first. You stay here. I'll just see how he looks and be right back."

I nodded. Sometimes I didn't understand Dolce at all. But a dead body can have a weird effect on the most normal people. Which was why I stood watching while Dolce strode purposefully up to the open casket. She stood there for a long moment, then turned and walked back. Her face was pale and her eyes wide.

"What's wrong?" I asked. "Are you okay?"

"I'm shocked," she said.

"I can see that. I should have gone with you."

"No, I had to do it by myself. To see for myself . . ."

"To see what?"

"If it was him. The man who came into the shop last week. And it was. It was him. It was while you were out to lunch."

My mouth fell open. "You didn't say anything."

"I had nothing to say. He came in and asked for advice. What to give the woman who has everything. I asked how well he knew her. He said very well. I suggested a set of gold and diamond bangle bracelets, a Josie Natori charmeuse silk robe or a pair of Pineider leather gloves, but he said nothing was quite right or good enough, he said it had to be perfect or else . . ."

"Or else what? The woman would be angry," I said, my mind spinning with this information. "So angry she might kill him. But who was she? Someone who's here today?" I looked around the room as if someone would stand out as the murderer.

"He didn't say who she was. He finally left without buying anything except an imported handkerchief with lilies of the valley hand embroidered on the edges." She shivered as if a cold breeze had blown in.

I didn't blame Dolce for falling apart. It was creepy to look at a dead body whether you knew him as a customer or not. But I had to do it. "Sit down and rest," I told her. "I'll be right back." I stood and walked slowly up the aisle to the front of the church where Guido was lying. There were two women standing there.

"Solid poplar, if I'm not mistaken," said the woman in a hat with a veil.

"That's fitting."

"How do you mean?"

"Grow fast but they don't last long. They usually use the wood to make cardboard boxes."

"That's not good."

"White crepe lining, very tasteful," her friend said.

"It makes me sad to think of what happened," said the

woman with the veil. She sniffed and pulled a handkerchief from her purse. I almost lurched forward and demanded to know, what happened? Or I could have snatched the hankie out of her hand. How many women use handkerchiefs? Was this the one with the hand-embroidered flowers? I couldn't tell. Before I could do anything, they left. I watched them walk back to find their seats, thinking they were so cool they might have killed Guido. But why? Because the hand-kerchief wasn't good enough? Because she expected a diamond bracelet from the famous chef?

Now alone, I swallowed hard and forced myself to look down at Guido. He was dressed formally in a Calvin Klein tuxedo with a black tie and vest.

From behind me the voice of Jack Wall said, "What do you think of the tux?"

He joined me at the coffin, and I took a deep breath before I answered. "I don't know. If I was a chef, I'd want to be buried in my toque and apron. That's what he was wearing when I last saw him."

"What about you?" Jack asked.

"What was I wearing?"

"What would you want to be buried in?" he asked.

"I feel like we've had this conversation at another funeral."

"It's possible," he admitted. "What do you want to talk about?"

"Clothes, of course. I would choose something simple," I said. "But not black. Maybe a wool dress by Missoni in dark green. I've been told that green brings out the flecks in my hazel eyes."

He stared into my eyes, and I felt my knees weaken. It could have been the overwhelming cloying scent of the flowers banked at the altar, or it could have been the look in his eyes, so dark, so intense. Even in ordinary, off-the-shelf clothes Jack would be more attractive than any officer of the law had a right to be. But today he looked especially disturbingly sexy.

"On the other hand," I said trying to stay on subject, "my eyes would be closed, so . . ."

"I assume you'd want people to say, 'What an unusual choice. Is it Marc Jacobs or Alexander Wang? No, wait a minute, it's Missoni.'"

Amazing how well the man knew me and my taste in clothes when I didn't really know him at all. "Is that wrong to want to be noticed at your own funeral? If not then, when?"

"Not wrong at all," he said. "I wouldn't expect any less from you."

I had a vision of myself lying in my coffin in a Georgette water-washed maxi dress from Nicole Miller, simple but elegant. Note to self: be sure to leave instructions to next of kin. So many people don't think ahead, as I did.

"I seem to remember your saying you wanted to have a brass band marching, playing 'When the Saints Go Marching In.' Have you changed your mind?" I asked Jack.

"That's what I want when we march through the streets of the city. But later at the cemetery . . ." He paused and looked thoughtful. But I didn't see him looking at Guido. Too disturbing? Maybe he wasn't as tough as he pretended.

"How about 'Nearer My God to Thee'?" I suggested.

"Why not?" he said.

I looked over my shoulder. "I wonder why no one else is coming up to view the body. Is it because you're here?"

"Could be. I have that effect on people."

"Even out of uniform and in plain clothes you are shunned? Not that your clothes are ever plain. Is your suit Fendi, D and G, or Bocci?"

"You're close," he said, but he didn't divulge the designer. I thought I was more than close, I had hit the nail on the head. But Jack wouldn't acknowledge it.

"Any luck finding the, uh, murderer?"

"I have some suspects."

I assumed he included me in his list.

I glanced at Guido, this time studying his face for a clue to his untimely demise. He looked so calm and peaceful I couldn't believe he'd died a violent death at someone else's hand.

"Hard to believe there's a bullet in his heart," I said. "Or is there? Did you find it?"

"How do you know about the bullet?" he asked.

"Just a lucky guess," I said breezily. "So where is it? If it's still in his heart, you're not going to let them bury him, are you?"

"Don't worry about it, Rita," he said curtly.

Okay, I would take another approach. "Have you given any more thought to my suicide theory?"

"More thought? How could I give it any thought at all when it's patently ridiculous."

I flushed angrily at the way he put down my ideas. "Fine," I said. "I will keep my suspicions and findings to myself."

"Forget about your suspicions and your findings," he said sternly. "Don't you have anything else to do?"

"As a matter of fact . . ."

I was about to remind him of my demanding sales job at Dolce's plus any upcoming self-improvement classes I might take, when two men in Bianco Brioni suits and sunglasses came up and kissed Guido on the forehead. Brothers? Father and son? I stepped back and watched. So did Jack. The two men muttered something in Italian either to each other or to Guido, I wasn't sure. I wished I could speak Italian because if ever there were suspects, these guys were it.

When they walked away, I tugged on Jack's sleeve and said under my breath, "They looked like mobsters or something, don't you think?"

He didn't say anything because at that moment a priest began chanting and altar boys came down the aisle and lighted candles. Jack walked off to the side of the church, and I hurried back to my seat. As I went, I felt many curious eyes on me, wondering who I was, how I was connected to the dead chef, or maybe some thought I was responsible for his murder. Or did they know it was murder? Maybe others like myself had other theories that were being dismissed out of hand by the police.

"What did Detective Wall say?" Dolce whispered when I returned to my seat.

I couldn't answer because the woman in front of us turned and shushed us. I was glad I was hiding behind my sunglasses.

The funeral lasted forever and it was mostly in Italian. My eyelids were so heavy and the atmosphere so heavy with the scent of flowers and so stifling, I almost fell asleep. Finally at the end various people got up to speak. That's when I wished I was in the front row where I could see where Jack had ended up. That way I might be able to read between the lines, so to speak. Some speakers didn't identify themselves and I had to guess. Friend? Relative? Competitor? Partner? Lover?

One woman who spoke was wearing a huge straw hat.

She was tall and thin and wore a vintage seventies royal purple fitted jacket. So much for black, I thought, and good for her for breaking the rules. But who was she, this woman who broke down at the end and cried when she talked about Guido? His wife? His mistress? She said she would miss the food Guido cooked for her, the *caponata*, the *panella*, the *maccu* and the *arancini*. It made my mouth water, and I wondered what would be served at the get-together afterward. I knew I was there to figure out who killed Guido, but there was no reason I couldn't eat too.

I made a mental list of the people I wanted to meet at the cooking school reception today, and the woman was at the top of my list, along with the woman with the handkerchief. The next speaker was a man who said Guido had taught him everything he knew. Like how to make *finnochio con sardo* with fresh sardines they caught in the Mediterranean. He raved about how creative and hardworking Guido was. Wiping the tears from his eyes with his handkerchief, he shook his head and left the podium.

After he spoke, a heavyset man dressed casually in a fisherman's sweater and baggy pants spoke with an Italian accent. He said he taught Guido everything he knew. That Guido was like a son to him. A man who loved life, food and fun. A man who didn't deserve to die. Then he broke down and had to be helped back to his seat.

I was confused. Who was the real Guido? A top-of-the-line celebrity chef followed around by sycophants? A man hated and envied by his peers? A fun-loving bon vivant who loved life, or a man who deserved to die because he did what? How was I going to finger a suspect if they *all* cried?

Finally the speeches were over and a woman wearing a dark brown Trina Turk sweater dress that hit just above the

knees and a pair of Christian Louboutin patent leather platform pumps approached me and asked where I got my
jacket. I was flattered, because her outfit was very conservative, very appropriate and very chic at the same time.
Whereas mine was a little bit out there. Not the dress of
course, but the jacket.

I took the opportunity to put in a word for Dolce's and
told her that many of the women in the room were wearing
Dolce fashions. She accepted my business card, which I
retrieved from my Kristin metallic leather hobo, and promised she'd come and see me at the shop.

When I asked how she knew Guido, she said she'd hired
him a few times to do her dinner parties and they were fabulous. I was envious. I would never be rich enough to afford
a chef. Even for a special occasion. The alternative was to
learn to cook, which I had tried. I knew learning to cook
would be a good addition to my attributes, but I didn't have
the time or energy to concentrate on it. I'd given one dinner
party, which turned out well, but afterward I was exhausted.
Otherwise, I was happy to have someone else cook for me,
like the Italians at the pizza place. It was time to stop waiting around for the men in my life to provide food for me.
But there was nothing wrong with reaching out to them to
let them know I was available.

Maybe today was a turning point. Maybe facing the death
of someone I knew would cause me to embrace life and look
for a new direction.

First I had to get this murder solved or I'd be spend-
ing all my time defending myself instead of finding the
new me. Meera was still on my suspect list. It was all I could
do to keep my mouth shut and not tell Jack about her.
One, he probably wouldn't take my theory seriously, and

two, I wanted to get credit for solving this crime myself. If there was a crime. I still liked the possibility of a suicide. No one had spoken of Guido's state of mind, but his buying that handkerchief didn't sound like a man ready to kill himself. I intended to sound out his confidantes after this funeral.

Dolce and I hopped in a taxi for the ride to Tante Marie's Cooking School on Potrero Hill. We were greeted at the door by a young woman wearing an apron over a dark dress. She didn't look one bit sad; in fact, she smiled brightly and welcomed us. Maybe she was the hired help for the day and had no connection to Guido.

"Have you been here before?" she asked when I commented on the tables set up around the room and a large banner that said "Farewell Guido—Buon Viaggio!" That was a nice touch. When I was last there, the chairs were set up facing the stove and the oven.

"I took a class from Guido," I said.

"Just one?" she asked.

"I wanted to take more," I said. I didn't explain how I had trouble following through on plans. The fewer people who knew that about me, the better. Although I was planning on changing. "But something came up."

She looked at me as if she knew my type. One cooking class, one knitting lesson, one swimming class at the Y, one workout at the health club and then I lost interest and moved on.

"But enough about me," I said. "Are you . . ."

"I'm Guido's niece," she said. "Maria Natali. My father Eduardo is also a chef. He'll be taking over the school."

"He teaches cooking as well?"

"He used to. They ran a school in Tuscany together, then

they split up and my father opened a restaurant here in San Francisco. Eduardo's."

"Is he here?" I asked.

"No, he has a banquet at the restaurant today," she said.

Dolce and I exchanged a look. He didn't come to his brother's funeral because of a banquet? Wasn't that strange?

I knew Eduardo's had been written up as a tiny gem of a restaurant serving expensive and out-of-this-world food, impossible to get a reservation unless you knew someone. So they said. I wondered if that was just a PR gambit. Maybe I'd give it a try just to see. Just as soon as I won the lottery.

"How amazing that they both ended up here in San Francisco in the food business," I said.

"Not so amazing. Their mother was a fantastic cook. At least that's what they say, and they use her recipes even today."

Two brothers, both in the same profession. I pictured them fighting over rights to the recipes. I smelled jealousy, envy, hatred and competition, even though I had no evidence. I had so many questions for Maria, but a crush of mourners were behind us at the door, waiting to get in. Dolce nudged me with her elbow, and we went into the large room where aromas of simmering sauces and roasting meats made my mouth water. My kind of funeral.

Five

·····························

Dolce was looking at a display of menus and recipes on the wall and I was heading for the buffet table when I noticed a tall graceful woman in a black pillbox hat with a silver metallic trim from the Shenor collection. She was dressed impeccably in a classic black Juicy Couture tropical wool jacket with a Roxy high-waisted pencil skirt and pair of T-strap Chanel booties. All of which looked familiar, which meant she was a Dolce's shopper. I told her who I was, and she smiled brightly.

"Rita," she said. "I can't believe we've never met at Dolce's. I'm Diana Van Sloat."

I couldn't believe we'd never met either. Dolce adored Diana and vice versa. According to my boss, Diana was super rich, super high society and super nice. Diana had been Dolce's numero uno client for ages. When times were tough, Diana had kept buying and bringing her friends into Dolce's to buy their clothes. She was still a regular customer but lately had been ordering outfits she saw in *Vogue* from Dolce over the phone. Which might explain why I hadn't ever met her in person before.

"Can you believe who's here today? Almost the whole town," Diana gushed. She proceeded to point out the city's various movers and shakers. Though in reality Diana Van Sloat was the biggest name there, at least in terms of the top level of San Francisco society. The Van Sloat family had arrived in California around the horn by boat from Holland after the gold rush. They'd given away tons of the money they'd made on everything from gold to real estate. They'd funded the major museums and contributed to the opera and the symphony. And not surprisingly, they'd hired the best chef they could find—Guido.

"Guido was the real deal, wasn't he?" I said. "Without the big ego that some other top chefs have, or so I hear."

She nodded emphatically. "Absolutely. I learned so much from just watching him. I don't know what we'll do without him, which is what I told the detective. I hear he's interviewing all Guido's contacts. Does that mean you too?"

"I've spoken with Detective Wall," I said. Was Jack really interviewing everyone who ever took a class or hired Guido to cook for them?

"So you took one class with him and that's all?" Diana asked.

"That's right." I tried to think of a good excuse. "I got busy at work. And I'm really sorry I had to drop out. I hope I didn't hurt Guido's feelings." Yeah, I was sure Guido had his plate full of San Francisco's richest patrons and had no reason to even know I was missing. "No time to cook or to take classes."

"That's too bad. Dolce's told me so much about you. How imaginative you are. What a great salesperson. I wonder if you'd be interested in my jewelry design workshop. Just a few good friends getting together to do something creative. But if you don't have time . . ."

Jewelry design? Diana was now a jewelry designer? I glanced at the pearl and amber choker she was wearing. "The necklace you're wearing is beautiful."

"You like it? I made it from some old pieces I had and never wore. I bet you have a drawer full just like I do, gathering dust." She laughed lightly. "Not that I'm gathering dust. Not yet. But my jewelry is."

A drawer full of jewelry just like hers? I didn't think so. "I'm all thumbs and I'm afraid I'd be terrible at it. Besides, what with working full-time . . ."

I wished I could say I was a brain surgeon and had no time for luxuries like jewelry making, but she knew perfectly well what I was. Even if she didn't know, I didn't look like a brain surgeon in my faux-fur jacket. But then again, even doctors don't wear scrubs all the time.

"We're all busy at something," she said. "I do volunteer work when I can. This fall I'm a docent at the zoo. I take groups to see the primates."

"How interesting," I said. First the jewelry, now I hear she is a docent at the zoo too. I felt like a slug by comparison.

"Onward and upward," she said with a cheerful smile. "If you can't make the jewelry workshop, why not join me at the zoo? Do you like animals? I'll give you the VIP tour. The baboons are such fun."

"I'd love to," I said. It was better for me to join her tour instead of signing up to make diamond and pearl necklaces. But enough of this interesting digression into Diana's life consisting of jewelry and primates, I was there for only one purpose, besides eating, of course. "Were you surprised when you heard about Guido being murdered?" I asked. "Or did he give you some kind of clue someone was after him? Did he seem nervous or anxious the last time you saw him?"

"Not at all," she said. "That's what the police asked me. They've been asking everyone. All of us, like those women over there. They're each holding Guido's cookbooks in their hands as a sign of respect. Of course I'm surprised. We're all surprised. Everyone adored Guido. Not just here but out there." She waved her hand toward the outdoors. By which I assumed she meant out there in the big wide world.

I looked at the group of four women all dressed appropriately in black. I thought I recognized them even though they all looked alike, each one holding a cookbook. Maybe the books were autographed.

"You say you've already spoken to the detective," she said. "The one standing over there by the door."

"Yes, just briefly."

"I don't know if this is de rigueur, but he wanted to know if I had any information, any sense of whether Guido had any enemies, anyone in the class who acted suspicious."

"And did you?" I asked.

"Not really. Except . . ."

I leaned forward. "Yes?"

"Well, one night a woman was in our class who definitely had an ax to grind. Everything he said, she challenged. If he said use unsalted butter in the sauce, she said what was the point if you salt the sauce anyway? She disagreed with everything he said. Finally he asked her to leave. She muttered something and stalked out. With people like that, you never know what's on their mind. Oh, there she is now."

I whirled around to see Meera with a frown on her face, chewing on something. "Oh no," I murmured. "I should have known."

"You know her?"

"Sort of," I said. "Did you mention this incident to the detective?"

"No, but I think I'll do it now while she's here."

I didn't know what to do. Make excuses for Meera, or let her get what was coming to her. A full-scale investigation. That was what she deserved. I excused myself and went to see Meera. As usual she was dressed in full Victorian garb: the high collar, the long sleeves, gloves and a matching hat with a veil. Why hadn't she told me about this incident?

"What are you doing here?" I asked.

"Paying my respects, of course," she said. "As I told you, I knew him rather well."

"I hear you had a set-to with him during one of his classes here. You didn't tell me about that."

"I don't tell you everything. I don't tell anyone everything. Nor should you. Everyone has to have a few secrets," she said. "It's no secret I had my problems with Guido."

"More problems than his stealing your recipes?"

"Isn't that enough?" she asked.

I decided to change the subject. If she killed Guido, she wasn't going to tell me.

"What do you think of the food?" I asked, glancing at her plate full of various antipasto items. Marinated artichoke hearts, prosciutto with melon, fresh mozzarella, roasted peppers and what looked like homemade garlic bread with tomato relish and cold shrimp.

"It's all right for an Italian funeral. But you should see a Romanian funeral if you want good food." She shook her finger at me and added, "But don't expect to attend mine."

Did she mean because she was a vampire and didn't intend to die? Or because I wouldn't be invited? I didn't ask. Instead, I left her and went to the table and filled my plate with some of the same delicious-looking food Meera had eaten but found lacking compared to Romanian dishes. In addition, I added some thinly sliced Genoa salami with Cacio di Roma cheese.

"Who is that woman in the long dress?" a man in a dark suit asked me as he reached for a stuffed artichoke. His eyebrows were raised at Meera and her unusual attire.

"She's a Romanian . . ." I almost said "Romanian vampire," but I caught myself in time.

"Friend of Guido's, of course," he said, looking over my shoulder in Meera's direction. "He collected the most unusual people, like your friend there."

"You mean in his classes," I suggested. I didn't want to explain that Meera was not Guido's friend at all. Not only that, there might be others here who were not friends. I wanted to know exactly who they were. That was why I was here: to find someone who hated him enough to shoot him.

"Everywhere. You know, he played Briscola down at the Italian Men's Club. That's where I met him. Hell of a card player."

"I suppose he was very popular there," I said. Please tell me about his enemies. Tell me someone threatened to kill him for cheating at cards. No, don't tell me, tell Detective Wall.

"Very popular," the man said. "He liked hanging out with the old-timers, and he always brought along some homemade biscotti to eat with coffee. Look around and you'll see the club members everywhere. I'm Lorenzo, by the way."

"Rita Jewel," I answered, and I set my plate down to shake his hand.

"You're not Italian, are you?" he asked me. "Jewel is *bigiu* in Italian."

"I'm not Italian, but I admire Italian food. I took a class with Guido. Wish I'd taken more. If I'd known . . ."

"That's the way, isn't it? If we only knew when we were going to die . . ."

"Guido sure didn't," I said. Or did he? Was that why he looked so nervous that night? Had he given me a clue and I'd missed it?

"I can't believe he was murdered." Lorenzo shook his head, his eyes wide with disbelief. Maybe a little too wide, I thought. As if he knew but didn't want me to know that he knew.

"That's what I heard."

"Il mio dio, quanto terrible," he muttered. "Let me get you a glass of wine." He turned and joined another man at the bar they'd set up next to the kitchen. The other man said something, then he looked straight at me. Why? Because of something I'd said? I wondered if they were talking about me, wondering if I'd killed Guido or wondering if I knew that they'd killed him.

When yet another Italian, an old guy named Antonio with steel gray hair and shiny black shoes, came up to ask me to contribute to a scholarship fund in Guido's name, I told him I'd be glad to. As if I was some kind of philanthropic type who had gobs of money to spare. Maybe my designer outfit made him think I was part of the moneyed crowd. "I had only one class from Guido," I said. "What about you?"

"He wanted us to take his classes, but never had the time," Antonio said. "I'm in the undertaker business. Never a dull moment."

"Really? Then you prepared his body?"

He nodded. "What did you think? Did I do a good job or not for my friend?"

"He looked good, but I was wondering, what about the bullet in his heart?" I didn't know if there was a bullet in his heart, but how else was I going to find out unless I put it out there?

"How'd your hear about that?" he asked.

"I, I don't know." I shrugged. "Word gets out. Such a shame. He was too young to die. Too talented."

"Well, the bullet's still there for all I know."

"But don't the police want it?"

"They do, but the family is protesting. They don't want him cut into."

"Even though he's already dead?"

"People are funny about death," he said with a sigh. "The stories I could tell you. But it made things easier for me. You interested in the undertaking business? More women should go into it. You know, when a woman dies they want another woman to prepare the remains. My family's been in the business for years. But my wife wouldn't touch a body. So there you have it."

I nodded as if I understood. I did understand. I wouldn't touch a dead body. I didn't even like looking at Guido in his coffin, and I was afraid I would have nightmares tonight.

"I don't blame her," I said. "I was wondering who's going to take over Guido's cooking schools in Italy and all of his TV gigs. He had a certain flair that made him stand out from all those other celebrity chefs."

"If you ask me, it's one of those two." The man pointed to a man and a woman in the far corner gesturing wildly to each other in true Italian style.

"I never know if Italians are arguing or just talking," I said. If they were arguing, maybe it had something to do with Guido's legacy or who was getting the blame for his death. If only I was a little closer, I might be able to hear them, although, except from their gestures, they looked like they were speaking Italian.

"Then you're not Italian," he said.

"But I love Italian food," I said. "And my last name translated into Italian is *bigiu*." Actually I loved all food, which was lucky for me. Then I took a deep breath. I was tired of making small talk; as pleasant as it was to chat and eat, I had to make some progress. I knew from experience and reading that the murderer is often a friend or someone who knew the victim very well, so didn't it stand to reason that the man or woman was here in this room? I couldn't leave without at least trying to find out who it was. Someone in this room knew. Someone at least had a suspicion. And I didn't mean Jack. Jack thought I'd done it. How preposterous was that?

"Tell me," I said, "who do you think killed Guido?"

He stepped back for a second as if I'd spoken the unspeakable. But why? Why wasn't everyone else talking about it? Was it wrong?

"You mean . . ." he said.

"I mean everyone knows he was murdered," I said. Why beat around the bush when it was common knowledge. Or was it?

"Do they?" he said. "But why? That's what I keep asking myself. He was such a good guy. Not your usual full-of-himself star. Everyone liked him. Who would want to kill Guido?"

"He must have had some enemies," I said. "Maybe someone who was competing with him? Someone with another cooking school, one of the other iron chefs or Food Network stars?"

"Non possibile," he said, giving me a dark look as if he didn't know what I was talking about, and then he walked away looking at least slightly offended. But that didn't stop me. I was determined to talk to as many people here as I could whether they were in denial or not. I was glad when Dolce found me. I needed a break from crime solving. She said she'd had some wonderful tiramisu, that traditional Italian cake. "Here, have a bite," she said.

"I don't think I'm ready for dessert yet," I said. But I couldn't resist tasting the traditional cake made of sweetened mascarpone cheese, ladyfingers, chocolate and coffee.

"It's wonderful," I said, "like heaven in your mouth."

"I told you," Dolce said, licking her lips. "Have you found out anything?" She looked over her shoulder to make sure no one was listening.

"I found out that everyone loved Guido—at least his students and his friends did. And I heard that everyone, including your best customer Diana Van Sloat, has been questioned."

"What?" Dolce said. "I didn't know that. Why Diana? She loved Guido. What possible motive . . ."

"I guess Guido being a high-profile personality, they are going beyond the pale. But I don't know about how far they've gone with his family. And then there's Meera. Surely she'll be hauled down to the station, if she keeps blabbing about how much she disliked Guido."

"The Romanian."

"Yes, she said he stole her recipes."

"So you're thinking maybe she's the killer."

"Maybe," I said. "But it's so obvious. That's not the way it works. It's always the person you least suspect."

"Well?" Dolce said.

"I have no idea who that might be, but I heard there are two people in this room who are taking over his classes in Italy. The thing is, they were probably in Italy when Guido was murdered." I looked around, scanning the room for suspects. "I'm not leaving this event until I do have a better idea. Somebody here knows something. I just know it. I'd give anything to know what Detective Wall is thinking at this moment. Look at him standing at the bar with a glass of dark red wine. He looks pensive, don't you think?"

"Maybe he's already solved the case," Dolce suggested.

"Maybe, but I'll be damned if I'll ask him," I said.

"What can I do?" Dolce asked. "Besides eating too much of this delicious food."

"Keep your ears open," I said quietly. "Who stands to benefit from Guido's death? Who inherits this place, for example?" I looked around. It was a nice place, but it was hardly the Cordon Bleu. Was it worth murdering for? Or was it something else that Guido had?

"But is money always the motive for murder?" Dolce asked as if I were some kind of expert. I guess after helping solve two murders in my recent past, maybe I was.

"Usually," I said. "Although there's also power, love, possessions."

"Possessions, like a cooking school or a famous recipe," Dolce said, "that someone wanted to get their hands on."

"Would you kill for this place?" I asked her.

She shook her head. "Not for a cooking school or the recipe for veal scallopini. But a boutique would be different."

"Your aunt died of natural causes, didn't she?" I asked. Not that I thought Dolce would have offed her aunt to get control of the shop.

"I was halfway across the country when she died, but I believe that pneumonia was the cause."

"What about revenge, anger and self-defense?" I suggested.

"Don't forget cheating or insanity," she added. "All popular motives."

"Sometimes I wonder if Meera is insane," I said. "You know she claims to be a vampire."

"She's definitely odd," Dolce said. "I notice your detective friend seems to be getting around." We both looked across the room to see he was now talking to Guido's Italian relatives.

"The Italians," I murmured. "Is that who he thinks did it? I need to spend more time with them. Maybe they had some unfinished business from the old country. All kinds of family disputes last for generations."

"You're right," she said. "I've seen a few movies about that. They carry grudges from generation to generation and on. It could be some motive we would never understand. Why don't you forget this murder and let Detective Wall handle it?" she asked. "It's probably more complicated than we think. Imagine Diana being called to testify. What could he be thinking?" She shook her head. "Come on, have something to eat and let the detective do his work. You're a fashion consultant, Rita, and a darned good one. You don't need to help the police. Especially if they don't appreciate your help."

"Did Jack Wall tell you to say that?" I asked. For all I knew, she and Jack had been talking about me behind my back today. I knew Dolce only meant to stop me from acting foolish and overstepping my boundaries, but I don't like to be told what to do outside of work, even by my beloved boss.

"Not exactly," she said. "Well, he may have said something along those lines."

"You can tell the detective for me that I'm not doing anything illegal or immoral. Instead of telling me to butt out of this business, he ought to be grateful to me. Never mind, I'll tell him myself," I said. I turned around and scanned the room, but he was nowhere in sight.

All day I'd seen him out of the corner of my eye either silently surveying the place or working the room, moving from group to group like just another casual mourner, no doubt picking up valuable pieces of information. Maybe he was getting ready to make an arrest, while I was moving in slow motion, learning practically nothing important. Why should I care if he was about to arrest someone as long as it wasn't me? Then I could go back to my real life, getting some modest exercise and selling clothes to the upper classes. But deep down I wanted to show him I could figure out a difficult problem like who killed Guido, and win his respect.

After a second glass of Prosecco, I gathered my courage and went up to the woman in the big hat who was holding a glass in her hand just as I was. "My name is Rita Jewel—that's *bigiu* in Italian," I said.

"Yes, I know," she said.

I didn't know if she meant she knew who I was or she knew what "jewel" was in Italian.

"Are you named for Saint Rita?" she asked.

"Probably, although I'm no saint," I added, in case she hadn't heard.

"I am Gianna."

I said I was happy to meet her, and then my mind went blank. I had questions to ask her, but what were they? Why did I think I could find out anything? Why did I bother? Jack was right: he was the expert. He'd been trained as a detective. I hadn't been trained as anything except as a sales-girl by Dolce.

"I just want to say how sorry I am for your loss," I said finally, even though I didn't know exactly who she was or how big a loss it was. "I took a class from Guido, and I thought he was charming."

"That's what people say," she said, "who didn't really know him."

I thought that was a pretty shocking thing to say at a funeral. Or didn't I understand? Or maybe she didn't under-stand. From her accent I knew she must be Italian, so I guessed she must be a family member. "Did you know him well?" I asked.

"I was married to him."

"I see," I said. So that's the connection. "I understand all the great chefs are temperamental."

"Have you ever been married?"

"You mean to a chef?" I asked.

"To anyone."

"No, I haven't."

She gave me a piercing look. I didn't know what it meant,

maybe that she wasn't surprised to hear that because from the way I looked I didn't have a chance at marriage. And she didn't even know me. Or maybe her look said it was good that I wasn't married because it's not an easy state to be in. And another thing, how many husbands would want their wives to wear an expensive feathered jacket to a funeral as I did? Us single girls can wear whatever we want and go anywhere we want, I thought. But that was just me being smug.

"Are you just here for the funeral?" I asked politely, though what I really wanted to know was, had she been here when Guido died and was she, by any chance, the one who'd killed him?

"I plan to stay a few days, but I came to see his body, to be sure he was really dead," she said.

"You don't mean you thought he might be a vampire," I said with a smile to indicate how ridiculous that was.

"No, but there's a woman here who told me she is."

"I think I might know who you mean," I said. "Is she wearing a long dress?"

"That's her," she said, pointing at Meera, who was holding a small plate in her hand filled with food. I thought she didn't like Italian food.

"Do you have any idea who might have killed your husband?"

"Ex-husband," she said. "It could have been anyone. He had more than a few enemies. That's why he left Italy."

"Oh," I said. I had to say I was shocked to hear it, although maybe that was just her opinion. "But I guess all those enemies are still in Italy, so they couldn't have killed him."

"I couldn't say," she said.

I wanted to say "Go ahead and say," but I didn't. I wanted her to give me a list of those enemies, but she didn't. Maybe because she was on the list too. And maybe she'd arrived in town earlier than she'd suggested. Early enough to have offed her ex so she could collect an inheritance? I looked at her, trying to picture her with a gun in hand, until she stared back at me. I then turned my gaze to the other people in the room with a new perspective. I was looking for an Italian who hated Guido for some reason but who had definitely been here the night he died.

"If you ask me who I thought killed Guido, as your detective did, I would say it was someone in his class. Someone who stepped up and asked too many questions."

Meera, I thought to myself.

"Guido didn't like to be challenged in front of the class by anyone. Or perhaps it was some married woman he was seeing and had a problem with. Maybe you haven't seen that side of Guido."

No, I certainly hadn't. "Are you saying he was a player, romancing his students on the side?"

She laughed a mirthless laugh but didn't answer.

"Where did you get your unusual jacket?" she asked in an effort to change the subject, which was fine with me. I loved talking about clothes instead of murder.

I took her question as a compliment, and I told her about Dolce's. "You'll have to drop in while you're in town. We have lots of wonderful clothes."

"I might do that," she said. "Then the trip won't be a complete waste."

"But I thought you came to make sure Guido was dead."

"That's right. But now that I'm here, I might as well make the best of it and do some shopping. Everything is much cheaper than in Florence." She gazed around the room. "For example, those Matteo and Massimo alligator-skin shoes on that gentleman over there." She nodded her head toward a man standing by the window. "Do you know how much they cost?"

I shook my head.

"Twice as much in Italy, I can assure you."

I didn't want to discourage her from shopping at Dolce's where she would surely find bargains compared to Italy, but maybe she should head for the mall instead for less-expensive clothing options. But I gave her my card anyway. For all I knew, she was rich enough to buy out the store and I'd get some points for steering her our way.

I thought this part of the funeral was simply Meet and Greet and Eat, but a few minutes later the Briscola-playing friend of Guido's clapped his hands, tapped his glass with a spoon and took the stage where Guido had once given his classes.

"Ciao," he said. "Everyone raise a glass to our friend Guido. As we say in the old country, *"Oggi in figura, domani in sepoltura."*

A voice in my ear translated for me. "Today in person, tomorrow in grave."

I turned to see it was Jack. "I didn't know you knew Italian," I said.

"Only a few phrases," he said. Which I didn't believe for a minute. I'd bet my aunt's antique jewelry collection he knew more than he'd ever let on. "But it comes in handy."

I'll just bet it does, I thought, but I kept my mouth shut for once.

Six

::::::::::::::::::

There were still more toasts, and then I was suddenly exhausted. There had to be even more information for me to find out, but I didn't know who or what to ask. Maybe it was the wine, maybe it was the food or the effort of concentrating, but after circling the room one last time, I'd had enough.

"Having a good time?" Jack stepped in front of me just when I was eyeing the door, wondering if it was time to go. He had a way of anticipating people's actions, which is why he was such a good detective.

"Wonderful time," I said. "Nothing like a funeral. But I have to leave."

"Learn anything?" he asked me.

"I learned that I have a lot more to learn. First on my list is to have dinner at Eduardo's where Guido's brother works. Have you been there?" I did not want to share what I'd learned from Guido's ex-wife. Or from Maria, Guido's niece.

If I said the ex-wife was suspicious, Jack would counter that she wasn't in the country at the time of his death, but how did he know? Had he checked the passenger list from Alitalia? Or did he take her word for it? If I were a detective, I'd look behind every stone for clues.

"That up-scale place downtown? No, I haven't. Why don't we go together?"

"Well . . ." If I went with Jack, he'd take credit for the clues we'd uncover, the suspects we'd meet and the information we'd gather. On the other hand, if he was paying . . . "All right. When? I hear it's hard to get reservations."

"Let's go tomorrow. I'll see if I can pull some strings."

"What does that mean, you'll use your police credentials to get us a table?"

"Don't worry about it. I'll be going undercover, so I'd appreciate it if you'd treat it as a date, an ordinary evening out."

"I'm not sure I know what that is," I said. An ordinary evening out with Jack? It wasn't possible. Never happened before and probably would never happen again unless . . . "You're using me, aren't you? You think I'll play the role of your date when I'm really just a foil."

"I hear the food is excellent," he said.

"Oh, all right," I said. "I'll go."

"Good," he said. "Now what else did you learn today?"

"Not much. What about you?" I waited expectantly for him to make some offhand comment and then walk away.

"Most people say they liked Guido," he said.

I couldn't believe he thought that was news. "Sure, they would say that," I said. "Isn't it wrong to say anything bad about the dead, especially at their funeral?"

"You mean *de mortuis nil nisi bonum*?"

As usual he'd one-upped me. "I didn't know you spoke Latin."

"I don't. I read it somewhere. A short story, or maybe it was *Lawrence of Arabia*."

"I assume you've had a few occasions to use it, being in the detective line of work," I said.

"I've been saving it to impress you," he said with a half smile.

I tried to roll my eyes to indicate my disbelief, but maybe he meant it. So I'd impressed Jack? Really? On that note I said good-bye and headed for the door where Dolce was waiting for me.

Fortunately there were a couple of cabs in front of the place, so we got into one and headed back to the shop. On the way I checked my phone messages, and this is what I heard from Dr. Jonathan Rhodes:

"Rita," he said. "You won't believe this, but I'm at home sick today. I mean, I can't believe: I have gallstones. I'll never lecture my patients again for complaining. Because it hurts. I'm in agony." He moaned loudly. "Give me a call. I've never been sick before and I'm going crazy. I need a distraction. Can you possibly come by?"

"Oh my God," I said to Dolce after listening to the message. "You won't believe this. My doctor is sick and he wants to see me."

"Poor Jonathan," she murmured. "You can't turn him down."

I punched in the number of his cell phone. "Hello?" he said, sounding groggy.

"It's Rita," I said. "What are gallstones?"

"They're small stones, about the size of a pebble, and they're located in the gallbladder."

"I thought so," I said. "But how did you get them?"

"I don't know," he said, sounding mournful. "Anybody else, I'd say it was too much cholesterol, but I'm pretty careful about my diet. I'm not overweight and I'm under sixty. I don't get it."

"What are they going to do? Take them out?"

"They've given me an experimental drug to dissolve the stones. If it works, then that's it. I don't want anyone cutting into me, so no surgical procedures. Not while I still have a breath left in me."

"Of course not," I said. But I wondered if he was afraid to go under the knife after what he'd seen in the ER.

"What can I do for you? I can come by and bring something. What can you eat?"

"The nurse told me to eat green soup and beets," he said.

"What?"

"I know, it sounds gross, but that's what she said. She heard about it from the dietitian. She gave me the recipe. The soup has parsley, zucchini, green beans and celery. Blend it up. That's all there is to it."

All there is to it? It sounded terribly complicated. "It really doesn't sound very tasty," I said, "but if that's what you need . . ."

"I need to see a real woman, not a nurse, not a dietician. Someone who wears real clothes, not a uniform."

"That's me," I said modestly. "I'll be over as soon as I can." I was afraid if I hesitated that beautiful blond nurse would beat me to it. She'd slip out of her uniform, and then she'd have an in with the hottest doctor in the city and I'd be out in the cold.

He gave me his address and thanked me, then hung up.

"Dolce, have you ever made a green soup and beets?" I

asked, with a feeling of anxiety in the pit of my stomach. It was my chance to take care of Jonathan, who'd done so much for me, but what a challenge. If I rose to this challenge, maybe he'd figure out a way to make me more a part of his off-time life.

"I don't cook very much," she confessed as the cab let us out in front of the shop. "But it sounds like a strange combination. If you're going to make soup for Jonathan, you'd better leave now. I'll run you to the grocery store."

She assured me she hadn't had that much alcohol to drink at the funeral, so we got into her car and went straight to the Safeway. I headed to the produce section while Dolce waited in the car. She said looking at all those groceries made her feel guilty for not making an effort to cook. With the green ingredients plus a bunch of beets in hand, I was grateful to my boss when she dropped me off at home.

"Rita," she said as I got out of the car, "be sympathetic. Remember, all men are babies when they're sick. Oh, they like to act macho, but deep down they want some TLC. And when he gets well, he won't forget how you came through for him."

I nodded and I wondered how she knew that. I knew so little about her past and even less about sick men. But Jonathan was worth cooking for and showing up when he needed me. He was what my aunt Alyce would call "a good catch." Besides being a doctor, he was really a great guy, kind, generous and caring. Even toward those, like me, who weren't even sick.

Once in my kitchen I spread the vegetables on the counter and stared at them, wondering how in God's name I was going to make a soup. I had no cookbooks. My eyes filled with frustrated tears. Why had I volunteered to make something for Jonathan? I was going to screw it up by giving him something that tasted so bad he wouldn't eat it. What was I thinking?

My doorbell rang. I wiped my eyes and pressed the buzzer. It was Meera. No matter my mixed feelings about her, I had to say I was glad to see her. Once I explained the problem of the green soup and the beets, she whipped out an apron from her large bag and tied it around her waist. Then she chopped up the vegetables, sautéed, blended, heated and seasoned the green soup with little packets she had in her purse. Don't ask me what they were, I have no idea. As for the beets, she roasted them in my oven and doused them with olive oil and vinegar.

"So they don't go together?" I said, pointing to the red beets and the green vegetables.

She shook her head vehemently as if I was too stupid to live or leave alone in the kitchen. Then I called a cab and she and I walked out to the front of my house. I was carrying the large pot of soup and the jar Meera had put the beets in. I offered her a ride, but she said no thanks. She wished me well and Jonathan a speedy recovery.

I never found out why she'd come to my house. If I'd asked, I had a feeling she would have said she knew I needed her. She was right about that.

The cab let me and my pot of soup and jar of beets off at a high-rise apartment building in the SOMA neighborhood. I stepped into the elevator and pressed the button for the tenth floor. The man who got in with me pushed the button for fourteen. He looked vaguely familiar.

"You're the woman from the funeral," he said. "I recognize your jacket."

That was the kind of remark I liked to hear. I knew it was

a stunning, unforgettable jacket. Finally someone had noticed it. I had meant to change clothes, but I hadn't had time. Luckily I hadn't spilled any green soup or red beets on it. Not yet.

"Yes," I said. "Are you a friend of Guido?"

"Was a friend," he said. "You his girlfriend?"

"No, I'm not. I mean, I wasn't. I didn't know he had a girlfriend. Who was she?"

"I don't know. All I know is he was trying to get rid of her."

"Really?" I felt like I'd seen a crack in a stone wall. Finally some decent information. "Why?"

"Oh, you know, the usual reasons."

I wanted to say "No, I don't know the usual reasons." But I didn't get a chance because we arrived at my floor, so I got out.

I found Jonathan's apartment, rang the bell and heard him shout, "Come in." He was lying on a couch, and even in sweatpants and a T-shirt with his spiky surfer-bum hair standing on end, he still looked to die for.

"Rita," he said hoarsely, "thank God you're here."

I set my soup on a small table. "How are you?" I asked, standing at the end of the couch, looking down at his pale face.

Instead of answering, he groaned and said, "Ever have gallstones? No, of course not. Nobody our age has gallstones. Why me?" he asked.

I shrugged helplessly. If he didn't know, how would I know? They say doctors make the worst patients, and maybe they were right, because Jonathan did not like being sick.

I tried to distract him by admiring the apartment, which was definitely upscale with ceiling-to-floor windows that offered great views of the Golden Gate Bridge and the Bay. He said he liked the location, near restaurants, museums and clubs. After recounting his symptoms to me—nausea, vomiting and pain—he finally asked how I was.

"Things are hectic," I said. "The shop is crazy busy, and I had to go to a funeral today."

He shook his head. Maybe I shouldn't have mentioned death to a sick man.

"What's that you brought?" he asked. When I told him, he made a face but agreed that was what he was supposed to eat. He pointed to the kitchen and I went in, found a small pan and heated the green soup.

I went back to the living room and asked, "Do you feel like eating?" I sure didn't.

"No, do you?" he asked.

"Not really. After the funeral, there was a reception at my cooking school."

"Who died?" he asked. "Maybe you told me but my mind is shot along with my gallbladder."

"It was the famous chef I told you about. They had a fabulous spread. All kinds of Italian food, frittata, marinated peppers, mushrooms and a delicious tiramisu."

"Stop," he said. "You're not helping. I'm not allowed to have anything delicious. Only green soup and beets."

"That's what I brought," I said. "Try the soup; it may not be as bad as it sounds. At least it's good for you."

I put some in a small bowl and brought it to the couch. He sat up and ate a few bites.

"I'm not very hungry," he said, holding the bowl at arm's length like it contained poison.

I set the bowl on the table. "Even though you don't feel

like it, you're supposed to eat something, aren't you? Something healthy."

"Maybe later. Did you make this yourself?"

"No, Meera did. She knows her way around a kitchen. In fact, I'm taking lessons from her soon."

He flopped back against the pillow and closed his eyes. "Who's Meera?"

"You met her at my dinner. She's an older woman who wears long dresses. She calls herself a vampire."

"You're taking lessons from a vampire?"

"She's a good cook," I said a little defensively. Me, defending Meera? What was the world coming to?

"There was a man in your elevator," I said, perching on a foot stool next to the couch, "who recognized me from the funeral. I wish I knew who he was because he said something about Guido, the man who was murdered. He lives on the fourteenth floor of your building. Do you know who that might be?"

"Can't help you," Jonathan said. "I just moved in here last month and I don't know anybody. I can't believe you're helping the police again."

"I wish I could, but as usual they don't want my help."

"Their loss," Jonathan said.

"Yes, well . . . What I found after circulating around the funeral and talking to people, the crowd seemed to be either pro-Guido or anti. In the anti group are the potential suspects like his ex-wife; his brother, who was his rival; and other chefs, whom he supposedly stole recipes from. There were way too many people who didn't like him. I suppose that's not unusual for a celebrity chef. Even one who's so successful. They say chefs tend to be emotional and difficult and edgy. So who knows?" I said, gazing out the window at the sailboats on the Bay. Jonathan's eyes were closed, and I was afraid I'd put him to sleep with my long speech. Maybe my voice had a soothing effect on him. I hoped so. Though I was hoping for a more stimulating conversation.

"How about a beet?" I asked after a brief silence.

"I hate beets," he muttered.

"I didn't know that. It's just that they're good for you. I'll leave them here. If you get hungry enough, you might want to at least taste them."

He shook his head.

I couldn't believe this was the same suave, charming doctor with the five-star bedside manner who'd treated me not too long ago.

I stood by the window, wondering how long I had to stay. Would I want someone hanging around if I felt terrible? Maybe he wanted me to leave but didn't want to hurt my feelings. "Who's filling in for you at work?" I asked to make conversation.

"Don't know," he said. "Could you hand me those pills on the table over there?"

I brought the bottle and a glass of water to him.

"Thanks," he said. He popped two pills and swallowed them with the water. Then he closed his eyes again.

"Will you be okay if I leave?" I asked.

He nodded but he didn't say anything.

"Don't forget to eat some soup and beets," I said as I went to the door.

"Wait, Rita." He propped himself up and managed a weak smile. "Thanks for coming. I appreciate it. I really do, and after this is over, I'll make it up to you. We'll have a night on the town like last time, only better." He paused, then he braced himself on one arm. "You're the best. And you look terrific in that jacket. If I wasn't sick, I'd tell you to take it off. Everything."

"Jonathan . . ."

"Don't worry, I'm delirious."

"Just get well. And if you need anything . . ."

He raised his arm and waved at me, then he sank back down on the couch with a groan.

I felt terrible leaving him alone like that, but what good was I doing standing around talking when he didn't want me around? But wait. He begged me to come here. He wanted company. Meera outdid herself with the veggie diet and now he didn't want it. I reminded myself that when I had my concussion and Nick kept coming by with Romanian food I just wanted him to go away. Maybe that's how Jonathan felt about me. It was nothing personal. I tiptoed out and closed the door softly.

I stood at the elevator and pressed fourteen, hoping I might be able to locate the man from the funeral. I felt that he had something to tell me and would have if we'd had more time in the elevator. Too bad I didn't know his name or where he lived. Too bad I hadn't followed him upstairs. But I wasn't thinking fast enough during that first elevator trip.

There weren't that many apartments on each floor of this high-rise, so if I just knocked on some doors, maybe I'd find him. It was worth a try. And if I found out something, I'd be one up on Jack Wall. The thought gave me a jolt of satisfaction.

When I got off the elevator on his floor, I knocked on the first door I saw. A woman came to the door wearing a floor-length gown and bright red lipstick and holding a cig-arette holder in her hand. I thought for a moment I'd stum-bled into an old movie.

"Yes?" she said.

I didn't know what to say. "I'm looking for a man I met in the elevator," I said at last.

"We're all looking for a man, honey," she said. "No man here, unfortunately."

I had a sinking feeling that unless I found Mr. Right in the next year or two, it was likely I'd end up just like her. "I met him at a funeral," I said.

"Really. So that's how you meet men these days. I've got to get out more."

I didn't want to get into a discussion about the unavail-ability of suitable men and where to meet them in San Fran-cisco, so I continued with my line of questioning.

"He was wearing a dark suit, and he may be Italian. I think he lives on this floor."

"Maybe it's Alfredo at number 1409. But I don't think he's your type."

"Thank you."

I went to 1409 and knocked, but no one answered. Maybe it wasn't Alfredo. Maybe it was someone who was visiting like me, who didn't live there at all. I sighed, and then I went from door-to-door on that floor, but had no luck. Until I got to 1418 and he answered, the man from the elevator. He was wearing a pair of dark Zanella slacks and a black Kenzo polo shirt.

"Hi," I said, "I'm the woman from the elevator. Rita Jewel."

"Gioccomo Parcisi," he said, shaking my hand. "You're the friend of Guido's from the funeral."

"Not really a friend. I was in one of his classes, and I was at the funeral. I wanted to ask you something, if you don't mind."

"Come in," he said with a sweeping gesture that, along with his name, made me think he had to be Italian. I know it's not good to stereotype people, but in this case, I couldn't help it.

Unlike Jonathan's, this apartment was done completely in stark ultramodern Italian furnishings. A huge white couch and large armchairs were facing the windows. The view was more spectacular than Jonathan's, and I gasped in admiration.

"Nice, isn't it?" he said. "Guido said it reminded him of Florence."

"The view?" I was puzzled. I'd never been to Florence, but I didn't think it was on the ocean or very hilly.

"No, the apartment. Probably because I had the same Piero Lissoni furniture in my place there."

"Guido was a good friend of yours?"

"Very good. I'm going to miss him," he said sadly.

I nodded. "Even though I didn't know him well, I knew he was an excellent chef and a fine teacher. Do you have any idea who killed him? You said something about a girlfriend."

"But why would she kill him?" he asked with a frown.

"Maybe she was mad because he tried to dump her. Didn't you say he was trying to get rid of her? That can be painful."

"You're not trying to excuse her, are you?" he asked.

"No, of course not. I don't even know her. I'm just trying to establish a motive."

"You sound like a detective."

I wished Jack Wall could have heard that. "I saw Guido

the night he was murdered. The police think I had something to do with it."

"Did you?" he asked.

"Of course not. I thought he was great. Of course, he's the only professional chef I've ever known, but still. I had no reason to kill him. I went to the school on Potrero to sign up for more classes. He acted nervous and didn't let me in. Then later that night I heard about it. I was just wondering . . ."

"Wondering if his killer was on his way?"

"I was wondering if you knew who his girlfriend was."

"I never met her," Gioccomo said. But he didn't really answer my question. Why not? "Maybe it was one of his students, like you," he said, pacing back and forth in front of the window. "It's too terrible. I can't believe anyone would kill Guido. He has had many girlfriends since his marriage ended, but I don't believe any one of them ever threatened him."

"What about his ex-wife?" I asked.

"Gianna? She might have wanted him dead after what he did to her, but she's not a killer, and she just got here. At least that's what she told me. I agree with you it might have been a woman, knowing Guido. He was irresistible to women—until it all fell apart, that is."

I waited, hoping he might elaborate. Or give me the name of his girlfriend. Had she been at the funeral today? Did he mean Guido had had tons of wives and girlfriends and cheated on all of them? He didn't say. And I didn't ask.

"So it's a case of *cherchez la femme*, as they say in France," I said.

"*Cerca la donna.*"

He stood at the window watching the street below. I

didn't want to leave without extracting every ounce of information from the man, and I still had another question.

"Do you know Guido's brother?" I asked.

"Which one?"

"There's more than one?"

"It's a big family," he explained.

"The one who's also in the food business."

"You mean Raymundo."

"Is he a chef at Eduardo's?"

"He's at Fior d'Italia. Didn't you meet him? He was at the funeral."

I thought I'd gotten around, but I'd missed one of the brothers. So they were all in the food business. Perhaps rivals. This brother was at another high-end Italian restaurant. All I could think was that I'd have to go and eat there too. I was starting to feel dizzy from the overload of information. Or maybe it was the altitude. This detective work was hard, but somebody had to do it.

"Which one was Raymundo?"

"He was wearing a dark suit."

Now that was helpful. What man wasn't wearing a dark suit at the funeral?

"So who works at Eduardo's?" I asked.

"Guido's cousin Biagio. But Eduardo is the owner."

Who was it I was looking for? Had I misheard? Were there still others I should look into?

"The other brothers are still in Italy," Gioccomo said.

That's when I said to myself that I'd gotten all I could digest for today. I thanked him for his time, and he saw me to the door. Probably relieved to get rid of me and my incessant questions. A lot of people feel that way about me. All

I've ever tried to do was get to the bottom of a murder and save my own hide at the same time. Either I'm stopped by the long arm of the law or by people who have something to hide or just want to be left alone.

It was not easy being an amateur detective. Now, if I were a professional like Jack, I could go anywhere, pull out my badge and ask any questions I felt like. Maybe in my next life. In the meantime I was happy to have a new nugget of information to share with Jack. Although I wouldn't be surprised to learn he already knew everything I knew.

....

The next day I realized how much I liked my own day job. I was no longer bored with it. I looked forward to it as a place I could relax and be myself and not worry about who killed who and why. I didn't even mind doing mindless jobs like hanging a shipment of metallic jackets on hangers, as long as I didn't have to wear one. All that glitter at nine o'clock in the morning was as much as I could handle. In total contrast I was wearing a pair of sleek, buttery, black leather Helmut Lang leggings I'd tucked into a pair of black, low-heeled Steve Madden boots, a black J. Crew tank and a long black Alexander Wang vest. Just the opposite of what was all around me at the moment. Maybe it was the funeral that had inspired me to wear so much black. Who knows?

When Dolce asked me how Jonathan was, I hesitated. I didn't want to sound heartless. "He was so sick," I said, "that he couldn't eat much of the beets or the green soup. I think he was glad to see me, but he seemed preoccupied." Maybe I was spoiled and I wasn't happy unless all attention was on me. I didn't want to admit it, but maybe it was true.

"Now, Rita," she said, "you know what I told you about men when they're sick."

"But he's a doctor," I protested. "And I'd gone to a lot of work for him. Or rather Meera had. She's the one who made the soup and the beets."

Dolce opened her mouth to tell me that he was a doctor second and a man first, but her words were interrupted when my cell phone rang. Normally I turn it off when I'm at work, but since there were no customers around yet, and it was Detective Wall, I took the call.

"Just wanted to remind you of dinner tonight at Eduardo's," Jack said. "Eight o'clock."

"Okay," I said. How like him to announce it instead of asking if that was all right with me. "Any instructions, warnings or tips?"

"We're going to see what we can learn."

"And eat," I reminded him. "Can I ask questions?"

"Can I stop you?"

"I'll take that as a yes."

"I'll pick you up at seven thirty."

"Dr. Jonathan?" Dolce asked when I'd hung up.

I shook my head. "Detective Wall," I said. "We're going to a restaurant tonight that is owned by Guido's brother Eduardo and where his cousin Biagio works. Neither one was at the funeral, which I think is strange."

Her eyes lit up. "Sounds like fun," she said.

"It's not a date really," I explained. "It's a hunting expedition. Hunting for clues to Guido's murder. That's all."

"Expedition or not, it's exciting to go out with such a good-looking man," she said. "And one who knows how to dress for the occasion." Then she got down to the nitty-gritty. "What will *you* wear?"

Seven

"We'll find something smart and low-key," Dolce suggested. "And make it look effortless."

The first thing she found was a short black Nicole Miller dress that hit me midthigh and was embellished with a bold design. I tried it on with black tights and I liked it a lot.

"It says glamour but it's not over-the-top," Dolce said, stepping back to get some perspective.

I agreed but when I looked at the price tag, I gasped.

"Don't worry about the price," Dolce said. "You can return it and we'll have it dry-cleaned. Unless you want to keep it."

Of course I wanted to keep it, but I already had a closet bursting with designer clothes she'd either given me or sold me.

"You'll be the best dressed in the whole place," Dolce promised.

"Except for Jack. He usually takes the prize with his

Armani suits, his Ferragamo shoes or his Marc Jacobs pants."

"You'll look great together," Dolce said. "I've always had a soft spot in my heart for that detective. I'm glad to hear he needs you as much as you need him. Or is he just looking for an excuse to see you?"

"I doubt it," I said. "He uses me to get information, and I use him for the same purpose."

"Sounds like a match made in heaven," Dolce said. "Unless you decide a doctor is the one for you. So you think Guido's brother or his cousin who works there are going to tell you something over drinks at the bar?" She sounded dubious. "If either knows who killed Guido, why haven't they told the police?"

"Maybe one of them did it or they're protecting someone else, like each other. I don't know. I do know Eduardo wasn't at the funeral, something about a banquet. If Biagio was there, I didn't meet him. Don't you think it's strange when close relatives don't show up to the funeral?"

"Maybe," she said. "But not if they've got work to do. If he's the owner, he's probably out chatting up the customers at his restaurant."

"I guess so," I said. "If they have the personality for it. If Eduardo is the chef and/or the owner, we'll go back to the kitchen on the pretext of complimenting him."

"And then?" Dolce said.

"I don't know. Jack will ask some questions. This is really Jack's job. He'll know what to do."

"Rita, you're too modest," she said. "You have a way of finding things out. You know you do."

I blushed at the compliment, but I had to agree I sometimes did get to the bottom of things because of my persistence.

I changed back into my all-black work outfit and hung the dress on a hanger. "I'll be very careful not to spill anything on it," I promised.

"It's too bad about your doctor," Dolce said.

"He was downright cranky," I said. "There's no other word for it. He's not a good patient."

"Doctors never are," she said. "Just don't give up on him. He'll get well and he'll be himself again. I'm glad to hear he's not the only man in your life. There's Nick the Romanian also. That makes three men in your life," she said.

I was about to protest that one was sick and grouchy, one was using me to uncover a murderer and the other was recovering from a broken engagement in Romania, but several customers came into the shop and we both sprang into action like the professional saleswomen we were.

That afternoon, Dolce insisted I leave early to get ready for my date. But I didn't want to sit around in my tiny apartment getting nervous about my so-called date. It wasn't really a date anyway; it was more of an assignment. The job was to find out something. If I didn't help Jack find out something, subtly of course, he'd be sorry he ever took me there.

I could see why he wouldn't want to go to a fabulous restaurant by himself on a Friday night. How would that look? It would look suspicious, I was sure of that. I couldn't go by myself either; not only would it look suspicious, but it would break my bank. Jack could either write it off as a business expense, or he'd pay out of pocket, and I knew his pockets were deep.

So I left work at the usual time and took the bus home.

I got dressed and studied myself in the mirror on the back of my bedroom door. Then I tried on a cropped velvet jacket over the dress because San Francisco evenings are cool no matter what the season. But the jacket hid the appliqué on the dress, so I grabbed a black hand-crotched shawl with a long fringe that I hardly ever wore. Finally an occasion that called for a fringed wrap. It was lined with black satin and felt wonderfully smooth around my shoulders.

When Jack came, he looked around the apartment as if he hadn't been there before, although he had.

"You were here one night when I was having a little dinner party. As I recall, you stayed for dinner."

"Thanks for inviting me," he said.

"I didn't. You crashed the party."

"Wait a minute. The older woman invited me."

"Older? You can say that again. Do you know how old she says she is? Almost two hundred."

"She looks good for her age," he said.

"She was at the funeral yesterday."

"I saw her."

"Did you ask her any questions?"

"A few," he said.

Would it kill him to tell me what the questions were? And more important, what were the answers? Like where were you on the night Guido was murdered? Did you have any motives for killing the chef? Do you know how to use a gun? Are you really a vampire?

"Since you and I are going to investigate a close relative of the deceased chef, I assume you have dispensed with the idea of blaming Meera for the murder."

"You know better than to assume anything," he said. Then he tilted his head to one side and changed the subject.

Could it be that I'd hit on the truth and that's why he said, "Nice dress."

"Thanks. You look very cool yourself." It was true. Jack was wearing a vintage Armani suit with double-pleated baggy pants in the fifties' style. Something only he could get away with. It was nice to go out with someone who not only wore stylish clothes but also appreciated what I wore too. If only this wasn't a setup to catch a murderer. Maybe someday Jack and I would have a real date.

Instead of driving his ultra-expensive sports car, Jack had a vintage Mercedes and driver waiting in front of my house. "This is Charlie," he said, pointing to the driver. "One of my parolees. I like to give him the business when I can. Keeps him out of trouble."

I said hello to Charlie, a hulking bald giant of a man with a jagged scar on one cheek. He'd gotten that either in prison or on the mean streets was my guess.

"Could double as a bodyguard, if you needed one," I mused. I hoped we wouldn't need one tonight. I wondered if Jack was afraid we'd discover the killer, who would pull out his gun and threaten us right in the middle of our crème brûlée, and that's why he was using Charlie.

Whatever Charlie's role was tonight he was a fine driver, taking the hills and the one-way streets with skill and nerve. Both of which were necessary for a career in crime or as a detective's driver. He pulled up in front of the restaurant, which was tucked away behind a storefront with no name on the door, and said he'd be waiting for us in the parking lot while he listened to the ball game. Jack said he'd have some food sent out to him, and Charlie did not fall all over Jack with gratitude. Instead, he just nodded as if this was the usual procedure.

"Does this happen often?" I asked Jack as we stood in front of the solid wood door.

"My going out to dinner? I like to combine business with pleasure. Eating with you—"

"It's all business. Don't tell me, I know." I knew he was using me, but deep down I thought he enjoyed my company too.

He held the door open for me and then put one hand on the small of my back. I felt a frisson go up my spine. There was no denying that Jack had an effect on me. He was tall, good-looking, smart and up front with his comments. With Jack you never got anything sugarcoated. The question was, did I have any effect on him? He was so cool I couldn't tell.

"You don't know everything," he said. He was right. There was a lot I didn't know, especially about him, but I was a fast learner.

The dining room was cool and sleek. I would have to say it was certainly minimalist with its stark white walls and white tablecloths. The bar was full of young professionals like us as well as a handful of oldsters having drinks. Jack ordered two French martinis, which were new to me. Turned out it was champagne and Chambord and totally delicious. We stood in the bar making small talk as if we were just another couple out on a date. I was so relaxed and into the atmosphere I almost forgot why we were there. Until Jack reminded me.

He leaned down and said, "Recognize the guy behind the bar?" His lips brushed my ear and I almost dropped my drink. I wondered if he knew how sensitive my ears were. I tried to conceal my reaction to his intimate gesture. I'd show Jack I could be just as cool as he was.

I pulled myself together and turned toward the bar to see

who he meant. I looked and looked again. I thought it was somebody from the funeral, but who? Guido's cousin or one of his brothers? He stopped pouring a drink and stared at me. But why? Of all those people at the funeral, did he remember me? I like to think I'm memorable, but not that memorable.

"Who is it?" I murmured.

"I think it's a cousin," he said. After we finished our drinks, a host in a tux came to show us to our table. I half expected him to be one of Guido's relatives too. Maybe he was.

"Lobster pot pie is one of their best dishes," Jack said, glancing at the menu.

"Sounds good. Do you come here often?" I could picture him bringing other suspects or informants here to soften them up before he threatened them if they didn't tell him what he wanted to know. Or did he bring dates here that had nothing to do with his work? Were they smarter than me? Prettier? Better dressed? More fashionable?

"First time. What about you?"

"Same, but I've heard a lot about it. What are we going to do?" I asked.

"First we'll order. Then—"

"I mean about the, you know . . ."

"We'll play it by ear," he said. "But just offhand I thought we would want to thank the chef in person."

I knew he'd have a plan. So the plan was to go to the kitchen to meet the chef, or maybe the chef would make the rounds of the tables. And if that didn't work, Jack would have plan B. If he thought a free dinner was all I wanted, he was mistaken. Of course I loved to eat. Who doesn't? But I love to get to the bottom of a puzzle, like who killed my favorite chef, even more. Or just as much. And I also wanted some romance in my life. Doesn't everyone?

When the waiter came, he lit the candle on the table with a flourish. The atmosphere was romantic, or it could have been if this had been a real date, me in my new dress and Jack looking gorgeous as usual by candlelight. But why not pretend? Why not act like we were a couple? Jack told the waiter we'd have the tasting menu with the sommelier's wine pairings. So that's why he'd had his chauffeur drive us: so he could drink without worrying. Not that I'd ever seen him worry.

"That all right with you?" he asked.

I nodded enthusiastically. It sounded divine and it was. The first course was a lobster salad with sliced Cara Cara oranges and caviar and with it a glass of Alsatian white wine. I thought I could die right then and there and go straight to heaven with no regrets.

"Not bad," Jack said.

I smiled. "Perfect," I said.

He leaned across the table and looked into my eyes. "See anything out of the ordinary?" he asked.

I was startled. Was I supposed to be looking around for suspicious behavior all the while sitting across from him, gazing into his eyes and eating this fabulous food? I guessed so. I took a deep breath and reminded myself why we were there. "Nothing yet," I told him. "Do you ever take a break? I mean, are you always on duty?"

"Pretty much," he said. "Especially when we have an unsolved murder."

"Like Guido's," I said. "Any new clues?"

"Forget Guido. Just enjoy your dinner."

"I am, or I was until you brought it up," I said pointedly.

The next course was the local petrale sole with a heap of local fresh peas and asparagus with garlic butter. After a few bites, Jack asked if I'd found a cooking teacher to take Guido's place.

"I'm not really looking," I said. "I don't have time. I take my job very seriously. Even when I'm not at the shop, I'm working. I'm looking and I'm studying what people are wearing. Take the woman across the room at the table for two."

He turned his head and raised his eyebrows quizzically.

"Well, she's wearing a pair of Christian Dior's latest blunt square-toed shoes."

"You're sure?" he asked, a look of surprise and what I assumed was admiration for my good eye and my fashion sense.

"Yes, I saw them featured in a magazine. I thought they almost looked like what a dancer would wear."

"If you say so," he said. "I'm impressed. No time for classes so you can concentrate on fashion."

"I also have to clear my schedule to solve the odd murder here and there," I reminded him. "In all modesty I confess to a system I call time management," I said, hoping he'd think my social calendar was packed full. "Then there's swimming at my club and the usual." I left the meaning of "the usual" up in the air. It could mean symphonies, the ballet, parties, cocktails, whatever. Let Jack assume whatever he wanted to assume that meant.

After we'd finished our main course and had been given the dessert menu, Jack was tapping his fingers lightly against his wineglass.

"Can't decide between the coconut pie with the caramel rum sauce or the handcrafted trio of ice cream?" I asked him as I studied the menu.

Just then the waiter passed and handed Jack a note. He glanced at the paper, stood and said he'd be right back.

I watched him stride across the floor toward the bar. I tell you, I could hardly stand to sit there, that's how consumed I was with curiosity. What was in that note? Was Charlie in trouble? Had he started a fight with the other chauffeurs? Or was there a break-in at the Bank of America and Jack had to take off? This was worse than going out with a doctor. At least they weren't on call *every* night.

Instead of reading and rereading the dessert menu until Jack came back, I got up and went to the ladies' room. To get there I had to go through the bar where I saw Jack in the corner talking to the bartender. He didn't see me.

Back at the table, I waited for him to return, then I asked, "What was it?" Of course I didn't expect him to tell me.

"I had to see someone," he said.

"The bartender?" I asked. "What did he want?"

I had to give Jack credit. He didn't explode and criticize me for spying on him. He didn't even look surprised. "Just a private word with me, that's all. Nothing to worry about."

"The least you can do is tell me who he is. Especially if he's connected with Guido."

"Okay, he's the bartender and he's connected with Guido."

I sighed, and the waiter came to take our dessert orders.

"I think I'll go with the pie," I said. "What about you?"

"Fresh berries."

"Very sensible and healthy," I said.

He leaned back in his chair. "Tell me how well you knew Guido," he said.

"I think I've already told you: I took one class from him and that's it."

"Except for the night he was murdered," Jack said.

"Well, yes, but that encounter was only a few minutes and we've already been through that."

"How many of your customers at Dolce's knew the chef?"

"Quite a few, I think. Do you want me to find out? Give you names?"

"That would be helpful," he said.

"On second thought, there aren't that many."

I hated to think of Jack summoning our customers down to the station to be interrogated, but what else could I do?

A few minutes later Jack told the waiter he'd like to meet Eduardo if possible, to compliment him on the wonderful food. Did that mean that Biagio was the cousin behind the bar?

The waiter said he'd ask him to come out but it was a busy night in the kitchen.

"What will you do if he says no?" I asked Jack while sipping the champagne left in my glass.

"He won't," he said. "Leave it to me."

I was a little concerned, but this was Jack's plan, not mine. So if Eduardo didn't come, let Jack figure out what to do next. I was still hoping I'd find out more about the bartender. Especially if he was Biagio.

When the waiter brought our desserts and coffee, he said he was sorry but Eduardo was too busy tonight. I have to say this for Jack, he didn't even raise an eyebrow, just said he was sorry too. Then he took his card from his wallet and wrote something on the back of it.

What was the deal here? First he got a note from someone, presumably the bartender, and now he was writing a note to someone else, probably the chef.

I could only imagine what he'd written. Maybe it was,

"You'd better cooperate with the police or you'll be in big trouble." Or maybe he'd scrawled, "I can arrest you now or you can play along with us." Or just, "Wonderful food. Kudos to the chef." If it was me, I'd take another tone. I'd be polite but firm. I'd write, "Please meet us after dinner in the alley to discuss the murder of Guido or else." But then no one asked me what I'd do.

Jack gave the card to the waiter with instructions to give it to Eduardo. I was glad this wasn't my plan because I wouldn't have enjoyed my pie as much if I'd been worried how it would turn out. But when the waiter returned, he looked worried. "The chef says this isn't a good time," he said and left.

Jack didn't look happy. He frowned and folded his napkin a few times.

"Oh well," I said cheerfully, "at least we had a great dinner." I leaned forward and whispered, "Maybe your note was too . . ." I never finished my sentence because the fringe from my shawl caught the flame from the candle, and in a second the fire had shot into the air above the table. With the flames licking at my shoulders, I stood and flung my shawl to the ground. Jack jumped up and stomped on the handmade garment, but it got away from him and rolled across the floor. The nearby guests jumped out of their seats and started screaming. Waiters were emptying pitchers of water on the shawl, which I feared would never be the same again.

The next thing we knew, a man in a chef's toque and a white apron came running out of the kitchen. Was this Eduardo or Biagio? As the waiter picked up the burned scrap of fabric, all that was left of my shawl, I picked up a scrap of paper from the floor and put it in my purse. The chef told everyone to calm down. He ordered champagne for every table and said he was sorry for the fracas. Then he came to our table. By that time I was sitting down again and Jack was still standing and watching the scene unfold.

"I'm sorry. Candles are very romantic but dangerous too," the chef said with a rueful smile.

I assured him the scarf didn't matter and our desserts were still intact.

I thought he looked like Guido, but I wasn't sure if this was his cousin, his brother or no relation at all. Maybe all Italian men looked alike to me. Whatever he was, why would he kill Guido to get his cooking school when he had a job as chef in such a place as this? It didn't make sense.

"You must be Eduardo," Jack said. "I don't believe I met you at Guido Torcelli's funeral. I'm the detective looking into his murder." He handed Eduardo his card. Now the chef had two cards, both from Jack.

Eduardo stared at the card, then looked at Jack.

"Very sad," said Eduardo, pulling up a chair. "He was a fine chef. I hope you catch the monster that did this to him."

"We will," Jack said, now back in his chair. "Were you close?"

"He was my favorite brother. We played together in Lucca when we were children. Our mother would let us roll the dough, mix the batter and taste everything."

"I'm Rita," I said, determined not to be left out. "I met your daughter Maria at the funeral." I hoped he got the message, which was, I met your daughter but I didn't meet you. Please explain why you didn't attend the funeral of your favorite brother.

"I couldn't make it," he said. That was it. No explanation at all. I thought that was strange. Especially for an Italian family member.

"It's no wonder you both turned out to be chefs," I said. Was he going to say anything about their relationship? Why they'd split up after working together? "I had a class with Guido a short time ago."

"How did he seem?" he asked.

"Cheerful and charming," I said. "He invited us to take some more classes at the family chateau in Florence in the summer."

"Yes, it's a wonderful place. You would have enjoyed it."

Eduardo shook his head, and I thought he might have a tear in his eyes. I glanced at Jack hoping he'd seen it too. Then Eduardo said he was sorry about the incident of the burned scarf and of course our dinner would be taken care of.

"You have a stunning restaurant here," I said. "The food was fabulous. Are you the owner?"

"Partly," he said.

I wanted to say, "Who else is part owner?" but he said he had to get back to the kitchen.

"Do you mind if I ask where you were the night your brother died?" Jack asked before he could leave.

I almost choked on my ice water. I should have known Jack would take full advantage of our meeting. But here in the restaurant?

"I was working," he said stiffly. "I don't have a day off except for Monday when we are closed."

I had to say that Eduardo didn't seem too upset that Jack had asked him for his whereabouts as if he was a suspect, so that was probably a good thing, at least for Eduardo. It made him seem like he wasn't worried about it.

After he left and Jack and I were drinking small cups of

strong coffee on a clean, fresh tablecloth, I looked around the restaurant. People were eating and drinking, talking and laughing. There was only the faintest scent of burned fabric hanging in the air over our table.

"It's almost as if nothing happened," I said. "The staff handled that well."

"So did you," he said.

What, a compliment from Jack? I almost dropped my coffee cup. Sometimes he surprises me that way.

"Was that intentional?" he asked.

"My setting myself on fire? No, but I would have done it for the cause of solving Guido's murder. That's the kind of girl I am," I said. "What did you think?"

"Later," he said.

He was right not to discuss the place and especially not the chef here on the premises. But I was dying to know. I was also dying to know what that slip of paper was I'd found on the floor. The original note from the bartender to Jack? I could only hope.

Jack left a hefty tip for the waiter, and after our coffee we went out to find our chauffeur.

Charlie was leaning against the car talking to another chauffeur. He held the door open for us and thanked Jack for the dinner, which he said was first class. "The risotto was fine," he said.

"Charlie's a vegetarian," Jack explained.

"I see." I was bursting to talk about the chef, but Jack shook his head and said to wait. It turned out that later meant at my house. He told Charlie he'd give him a call when he was ready to leave, and Charlie drove away in the Mercedes.

I offered Jack more coffee from my kitchen, but he turned

it down, probably figuring it wouldn't compare with the espresso we'd just had, which was correct. Or maybe he didn't need another stimulant tonight.

He sat in the one comfortable chair in the living room with his legs stretched out in front of him, and I sat on the couch with my feet curled up underneath me.

"At least we got a free dinner out of it," I said.

"Thanks to you," he said. "Sure you didn't do that on purpose?"

"I could have if I'd thought of it. You don't think Eduardo had anything to do with the murder, do you?"

"Sounds like he had a good alibi," Jack said.

"Unless he could have slipped away between courses and went across town to kill his brother. But why? A food fight? A dispute over a recipe? Family matters? And why didn't the brother go to the funeral? I didn't buy his excuse. There was something going on between them, and it wasn't good."

"What about the others?" Jack asked.

"Others as in the bartender?" I asked. "Who I assume is his cousin."

"Forget the bartender," he said. "There's nothing there."

"If you say so," I said. But if there was nothing there, why didn't he share that nothing with me? "It has to be family. It's always family. If it wasn't his cousin or a brother, then how about his ex-wife?"

"Who, I understand, was in Italy when Guido was murdered."

"That's what she said, but we have no proof, do we?"

Jack didn't answer. I took that as a no.

"Who was the woman you were talking to at the reception?"

"The one with the hat? It was Diana Van Sloat. Wait a

minute, she told me you'd interviewed her and now you're asking me who she is?"

"Couldn't recognize her with that hat."

"It was a pillbox," I reminded him. "No brim."

He shrugged, but I thought he wasn't being straight with me. The question was, why?

"She say anything interesting?" he asked casually. A little too casually.

"Many things interesting. She invited me to join her jewelry workshop and her tour of the zoo. She's one of Dolce's best customers. I assume you'll be interviewing all the customers as well as her relatives." I paused. He didn't confirm or deny it. "Am I right?"

"We don't publish the list of persons of interest," he said with a half smile. "To protect those like yourself."

"I'm still a person of interest?" I demanded. "When you know perfectly well I couldn't kill a fly. And neither would Diana." I took a breath before I continued, though sometimes I wonder why I bother. "What about any disgruntled students? You have a list, don't you?" I asked. "Guido was a wonderful teacher, but he demanded the best from us. Maybe there are some people who take cooking classes as a lark. Guido wouldn't approve of that. He could be critical. Some people can't take criticism. They have thin skin. As a teacher, he gave his all to fine cuisine and he expected the students to take it seriously."

"Are you saying someone didn't and they got into an argument with him?"

"Isn't it possible? Is it a coincidence the murder took place right after his class? You have the class list; who's on it?"

Jack didn't answer. Of course not. He didn't want me to

go knocking on doors asking the members of that class if they'd shot Guido with their antique pistol because he'd insulted them. Instead, he'd do it himself because that was the logical thing to do.

He gave me a long thoughtful look. I admit even in the midst of this murder investigation those looks had the power to curl my toes. I tried to think. Was it something I'd said that resonated with him? If so, why didn't he say so and give me credit? Because he didn't want any compliments to go to my head, that was why. No danger there.

Then he stood and said he had to leave. I walked him to the door, and he thanked me for my part in the investigation. It was about as romantic as saying good-bye to your buddy after doing the graveyard shift. That's how eager he looked to be leaving.

"And thanks again for setting yourself on fire," he said.

"Anything to help the investigation," I said.

"I'll get you a new shawl."

I was about to say forget it, but then I remembered that Jack was not poor and I was. So I said, "Come by the shop. We have some."

For a long moment we stood at the door looking at each other, and I felt the tension rise. Would he or wouldn't he? Was he using me or wasn't he? He finally took me by the shoulders and kissed me. Not once, not twice, but many times. I kissed him back. My knees shook, my head spun. After an eternity, he said, "Be careful," and left. I could swear I heard him whistling as he walked down the stairs. The kisses were as hard to figure out as Jack himself. Did they mean thank you? I like you? I wish you would stay away from murders so we could get something going? Or all of the above. And why did he tell me to be careful? Of what? Of whom?

I went into the bathroom and looked at my face. My lips looked bruised, and I felt like I'd been stung. The man could kiss. The question was how many other women was he kissing? And where was he going from here? To the Fior d'Italia to interview Raymundo, the other brother? Wherever it was, I wasn't invited. I didn't like being left out. Jack knew that. Was that why he kissed me, to distract me? It almost worked.

....

I sat down on the edge of my bed and fished out the paper I'd found at the restaurant. It said, "I have to talk to you." I turned it over and over. No signature. If it had come from the bartender, how had Jack known that? And what had he said when they got together? Damn Jack for not confiding in me after all I'd done for him, including setting myself on fire. Kissing was fine, more than fine. But as usual, I wanted more.

Now what?

Eight

Naturally Dolce wanted to know how it went with Jack. I told her we'd accomplished what we set out to do.

"You got to know each other better?" she asked anxiously as she stopped pushing a wheeled rack of coats from the hall to the great room.

"I'm not sure about that," I said. "But we did get to meet Eduardo, the chef who is Guido's brother, thanks to my setting my shawl on fire. Otherwise I don't think he would have come out of the kitchen."

That information caused Dolce to sit down on a velvet chaise and fan her face. "I hope Detective Wall appreciated your gesture."

"Hard to tell with him," I said, feeling my face heat up with the memory of his kisses. "But Eduardo said he was at work the night of the murder and at work the day of the funeral. So there we are. Nowhere. Unless . . ."

"It's true that chefs work long hours," Dolce said.

"Isn't it true that they take breaks also?" I asked. "Step outside for a cigarette or a quick trip across town to knock off a rival? And who would notice?"

"You're letting your imagination run away with you," Dolce said.

"It wouldn't be the first time," I said. "The strangest thing was that Jack kept asking me about Diana Van Sloat. When I'd only just met her at the funeral."

Dolce frowned. "Funny you should say that. She just called me and said the police want to talk to her again. I assured her all of our customers were being questioned so she wouldn't worry, but of course they aren't."

"I don't understand," I said. "What's the reason they're focusing on her all of a sudden?"

"I told her you might be able to find out."

"I wish I could. Sometimes I think Jack tells me less than he would if we, if I . . ."

"If you two weren't romantically linked?" she asked.

I nodded.

"I just don't want any other customers to hear she's a . . . whatever she is," Dolce said.

She didn't want to say "suspect," or "person of interest," but what else could we think? Of all the suspicious people at the funeral with their various motives to kill Guido, Diana was the last person I'd ever question. What was wrong with Jack?

"This may be off the subject," Dolce said after a long silence, "but I have to ask. Which of the three men—the detective, the Romanian or the doctor—do you prefer?"

I was relieved she'd focused on me for a change, and not on the murder. "As if I had a choice," I said. "I don't. Besides that, the trouble is there's something wrong with each one of them. Dating a doctor is hard because even if they're off duty, they are responsible for the life and death of their patients. Plus they're often on call and a date could be interrupted at any time. Not that I'd mind. After all, who wouldn't want to see Jonathan when they're sick? I do have an excuse to get in touch with him now, so I will. Then there's Nick. He's different and athletic, but he's hard to figure out. Maybe because he's foreign and his aunt is a zombie. I should call and invite him over for dinner or something. As for Jack Wall, I see him often enough, but he may just be using me to solve this murder for him." I sighed.

"Rita, you should definitely not sit back and wait for them to call. Besides, there's something wrong with each one of all of us," she said. "If you're looking for perfection, you're looking in the wrong place. There's no such thing in the human race."

"I know," I said. Was that my problem, I was expecting too much from people? I wished that was all it was. But what really worried me was that none of the three had indicated that I was number one on their list. Dolce was right. It was up to me to call them and get something going. This wasn't the seventies; this was a new century, and I should take advantage of being a woman and in charge of my own destiny.

I waited on customers all morning, showing more and more long dresses.

"There's long and there's longer," I explained to Patti French, one of our best customers. "Celebrities have been wearing long skirts for years. Now we're finally catching up." It's a real break for the shop when a new item comes along. Everyone has to have one.

As usual Patti was one of the first to jump on the bandwagon. She could wear anything and look good, but these long dresses were made for her.

"These long skirts were made for me," she said, looking at herself in the full-length mirror, pleased with the pleated Catherine Malandrino maxi skirt she'd tried on. "Don't you think?"

I agreed. "It's a timeless silhouette," I said, "that elongates the body. Not that yours needs elongating," I assured her. "You can wear flats or flat boots with that. I would also suggest bangles and big earrings."

Patti looked at her pal Sadie, whom she'd brought along today to give her opinion. "Rita is just the best," she told Sadie, and I smiled modestly. "She knows everything about clothes and accessories, and she even found out who killed my poor sister-in-law."

"Well," I said, "that was just a lucky break."

"For you, yes, but what about that poor chef who was murdered last week? Know anything about that? If I were the police, I'd be pounding on your door asking for your help."

"I have been called in on that case," I admitted. I didn't mention that I'd been called in and warned to stay out of it. No one else needed to know that. After all, I had my reputation to think of.

"Any idea who did it?" Patti asked, slipping on a pair of Bloch luxury ballet flats I'd brought out. "You can count on me to be discreet."

"No idea at all," I said. Occasionally I do know how to keep my mouth shut. Telling Patti anything would guarantee the word would be all over town in minutes.

"Come on, Rita," Patti said with a playful poke to my

ribs. "You have an in at the police department. You must know something. The word on the street is that someone who buys her clothes here at Dolce's is a suspect."

I fought the urge to blurt out something like, "Where did you hear that?" Or, "Who are you talking about?" Instead, I laughed lightly as if her suggestion were the most ridiculous thing I'd ever heard. Then I changed the subject.

"I met Chef Guido when I took a class from him. I thought he was absolutely inspirational. I can't imagine who would want to kill him. He made me want to master the art of fine cooking. Unfortunately I haven't made much progress," I confessed.

"How about this?" she said. "I'll mention a few names and you just nod if I'm getting close. Then you won't be guilty of spilling any beans, if you catch my meaning."

So she hadn't forgotten her quest for the suspect after all.

"Molly Green," she said, looking me straight in the eye. As if this game of hers wasn't bad enough, she was now joined by two of her best pals, who were all ears and just dying to see what they could learn. "Jenna Lindon, Mavis Brown, Diana Van Sloat." She paused dramatically, and the three of them looked at each other, then at me.

"I really have no idea," I said as calmly as I could, though my mind was spinning. I tried to keep my face emotion-free, as if I'd had a shot of Botox.

"Really?" Patti said. She wasn't buying my innocence at all.

....

Desperate for a way out and eager to escape this trio, I went to look for another long skirt with which to distract Patti. I suggested she wear a belt with a full skirt and tuck in the shirt for contrast. "But if the skirt is form fitting, then I'd wear a long knit sweater or a fitted tee or tank with it."

I did such a good job of changing the subject and selling her the full skirt, and a long knit Alarice sweater with bold stripes and a sporty V-neck silhouette, a wide Ralph Lauren cross-grained D-ring belt and a pair of Marc Jacobs pilgrim shoes, that I talked myself into shopping for a new outfit. Before she left, Patti put on the shoes and I told her they were the latest trend and with socks they would not only be comfortable but would also stand out in any crowd. Fortunately Dolce hadn't heard the gossip about her best customer or she would have been upset. I was upset enough but also smart enough to keep it to myself. It was just gossip, I told myself. Tomorrow there would be another suspect everyone was talking about.

Dolce was all for my finding a new outfit. She said I was a walking advertisement for the clothes we sell. So when we had a quiet moment, I looked for something new for myself. A dress was what I wanted. A dress makes it easy to look put together without too much effort. I went with something I could wear every day: a bright blue and white lightweight knit dress by Tory Burch, a pair of casual Florian sandals with high, chunky heels, and a set of Lydell bracelets.

Dolce added a slouchy shoulder bag, and I was ready to go anywhere. Unfortunately the only date on my calendar was jewelry-making class. Me, the klutz, noncook, the girl who loved to wear clothes and jewelry but had no idea how to make them. Me, the girl who would rather solve mysteries than slave over a hot stove or make craft items. But taking a class at Diana's would give me a chance to make sure, with a small amount of amateur sleuthing, she was as innocent as I believed her to be.

True to my plans to find Mr. Right, I put in a call to my doctor, and Jonathan said he was feeling better. So much better he planned to go back to work the next day. I asked him if he'd eaten the soup or the beets, and he didn't say yes or no, he just thanked me again for coming by. Then he said one of the nurses had stopped in to see him.

I gritted my teeth, thinking it was probably that skanky flirt I'd seen in the cafeteria who probably had a better bedside manner than I did.

"What did she do for you?" I asked.

"She brought some kind of rice pudding made with egg whites and flaxseed oil."

"Was it good?" I asked.

"Terrible. Nurses can be a real pain," he said. "When you're sick."

I agreed. When I was in the hospital with my concussion, I'd met two of them. Two too many.

"I hope you'll be well enough to come to my next dinner party," I said.

"Why wait?" he said. "As soon as I'm well, we'll hit the Indian Grill in the Mission. Ever been there?"

No, I hadn't been there, but I would *love* to go. "It sounds wonderful."

"Then let's go. How about tomorrow? I have the day off."

"But I thought you were sick," I said.

"I'll be better by then, and I need a change of scene," he said. "Doctor's orders.

So I told him I was free without looking at my calendar. This was a date too good to pass up. Interesting food and an even more interesting man to eat it with. I loved going out for lunch or dinner or any time at all. I knew I should work on my hostess skills to boost my confidence, and I would as soon as this murder business was over.

"See you then. I've missed you, Rita."

I smiled into the phone. It sounded like Jonathan's sickness had affected his feelings for me in a good way. Then he had to hang up because someone was at the door. Another nurse on the prowl, I thought. They were a determined bunch, and no wonder. Jonathan was a man worth pursuing, especially when he wasn't sick and crabby. He sounded much better, and I was encouraged that he wanted to get out and take me with him.

When Jonathan came to pick me up at noon, he was wearing casual slim Ludlow suit pants in fine-stripe cotton with a crisply tailored cotton shirt. He took a good look at me and told me I looked terrific. I returned the compliment. He'd bounced back from his illness with determination, and although a little pale, he was still a head turner.

....

We drove to a garage on Seventeenth Street to park his vintage Maserati, and took advantage of the good weather to stroll around the colorful Mission district, admiring the small shops and restaurants. We passed several burrito joints that smelled so good I could hardly resist stopping for one.

"Next time we'll come for Mexican food," Jonathan promised.

It was good to know he was already planning on another date. Because what they say about these burritos is true. They're huge and everyone loves them. Basically they are tortillas stuffed with meat, cheese, rice, beans and everything else you can imagine. Knowing we were heading toward a gourmet Indian lunch, I used my willpower to hold off. When we finally arrived, I thought the restaurant looked like a large, imposing box from the outside. Once inside I realized it was gorgeous, though a bit dark.

From the first look at the menu, and the attentive waiter and the soft music, I knew I was in the right place. All that and Jonathan too, with his sun-bleached hair, his vibrant good looks, his quick thinking and his natural charm. I thought I must be in heaven.

The food was heavenly too. We started with assorted tandoori appetizers like chicken tikka and samosas pakora, then moved on to the curries and basmati rice. For dessert we had mango lassi, a refreshing drink.

....

After lunch we continued our walk around the neighborhood. Jonathan wanted me to see the old Mission church, so we stopped at the small adobe building that dated from 1791, and observed it from the outside while he described its history.

"You know these twenty-one missions are located up and down the coast of California at approximately one day's horseback ride from each other. They were not just churches but communities with sheep and cows and other livestock. Ranching and farming were done all along a beautiful clear creek. And there was always a hospitable place to stop and rest for the travelers."

I gave Jonathan a surprised look. How strange it was to have a guy who spent many hours taking care of sick people explain California history to me, who had lived here longer than he had. He was so proud of his role as tour guide, his once pale face positively glowed in the afternoon sunlight. What a contrast between now and just a few days ago. Of course, no one could blame an invalid for being out of sorts. Did nothing get him down except being sick?

"But what about the natives?" I asked. "I heard the Spanish settlers used them as slaves and treated them badly. If they tried to run away, they were beaten and imprisoned and often worked to death."

Jonathan frowned. Maybe he didn't like that part of the American frontier fairy tale. None of us did.

He was spared from answering my question when my phone rang. I fished it from my bag and when I saw it was Dolce, I walked to a nearby bench and sat down.

"Rita," Dolce whispered breathlessly, "you'll never believe who just came to the shop."

"Dolce, I can hardly hear you." Why was she whispering? And why had anyone come to the shop on Sunday?

"That's because I'm in my office and she's in the shop."

"She, who? Why did you let them in when you're closed?"

"That woman from the funeral, the chef's ex-wife. I couldn't say no. She came all the way from Italy."

"You mean Gianna? How strange."

"It's all right. She's buying up a storm. She says everything is less expensive than in Europe. Still, as you know, our clothes are not cheap. She said she is going to inherit some money soon, so she wants to celebrate."

"Celebrate? She's celebrating someone's death, and I think we know who. But why would Guido leave her any money if they were divorced?"

"Do you want me to ask her?" Dolce said. Because she was whispering, I couldn't tell if she was serious or not.

"Sure, go ahead," I said. What did we have to lose? "Should I come there? Do you need any help?"

"No, I just wanted you to know. I hope you're having a nice time."

"Very nice. Jonathan and I are walking around the Mission after a delicious lunch. Let me know what happens."

When I hung up, I noticed that Jonathan had disappeared and there was a bride and groom standing on the steps of the basilica, which, unlike the old mission next door, was a combination of Moorish, Corinthian and Mission styles. The couple was surrounded by what appeared to be their wedding guests. The men were in dark suits and ties and the women all in dresses and hats. I tried to identify the dress designers while a photographer snapped pictures of the bridal party. Several shots with their parents, many others with the attendants and small flower girls. I had a twinge of envy as the groom put his arm around the bride and kissed her. They looked so happy. I wondered if that would ever be me standing at the door of the church after my wedding, kissing my groom. And if so, who would the groom be? One of the three men in my life or someone I hadn't met yet? If I didn't learn to cook soon, why would anyone marry me? That's the question my aunt Alyce would ask.

Nine

When I stopped feeling sorry for myself and my single status, I noticed Jonathan was standing off to the side, staring intently at the young couple with a smile on his face. No reason to assume he was regretting his single state. Though for some single people, there was nothing like a wedding to make them feel alone in the world.

I walked over to him. "Anyone you know?" I asked. Maybe that's why he was so interested.

"One of my patients. I'm glad she recovered enough to get married."

"Let's go inside the church and look around. I think it's just a museum now."

Next we wandered into the oldest building in San Francisco. After giving a small donation to the building's restoration fund, we read about the place from a brochure as we walked around.

"The rough-hewn redwood timbers are lashed together with rawhide," I said, "It's the only intact chapel left of the twenty-one churches built under the direction of Father Junípero Serra." I didn't mention how many slaves lost their lives during this era and how Father Serra was blamed for the way they were treated. Everyone knew that.

"It's a miracle the mission survived the 1906 earthquake," I said. "It says the ground settled but the building stayed standing."

"Like me," Jonathan said. "I was so sick, I thought I'd never get well, but here I am still standing. I can't say it wasn't good for me, because I finally know what my patients are going through. Thanks to you for coming by to cheer me up."

"It was my pleasure," I said. "You're a survivor just like the mission. Shall we go?" I said.

He nodded, and we went back outside the thick adobe building into the sunshine. Enough of dwelling on the past.

"What about some coffee and a donut?" I suggested. "I heard there's a fabulous donut shop somewhere around here."

Jonathan agreed, so we asked someone and were directed to the place I'd heard about and was dying to try.

We sat at a sidewalk table outside the small donut shop, ordered coffee, then poured over the menu trying to decide what kind of donuts to order. Chocolate saffron? Apricot cardamom?

A couple at the next table were drooling over maple-glazed bacon apple. Bacon, in a donut? Really? My eyes popped open as I listened to them rave about it. Jonathan looked more like his old self sitting out here in the sun with the prospect of a donut in sight. We ordered a half dozen different kinds. After all, we didn't have to eat them here on the spot. We could take some home.

When we got our order in a cardboard box, I took a tiny, tentative bite of chocolate rosemary almond and shock waves went through me. I was in heaven. Paradise.

Jonathan smiled indulgently. I knew there must be some doctors who would look askance at the eating of donuts, but not this doctor. I sighed happily, and he tried the apricot cardamom. He said it was great and ate another. "It's good to feel hungry again," he said. "And who was that you were speaking to on the phone?" he asked. "You looked disturbed."

"You mean back there at the church? Dolce called to tell me she had a surprise customer today. "

"Isn't the shop closed?" Jonathan asked.

"That's right," I said. "The customer is a woman I met at the funeral of my cooking teacher, and she acts as if she has a sense of entitlement about her. That doors should open, money should come and people should cater to her. She just marched up to Dolce's and knocked on the door. It happened that Dolce was there, so she let her in. Not that she minded. Dolce is always willing to make a sale."

"That's what makes our country great, the entrepreneurs like Dolce, and you too."

"Of course, I want to sell clothes and accessories any day of the week," I said. "But even shop owners need a day off to refresh the merchandise and themselves."

"You look very refreshed," he said with the sexy smile I was glad to see had returned. I wanted to believe he was himself again after what he'd been through.

All in all it was a good day. Jonathan and I continued our

tour of the Mission district by buying a map of the murals painted on the walls of various buildings. We strolled and looked and read about them. Some were cartoonlike pictures that looked like they'd been drawn by children; others treated serious subjects, like people who'd died of AIDs. Another honored the artist Diego Rivera and his wife, the painter Frida Kahlo.

Finally I couldn't look at another painting or drink any more coffee or even eat another delicious donut, so Jonathan drove me home. He said he wanted to look in on a few of his patients this evening. He insisted I take the leftover donuts with me, and I didn't resist. He looked more and more like his old healthy self, and I hoped that our tour of the district along with my company were part of the reason.

When I got home, I went out on my deck to catch the last rays of the sun and to gaze at the view of the Bay at dusk. I bundled up in a warm Ralph Lauren Blue Label cashmere shawl cardigan. I often have a hard time finding a good sweater. Either they're super stylish but don't keep you warm, or they're dumpy and easy to snuggle up in. Hard to know which is best. This cardigan was perfect I thought as I called Detective Wall. After all, didn't he tell me to keep in touch? Or was that wishful thinking?

When he answered on the second ring, I was glad I didn't have to leave a message. He might not have returned my call unless I exaggerated my news.

"Don't you ever take a day off?" I asked.

"Not when there's a high-profile murder on the books."

"So the Guido case comes under the heading of high-profile, or are you working on another murder?"

"Just this. Have you got something for me?" He sounded

impatient, so I organized my thoughts so as not to ramble and lose his attention.

"I might. I heard from Dolce that Gianna was in the shop today."

"On Sunday?"

"Yes, Sunday," I said impatiently. "The important thing is that she said she was going to inherit some money. What do you make of that?"

"I have no time for Q and A, Rita. Just give me the facts."

Honestly sometimes I wonder if Detective Wall appreciates me.

"I did. Gianna is Guido's ex-wife, as you know. Now we know she had a motive for killing him. His money."

"Is this news?"

"If you'll give me a chance . . ."

"Sorry, I have an Italian relative of Guido's here who is waiting to see me. He says he knows who did it."

"I guess you can't tell me who it is. His cousin? His brother?"

"No, I can't. Now, you were saying . . ."

"That his ex-wife said she'd only arrived in time for the funeral, but it seems that she was here before he died and I just wondered—"

"You wondered if she'd killed him? Is that what you're trying to say?"

"She had a motive," I insisted. "They weren't getting along, and today she went to Dolce's and bought the store out. She said something about inheriting some money. Am I making myself clear?" How many times did I have to say it?

There was no point pussy-footing around the basic questions. When you wanted to find out something from Jack, you had to ask point-blank.

"You may have something, and I appreciate your call. Now I really have to go."

I bit my lip in frustration. *You may have something.* That's all he could say? I was sure I had something, and if he wasn't going to follow up, I would. I didn't know how or when, but I knew I would try. I knew I should hang up then and give up, but that's not my style.He thanked me politely and hung up.

I won't say I was discouraged by that conversation; I will say that after I hung up, I decided to focus on improving myself instead of helping the police. Sometimes I'm just too unselfish for my own good. So the next day I did something for myself and only my own self-esteem. I decided to attend the jewelry camp that was scheduled to be held at Diana's spacious house in Pacific Heights. Even if I didn't learn how to make unusual artsy bracelets for myself, I would have a better appreciation for those who did make jewelry, which we then sold at Dolce's. It seemed to be a win-win situation for me. I might learn a craft, and even if not, I might further my sales career by understanding what goes into designing original pieces and impress our customers with what I knew. If nothing else, I'd get a chance to see how the rich live and spend their leisure time.

I arrived at Diana's house on Wednesday evening at five. Dressed for a hands-on project under my black stretch-cotton Theory jacket, which was a pitch-perfect choice for casual layering, I was wearing a Parker minidress with batwing sleeves and a wide boatneck. I'd paired it with charcoal leggings and pair of Prada woven platform oxfords. They were expensive but so comfortable they were worth every penny I'd paid for them.

I'd had to leave work a little early, but Dolce was fine with that. She thought my learning to make bangles and beads would help me sell jewelry, and besides, it's always good to get to know our customers better socially. Especially Diana, who was customer numero uno.

I shouldn't have been surprised to find Diana lived in a mansion on one of the city's poshest streets in Pacific Heights. After all, she spent freely at Dolce's, and I thought I'd heard her husband was a venture capitalist. But I was surprised when Patti French joined me to gape wide-eyed at the four-storied house behind the brick walk and the acres of flowered gardens that surrounded the mansion. Like she didn't have one just as large and just as gorgeous as this? Tonight she was dressed appropriately for a jewelry design workshop in a belted Donna Morgan shirtdress and a pair of yellow leather Miu Miu peep-toe platform heels.

"Nice, isn't it?" I said, not wishing to seem overly blown away by all the opulence.

"'Nice' isn't the word," Patti said as a breeze tossed her carefully streaked well-coiffed hair. "This house is a Grand Tudor Revival from 1922. I know because it was on the house tour last year before the Van Sloats bought it."

"Mr. Van Sloat must be doing well," I said, hoping she'd elaborate.

"I guess he is. I only met him once. He's older than Diana, and he seems to adore her. Hanging on her every word. Okay, I'm jealous. My husband takes me for granted," she said with a sigh. "Maybe you'll get to meet Weldon, although he didn't strike me as the kind of guy who hangs out in the craft room handing out advice or compliments."

"If I was rich," I said, "I don't know if I'd bother with making my own jewelry when there are so many talented designers around. I think I'd just find one and tell her to accessorize me."

"Oh, come now, Rita," Patti said with a smile. "You know you want to be able to say, 'You like it? I made it myself!'"

"That would be satisfying," I admitted. "Anyway, Diana seems motivated, and I appreciate her inviting me. Heaven knows I'm all thumbs and I could use some one-on-one lessons."

Patti said she too was looking forward to the class. "Diana told me she has a surprise for us. A real live well-known jewelry designer will be here to show us how he does it."

"I didn't know that," I said. How like Diana to hire the best in the business. If it wasn't a famous chef, it was a famous artisan. Now I was really nervous. What if I made a mess of it and this designer threw up his arms in disgust?

"It's a secret," Patti said, holding her finger against her lips. "I have a gazillion friends' birthdays coming up, and what better to give than something original I've made myself, right?"

Even with a designer's help, I could just imagine what my friends would say when I handed them a weird-looking bracelet constructed of leather and twine and resembling something I might have made in kindergarten. "Rita, you made this? You shouldn't have! Really." Then they'd make an effort to say something nice, like "How amazing! How artistic! How different!"

Patti looked over her shoulder. "Are we the only ones here?" Just then a small sleek Porsche 911 Turbo pulled up and Maxine, the newbie in town, stuck her head out the window. "Is this the place?" she called.

I told her it was, and instead of leaving her car in their

driveway, she drove down the street to find a parking place while we waited for her. That was like Maxine not to want to intrude on their space. I was glad to see her expanding her horizons just as I was.

Speaking of horizons, Patti, who'd been there before on the house tour, told me to expect nothing less than extraordinary views from every room. "Wait until you see the Bay, the Golden Gate Bridge and Alcatraz. And notice the moldings and the leaded glass windows. They just don't make interiors like that anymore. Of course you'll see beaucoup gorgeous houses on the home and garden tour next week, but Diana's house is one of a kind."

When Maxine joined us, we walked up the brick path toward the house, which was set way back from the street for privacy and quiet. After a quick look, I noticed Maxine was wearing a Lafayette canvas skirt in an animal print with a loose, classic Eileen Fisher shirt in silk georgette.

"You have to see the black-bottom pool and spa behind the house," Patti said. "They are to die for." With that, she opened the gate and waved us around to the back of the house as if we were on tour. I hoped that Diana wouldn't mind us making ourselves at home on her property.

We stood at the outside of the pool house gazing not at the sapphire blue pool but off in the distance at the sweeping views of the whole Bay area. Since it was dusk, the lights of the city in the foreground were just now sparkling like diamonds. For a moment no one said anything. Even though the other two women both had houses of their own that I assumed were not too shabby, they were just as speechless as I was. There was the house, the views and then the silence, which was suddenly broken by the sound of voices coming from the house.

"You told me it was a woman," a man's voice said. I looked at Patti. She looked at me. Maxine turned to look at the house. None of us knew what to say, so we said nothing, frozen in place as if we were statues.

"She couldn't come so she sent her uncle. He's an Italian. And rather famous in certain circles. I was lucky to get him."

"Where is he?" the man shouted. We heard a crash, and then a door slammed.

"Servants," Patti said lightly after a moment. "Can't live with them. Can't live without them."

I smiled as if I agreed completely. Though they both must have known that as a humble salesgirl I didn't have any servants. But didn't the word "Italian" refer to our teacher? So what was that crash? And who was that shouting? Maybe we'd soon find out. Without saying another word, the three of us headed back around the house to the massive double doors out front. We stood under the arched portico and rang the bell as if we'd just arrived and hadn't heard a thing.

Unaccustomed as I was to living with servants, I had no idea if a butler would answer the door dressed in a tuxedo. It turned out Diana herself opened the door, her face flushed as if she'd been slaving over a jeweler's torch already. Her slim Rachel Roy snake-print crop pants with a simple cashmere boyfriend cardigan from J.Crew were partly covered with a retro fifties designer apron. But most striking was her jewelry. She wore a texturized copper bracelet and a sunstone bronze tree-branch ring. On her ears were jellyfish shaped earrings studded with freshwater pearls. I wanted to ask if she'd made them herself, and more important, would I be able to make them after this class. But I didn't.

"Come in," she said, looking around and over our heads as if expecting someone else. More students? Our teacher, the designer? "Did you see anyone out there?" she asked.

I wanted to say, "No, but we heard two people having a heated discussion in your house, and what was that loud crash?" but of course I didn't.

"Armando, the designer I snagged for our session tonight, is running a little late," she said, wiping her hands on her spotless apron. "But I have everything set up in the craft room, so we can get settled while we wait for him."

We followed Diana into the foyer then to the great room with its high ceilings and the French doors that led to the walk-out courtyard. I could just picture swanky cocktail parties in that courtyard, with servants serving drinks and hors d'oeuvres to crowds of guests draped in designer clothes and handmade jewelry. I knew I would never be a part of that scene, but it was fun to imagine the kind of lives these people led.

The kitchen was like something out of *House Beautiful*. It was out of the past but yet still up-to-date. The floor was wide white oak planks with mahogany finish that Diana said were original but well-worn and refinished many times. To me they looked like you could slide across them in your bare feet. There were bowls of giant prawns on ice on the Italian marble counter, along with a jar of saffron and various other herbs and spices. I thought I smelled curry in the air, although there was nothing simmering on the stove with the pale blue glass backsplash, which matched the leather bar stools and the furniture in the living room. I was envious, and my stomach rumbled. I wondered if there would be snacks and drinks along with the jewelry-making lessons.

"We faux-finished the walls with a yellow glaze," Diana

explained when we admired the kitchen. "Yellow and blue are my favorite colors. They're so cheerful. Then we painted pictures of country scenes on one of the walls. And of course I needed a walk-in freezer." She pointed to a door at the far end of the kitchen.

I think I mumbled, "Of course," but I'm not sure. I was absolutely stunned at the way it had turned out. The kitchen had a homey yet elegant look, and the artwork was professional and beautiful. "You did this yourselves?" I asked.

"Oh no. I had a crew do it after I saw a similar kitchen featured in an architecture magazine. Do you like it?"

Everyone murmured their admiration, and I said I loved it. "It's just what I'd do," I said. "You and your husband have exquisite taste."

"I wish Weldon could hear you say that," she said. "But he's upstairs in his home office. Poor man. He never gets any time off. And he travels on business. So he leaves everything in the house to me and whoever I can get to help me."

I wanted to ask if that was him we'd heard when we were in the garden, but I wisely kept my mouth shut and so did the others.

"I'm going to run out in front to see if Armando has arrived," Diana said. "There's a pitcher of martinis in the fridge. And a bowl of jumbo shrimp with a dipping sauce. Please help yourselves." She waved her arm at the double-wide, subzero refrigerator with a glass door.

"What a kitchen," Maxine said, gazing around at the six-burner Wolf range, the hammered copper double sink and the built-in pizza oven. Patti had just opened the heavy door to look into the wood-burning pizza oven when the kitchen door opened and a short man in shirtsleeves burst in.

Patti let the oven door slam with a bang, she was so startled at his sudden appearance.

"Hello, ladies," he said. "Welcome to our humble home. I'm Weldon. Where is Diana?"

Humble? Was he being ironic? It didn't look that way.

"She went to look for Armando," I said. "I'm Rita. This is Patti and Maxine."

He shook our hands. "Glad you could join my wife in another one of her adventures. She's very artistic and always has been, from furniture to painting to decorating. And now it's jewelry." He shrugged. "That's my Diana," he said.

That's what I wanted, a husband who'd brag about me. Maybe not as short as Weldon, but someone who'd buy a house like this would be nice.

"So the teacher is late," he said. "As usual. I guess we have to excuse these crafty types. They're not like us. They operate on their own time. They're creative, so if they're late, they've always got an excuse. They can't be expected to follow the rules and arrive on time like us ordinary people. Sometimes lessons start late and end late too." He shook his head.

I doubted that Weldon was ordinary at all. But at least he was understanding of the nature of the artists and their "flexible" schedules. "I hope she hasn't left you alone here."

Patti shook her head and assured Weldon we were just fine and that Diana had left us martinis and we didn't mind waiting at all.

"I'm so happy to be invited to join the group," Maxine said. I knew she meant it. As an outsider, she wasn't always invited to the inner circle's doings. This was a breakthrough. Maybe now she'd feel like she belonged.

"I must apologize for my wife," he said. "She should not have deserted her guests this way."

"We're actually having a lovely time," I said. "We're not really guests, we're students. And we're going to learn how to do some creative work tonight."

"I'll go find her," he said. "These artsy-fartsy types are not to be trusted. They're too temperamental. Keep their own timetable. I thought she'd learned her lesson with that Italian."

I imagined he must be referring to Guido. What lesson had Diana learned from him? He'd never seemed temperamental to me except for that evening when I'd stopped by. But I couldn't blame him for that. He hadn't been expecting me. He had been expecting someone else, however. Did Weldon know that Diana's other guru had been murdered and that's why she was concentrating on jewelry? Of course he must know because Diana had even gone to the funeral.

Weldon left the kitchen, presumably to find his wife, who was probably at the front door waiting for our leader. The three of us said nothing. But I opened the refrigerator and took out the pitcher Diana had told us about. I poured the mixture into three glasses on the counter, and we each silently toasted each other. In a few minutes Diana was back with a man who had to be Armando. Weldon came too. He was looking at Armando with great interest. Maybe he too would join our class, though I had to think that as a venture capitalist he might have some homework to do instead of gluing tiny pearls to silver or however you attached them. I really had no idea.

All I could think was that Armando was Guido with an even more authentic Italian accent. Tall, good-looking and charismatic, just like Guido. Just what you want in a guru of any kind. Was that why Diana had chosen him, because he reminded her of Guido?

"Everyone, this is Armando," Diana said with a huge smile. Why shouldn't she smile? She'd hooked a real artist of high-end jewelry to come to her house for a private lesson. Of course, he might have come thinking Diana's rich friends would turn around and buy jewelry from him or at least jewels from which to craft their own pieces. "Welcome to jewelry camp."

I glanced at Patti and Maxine. They were staring at him like I was, wide-eyed and ready to follow him wherever he wanted to go: chunky watches, cocktail rings or diamonds for daytime. Diana, our hostess, was beaming at him like she'd discovered him herself. Maybe she had. At least she'd scored a coup by bringing him here tonight. I was grateful to her for sharing him with us. Weldon, apparently having ascertained that Armando had arrived and we were about to start some serious creative work here, excused himself to go to his home office. He wished us all a good evening and left the kitchen.

With our drinks in hand, we followed Diana to the craft room between the kitchen and the living room. We all gasped in awe and admiration when we saw not some nook or cranny formerly a laundry room or a closet. This was a huge room furnished simply and elegantly with craftsman furniture that must have cost a fortune but still looked like it belonged. The space was not filled with wrapping paper and spools of ribbon the way an ordinary craft room might be. No, this was a craft room for the serious craftsperson. Was that Diana? Apparently it was. The floor was a dark mahogany; the walls were white with black accents. On the walls were shelves full of bins, but not the plastic kind.

These were polished wooden boxes filled with supplies. It shouted out sophistication and, yes, money. Both of which Diana had in spades.

"Do you like it?" Diana asked, standing in the middle of the room. She must have noticed how all three of us stood there gaping. "It took me six months to remodel it. This room was totally worthless and unusable. I don't know what the previous owners did with it. Nothing is my guess."

"Like it?" Patti asked. "It's awesome. Seems like there's nothing you couldn't do in here."

Diana hesitated just for a moment, then she smiled and shook her head. "I get inspired just coming into the room."

"This is a dream craft room," Maxine said, running her hand over the surface of the worktable.

"How do you keep it from getting messy?" I asked. I knew if it was mine it would be piled high with stuff. What kind of stuff I didn't know, since I'd never made a single item.

"It takes discipline," Diana said. Then she opened two drawers from the far wall and put them in the middle of the worktable. All three of us hopped up onto the stools and leaned over the table. There in glass containers were the raw materials I supposed we'd be using tonight.

Imagine such a group at my house where there was no extra room to be had. The kitchen was barely big enough for me. Which wasn't really a problem, since I hardly ever cooked anything. Maybe I should turn it into a craft room. After I learned a craft, of course.

With a flourish, Armando opened his jewelry case on the worktable and put out strips of leather and lengths of sterling-coated wire, talking as he arranged the materials in front of us. Then he held up a finished bracelet and twirled it around his fingers. I was blown away, and I thought the others were too. The bracelet was simple in form but made of such unusual materials it would stand out anywhere, even at Dolce's. It was different from anything I'd ever seen before.

"Bright bangles piled on or worn by themselves are an easy-fix accessory," he said.

I wondered if "easy-fix" meant easy to make. I hoped so. I pictured myself wearing these bracelets on my wrist and up my arms in a tangle of leather and wire never seen before. The customers would demand to know where they could get such unusual, handmade accessories. I would smile modestly and admit that I'd made them myself.

Armando and Diana stood on the other side of the counter demonstrating the technique of bracelet making as if they'd been working together wrapping hand-knotted leather around wire for weeks. I expected Armando to be professional, but not Diana. How had she gotten so good at this?

We spent an hour making bracelets in different colors. Even I caught on after only a few mistakes where the leather fell off the wire in a twisted mess. But with Armando's help I finally had an arm full of bracelets, each one in a different color leather. One was Kelly green, one hot pink and one pale blue.

"You see," Armando said as he held my arm up. "These colors pop with everything, from neutrals like the ones you're wearing, to a mishmash of prints."

"Those bracelets look fabulous on you," Diana said. "I wish Weldon could see what you've accomplished." She swept her arm around the table to include everyone else. "But he has too much work to do." She sighed. "It's always like that. He works too hard. Thank God I have my own life and a new creative outlet. If only Weldon understood how important my interests are to me." Her lower lip trembled as if she was going to cry. I had never realized how emotional Diana was, but maybe I'd be teary too if my favorite chef had been murdered and my husband was a workaholic.

Seeing how disappointed Diana looked when discussing her husband, I decided maybe I shouldn't be so envious of her life. Despite her gorgeous house, the well-appointed kitchen, the views and the gardens, and private jewelry lessons in her to-die-for craft center, her husband seemed either overly hands-on, as when he'd come into the kitchen, or not interested at all. And who had been shouting before we came into the house? However, she seemed to be making the best of the situation by insisting we all have a cappuccino, which she whipped up in her kitchen and brought back to us on a hand-painted tray.

"I'm so glad I waited to have this session until I'd finished redecorating," Diana said, looking around her craft room with justifiable pride.

"You did the right thing," Patti told her. "But you know that no house is ever finished no matter how hard you try. There's always something else to do. We are adding a sauna. I've always wanted one. And think of the money we'll save by not going to Scandinavia this year."

"Take our house," Maxine said. "The painters are there today because I couldn't stand the color of the bedroom walls. Who paints the bedroom bright red? It gives me a headache."

"You're right," Diana said. "Although Weldon leaves everything to me, which makes changes easy." I tried to imagine having enough money to call in the painters to redo my walls. Maybe I could if I married someone like Weldon.

For some reason, I'd gotten some negative vibes from him. No matter how much money he made or how much he indulged his wife in her interests.

We all trooped out the front door at the same time, except for Armando, who was packing up his leather, his wire and his jewelry knives in the kitchen.

Maxine drove me home. At the corner of Van Ness and California we saw an ambulance with its lights flashing turn onto California and head west.

"An accident," I murmured. "Or maybe a heart attack."

We talked about the class and Armando and Diana and her husband all the way. She was as impressed as I was with Armando and with Diana's house. She was just as determined as I was to try to make jewelry on her own.

"Do you think you learned enough tonight to do it on your own?" I asked.

"I can only try," she said thoughtfully as she put the car in second gear and started up steep Telegraph Hill toward my house. "I mean, it's easier with the artisan right there in the room with us." After a few moments of silence, Maxine abruptly changed the subject. "What did you think of Diana's husband?" she asked me.

What could I say? He was weird? Or maybe all VC's are like that? "I've never met a venture capitalist before, so I didn't know what to think," I said. "It must be nice to have a husband who indulges you in everything." I sighed. "I wouldn't know."

"Spoken like a swinging single girl," she said with a smile. "So do you think tonight's chef was single too?"

"He wasn't wearing a ring," I said. "I couldn't help noticing."

She pulled up in front of my house and that was the end

of the conversation about our class. She asked if she'd see me at the house and garden tour. I said I wouldn't miss it. I went inside telling myself I must master some type of craft, since I was a washout as a cook.

After a hot soak in my very own claw-foot tub, I thought about poor Jonathan and the unappetizing health food I'd brought him when he was sick. I doubted that he'd eaten it even though I'd gone to a lot of trouble to shop and then bring it to him, to say nothing of Meera's effort to cook it for him. I wrapped myself in my terry-cloth robe and called him on his cell. I figured if he was in the middle of an emergency, he wouldn't have his phone on, and if he was just sitting around the doctors' lounge trading stories about patients with bug bites, stings, sudden chest pains and shortness of breath, then he'd pick up.

He did pick up. I asked him how he was feeling.

"Much better. Those drugs finally kicked in."

"Maybe the food I brought helped." If he'd eaten it, which I doubted.

"Maybe," he said, making me conclude he'd thrown it down the garbage disposal after I left. "I really appreciate your coming by. I was completely down and totally out of it. You saw me. You know. Sorry I was such a terrible host. I owe you. As soon as I get a night off, I'll have you over for a real dinner. I'm not cooking, don't worry. There's a local restaurant around the corner that delivers. I ran into the delivery guy in the elevator, and he gave me the menu. Sounded and smelled pretty good. What are you up to?"

"Actually tonight I had a jewelry-making class."

"Don't tell me it was with a guy named Armando."

"Why, do you know him?"

"I know he had an accident tonight. Came into the ER a

couple of hours ago. Just bandaged him up and sent him home in a taxi. No stitches required. Was he relieved."

"Was it a car accident?" As we were leaving Diana's house, I'd noticed an SUV parked in the driveway that I'd assumed was Armando's. It hadn't been there when I arrived.

"He cut himself with his own knife. Can you believe that? A professional jewelry maker. Maybe it happens a lot, but not on my watch."

I felt a shiver go up my spine. I'd seen Armando's knives. I'd used one of them tonight to cut the leather for my bracelets. They were so sharp, they looked like they could cut right through an artery. "Did he cut through an artery?" I asked. Then I remembered that Jonathan had said he didn't require any stitches. "No, I guess not," I added quickly so as not to seem clueless.

"Just a superficial cut, but he was freaking out. Came in an ambulance. He was in minor shock. The sight of their own blood, you know, does it to some people. Low blood pressure, cold clammy skin, dizziness. I treated him, but sometimes a doctor's job is just reassurance. Someone to say you're okay. I'll fix it. Don't worry. Nothing serious."

I knew Jonathan was the perfect doctor to soothe a nervous bleeding patient. But Armando nervous from a superficial knife wound? Didn't seem possible. But what did I know? Stranger things happened every day. Who would have imagined Jonathan suffering in the unfamiliar role as a patient. Although he was always kind and caring, which I should know, since I'd been his patient at one time. I really had to be grateful to the woman who'd pushed me off that ladder, which had landed me in the hospital and into Jonathan's hands with a concussion and a sprained ankle.

Otherwise, I would never have met him. Not the way my social life was going. I would thank her if I could, but she'd been murdered shortly after our encounter.

"I don't blame the man for being nervous," I said. "Seeing your own blood is a downer." Like I would know. I'd had a lot of pain but no loss of blood.

"So you know this guy?" Jonathan asked.

"I just met him tonight. He was fine the last I saw of him. I'm glad to hear he recovered so fast, thanks to you, I'm sure. He taught us how to make some dynamite pieces of jewelry. I'm dying to make something on my own next."

"Good luck with that," he said. Then he said they were paging him and he had to go.

I couldn't get over the vision of poor Armando cutting himself and bleeding all over the kitchen. I wanted to call Diana, but it was too late. She must be freaked out to have had that happen at her house. Not that that would be her first concern. I was sure she was worried about Armando. Maybe she took him to the ER. No, he'd gone in an ambulance. But who drove him home from there?

And who cleaned up the blood in Diana's once-spotless kitchen? I shouldn't worry about that. She could call a cleaning service, who'd have it like new again. What did her husband think? Would he put the kibosh on future jewelry-making classes? I could tell Diana loved being creative. Apparently she loved to share her house and her favorite experts. Like at our class.

The next day I dressed carefully, as usual. I wore a short Emilio Pucci print skirt, a French striped T from Saint James with a double-breasted, cropped Rudsak trench over it, tights and a pair of two-tone Chanel ballet flats. I didn't wear my new bracelets, and I didn't say anything to Dolce about my lesson in jewelry making. Even if I'd wanted to, she was preoccupied, worried about our sales, which she said had been slipping. She was going through catalogs and on the phone with distributors when I arrived.

"We're going to expand our shoe and jewelry sections," she announced when she got off the phone. "I'm tired of seeing our clients buy an outfit here and go somewhere else for their footwear and their cultured pearls, their cocktail rings and the latest earrings. We've got to be a one-stop shop."

That's when I almost blurted out, "I know how to make some stunning custom bracelets you could sell." What if they didn't sell? What if it took me hours to make one bracelet and then it looked amateurish? Better get some more practice before I went pro.

Some people cut back when business isn't good. Dolce's philosophy was to expand, and so far it had worked. I already thought we were a one-stop shop. It was disturbing to hear our customers' loyalty was slipping. I vowed to step up my salesmanship. Giving free advice and fashion tips was not enough. Not in these trying times. I had to put a little pressure on, in a tactful way, of course.

Dolce opened a catalog and showed me the shoes she'd ordered in her new favorite color—traffic-stopping red.

"You'd look great in these Aldo's," she said, pointing to a pair of red suede wedges. "Or these patent leather and wicker wedges."

When I didn't look enthusiastic enough, Dolce said, "I am truly, madly, deeply in love with wedges. They are a heel lover's best friend."

"I agree," I said. "They were hot this summer."

"And they'll be hotter this fall. You'll see."

"They are stunning," I said, referring to the red shoes she'd showed me. In those shoes my feet would be stunning, but what about the rest of me?

"So how was your class?" Dolce asked after she'd taken her pen and circled the picture of the fire engine red shoes.

Ten

....

I took a deep breath. I was dying to talk about the house and Armando the artiste, Diana and Diana's husband, but how much should I say about what happened after we left? Maybe for once I should keep my medical horror stories to myself. "It was fine. We made some unusual pieces I want to show you. The house is incredibly gorgeous. Apparently it's on the house and garden tour that's coming up."

"Is it?" Dolce said. "I bought the tickets, of course, but I haven't had time to look at the schedule. All I know is that there are five houses featured and a tea at the last one on the list. We can go together."

I breathed a sigh of relief. As usual, Dolce made it possible for me to mix socially with the upper class and enjoy the same perks they did, like house and garden tours or designer shoes, the kind of things I couldn't afford to do on my own. Even though the tour wasn't until next week, Dolce

said we should put our outfits together right then while we
weren't busy waiting on customers. When I said something
about wearing an outfit already in my closet, she shook her
head emphatically.

"I've said it before and I'll say it again," she said. "We
are walking advertisements for our shop, you and I. We will
be seen all afternoon as we make the round of the houses.
Not only will we see how our customers live, but we'll also
see everyone who's taking the tour and they'll see us. Some
of whom may have never even been in this shop, if you can
believe that."

I shook my head in dismay. Someone in the social scene
who hadn't been to Dolce's? I had to feel sorry for anyone
so out of touch.

"Too bad we can't wear signs that say 'Dolce's' with the
address," I said jokingly.

"No need for signs," she said seriously. "We will get the
message across with the help of our regular customers. I've
been on these house tours. There's just so much you can say
about the molding and the energy-efficient light fixtures and
the antique porcelain doorknobs, then the talk turns to fashion." She turned to a rack of pants and tops that had just
come in. "What do you think, long and lean or flirty and
feminine?"

I didn't know what to say. I was having a rare moment
of fashion indecision. Fortunately Dolce stepped up to fill
in the void. "You know, prints can be fun without being
overwhelming," she said. "How about something flowy in
a wide-legged pant?"

Taking her suggestion, I found a pair of wide print pants
by Alice and Olivia that I liked, then went to look for something to go with them.

"Nothing voluminous on top," Dolce warned, "or you'll look sloppy, especially if the top is on the long side."

"What about a body-conscious, form-fitting Tory Burch cashmere sweater?" I asked, riffling through a pile of sweaters for one in my size.

Dolce had cocked her head to one side as if to get a better look at the ensemble, which I hadn't tried on yet. She waved one arm as if to say "Go ahead and try it on," which I did. A few minutes later I came out of the dressing room.

"It looks like you," Dolce said.

"Is that good? Shouldn't I try to look like someone else sometimes?"

"How about wearing it with a pair of red and black striped Prada heels with the strap?"

"Print skirt and striped shoes?" I said just to be sure I'd heard correctly.

"Why not?" she asked. And she went into the alcove to find the shoes she said had been waiting for me to come along.

That's the thing about Dolce: she's always turning fashion rules on their head, which is why she's such a great saleswoman. What would the world be like if we all followed the rules every day?

She was right; even though the pants were so long I almost tripped on them, the shoes peeped out and gave the whole ensemble a jolt of surprise. The top clung to my torso, and the print pants swished against my skin like cumulous clouds.

"What will you wear?" I asked her.

Dolce bit her bottom lip as she always does when she's thinking. "I'm thinking head-to-toe solids," she said. "One of those Akris Punto skinny pantsuits we got in the other day. I love this shade of gray." She held up the suit for me to see.

"With a chartreuse blouse and a pair of those red shoes you love," I suggested.

"Rita, that's brilliant," Dolce said.

I was amazed that Dolce was going so far to be trendy. Usually she's more conservative than I am, but not today. Maybe it was because of her financial situation that she was willing to take more chances.

"I think you'll surprise everyone."

"Too much of a surprise?" she asked, the pale gray jacket in one hand and the shoe box in the other.

"Not at all. We don't want to be taken for granted, do we?"

Before she could answer, the phone rang in the office and Dolce asked me to answer it because some customers had come in.

It was Detective Wall calling, and of course he wanted to talk to me. And it wasn't a personal call. I sighed and wished I hadn't answered.

"Were you at the house of Diana Van Sloat last night?" he asked.

I clenched my teeth, expecting to be accused of something. What was it this time?

"I was at a jewelry workshop. Don't tell me that's a crime?"

"I understand there was an accident involving a knife."

"Not when I was there. No accidents. The only knives were used for slicing leather. We made some very interesting bracelets, which I'd be happy to show you. Don't tell me you're out looking for danger again."

"I don't look for danger, Rita," he said. "Danger looks for me."

"You're not complaining, are you?" I asked. "Because I would think as a cop it goes with the territory."

"Thanks for that tip," he said dryly. "Is there some reason you're being evasive?"

"About what, the dangers of police work? I'm in the fashion business. Now if you want to know what everyone was wearing last night . . ."

"Stop right there. I want a list of participants."

"Why don't you ask whoever told you I was there?"

"I did. It's called cross-checking."

"Well, if you want to know about cross-dressing, I could—"

"Are you going to help me or not?"

"If I don't, you'll call me in to the station, won't you?"

"Rita."

"Okay, okay. There was Maxine Anderson, Patti French, me and Diana, of course, and the jewelry guy, Armando. I don't know his last name.

"That's it? What about Mr. Van Sloat?"

"I thought you meant who was in the class. Diana's husband was there briefly. But he wasn't—"

"I understand he wasn't in the class. Anyone else in the house?"

"I don't know. It's a big house. There could have been a whole family living in the wine cellar for all I know. It's huge. You should see it. If you want to see it, it's on the house and garden tour coming up next week."

"Are you going?"

"Of course. Dolce and I will be there drumming up business for the shop, in a subtle way, of course. Can I ask why you're so interested in my making bracelets?" I didn't have a hope in hell he'd actually tell me anything. He never did unless he was desperate for information and he thought he could get it from me.

"We had a report that there was an injury at the Van Sloat house last night."

"What does that have to do with me?" I asked. This was not a rhetorical question. I really wanted to know. And more important, how had he found out? Had Jonathan told the cops about the injury? If so, why? When I'd come in by ambulance with my concussion, no one called the police.

"That's what I want to know," Jack said. "Is there something you aren't telling me? It's in your interest to tell the truth and the whole truth while you can."

"*I am!*" I said so loudly that Dolce opened the office door and looked in with a worried frown.

I nodded at her and held up my hand. Then I told Jack I had to go to work. "I have a job, you know," I said stiffly. "And you are interrupting my work."

"Helping rich idle women spend their husbands' money," he said. "You call that a job?"

"That is a sexist remark," I said. "How do you know it isn't *their* money? And for your information, I am helping women look their best, which is good for their mental health."

"So now you're a therapist as well as a salesperson."

"I do what I can," I said sweetly. It was no use getting into an argument with Jack. It was a no-win situation. I wasn't sure what he wanted from me. What did he think went on at the Van Sloat house last night besides a workshop and a minor accident with a knife?

Sometimes I felt like making up stories to tell him just to lead him astray so that I could then solve the problem myself, whatever it was. This time it had to do with Armando's injuries, but why? I was always trying to figure out the answers to Jack's questions before he asked them. Which was ridiculous. I couldn't even figure out the answers to the questions he asked. Not without giving away too much information.

"Does this line of inquiry have to do with the death of the chef?" I asked.

"You know I'm not going to divulge any confidential information regarding a pending criminal investigation, don't you?" he said.

I didn't want to answer, so I said good-bye and hung up. He couldn't get away with taking me from my important job of retail therapist to the rich and well-dressed.

What was left of the week flew by. Sales picked up, which was good for business, and Dolce looked happier. A week from Sunday we met at the shop in the morning for the house and garden tour. First we admired each other's outfits. Dolce looked great in her slim gray suit with the dynamite shoes. The unicolored outfit made her look taller and thinner than usual, which is what I told her.

She smiled and said that the print wide-legged pants were made for me. Before we left, she chose an eye-catching necklace with three graduated gold-plated brass tubes to hang around my neck, which was just what I needed against my black sweater. I thought about wearing my handmade bracelets, but decided not to.

Dolce drove up Van Ness to the breathtaking Pacific Heights neighborhood where gazillion-dollar mansions, painted Victorians and faux chateaux like Diana's lined the wide streets. On Jackson Street, Dolce miraculously found a parking space. It was a gorgeous warm fall day, which would have reminded us of summer anywhere else. But June and July summer days in the city are likely to be foggy. On our way to the first house on the tour, we stopped to admire views of the Golden Gate Bridge, Alcatraz and the sparkling blue waters of the Bay.

"The neighborhood was first developed in the 1870s," Dolce read from the brochure. "With small Victorian homes. But after the earthquake in 1906, they were replaced with larger, more substantial houses."

"You mean mansions," I said, gazing at the houses on both sides of the street.

"There are a few Victorians left," she said, pointing to a tall pale green three-story house with a steep roof and lots of gingerbread detail. "But the rest are Edwardian, Mission Revival and Chateau."

"Wait until you see Diana's house," I said. "I believe they call it Grand Tudor Revival. It's not as old as the Italianate Victorians or the ordinary Victorians or the Queen Anne's, but it's . . . well, you'll see."

"Here's the description of their house," Dolce said, consulting her brochure. " 'Built on four levels. Vast formal grounds. A sense of privacy.' Is that what you liked about it?"

"I liked everything," I told her. Everything except for Weldon, her husband. "But I really didn't see much except for the kitchen and her craft room, which are both wonderful. Even a person like you who doesn't do crafts would appreciate what she's done to the house."

But first we visited an enormous mansion up the street from Diana's, built in 1910 but recently remodeled by some famous architect. We joined some other women who were well-dressed, though we'd never seen them at Dolce's. I couldn't help staring at their outfits trying to decide who the designers were while Dolce's eyes were on the details of the living room, like the molding around the French doors, the gigantic fireplace, which was blazing even today, and the floor-to-ceiling leaded glass windows. We checked out the morning room across from the formal dining room.

"I don't know what I've done without a morning room all these years," Dolce said with a twinkle in her eye. We faced the fact that some people lived lives beyond the dreams of ordinary folks. Of course we knew that, but today we had a glimpse into the lives of the really, really rich. I appreciated Dolce's world view. Though she dealt with the super rich every day, she appreciated her good fortune in owning a house where she worked and lived under the same roof, and never seemed to envy the women who had enough money to afford fancy cars, multiple houses, and the expensive clothes they bought from her. I hoped someday to be more like her, because sometimes, like today, a wave of jealousy crept up and threatened to undermine my equilibrium.

We walked all the way up to the fourth floor of house number one where we stepped out onto the sun-drenched terrace facing west. I gasped at the view, at least one hundred and eighty degrees. The green trees of the Presidio, the historic military base; the bridges; the Bay were all laid out before us. Dolce saw someone she knew, so she went to speak to the woman while I braced my arms against the railing and stared out across the water to the Marin Headlands.

"Nice view." A familiar lightly accented voice interrupted my dreams of living like this. I whirled around. I should have known I'd run into someone I knew, but Meera? On a house and garden tour?

"I'm surprised to see you here," I said.

"I always attend historical tours," she said. "To see what they've done to the old houses in the name of modern comfort." She wrinkled her nose to show her disapproval. I assumed that meant she thought everything should be left as it was one hundred years ago to match the clothes she wore.

"Your dress is authentic, I suppose," I said, taking in the long dark brown satin gown, the bustle and her leather lace-up shoes. "And it suits you."

"Thank you," she said. "If I may quote Thomas Carlyle, who was an acquaintance of mine some time ago, 'The first purpose of clothes was not warmth or decency but ornament. Warmth was found in the leaves of the tree or in the grotto, but for decoration, one must have clothes.'" She paused and looked over my outfit, which she didn't seem too excited about, but then, it was hard to read Meera. "Don't you agree?" she asked.

"Definitely, since I'm in the clothing business," I told her. "So you knew this Carlyle?" I probably shouldn't have asked because she was bound to bring up the past, and with Meera, the past was definitely the long-ago past and went on and on. Sure enough, she had to tell me about it.

"Yes, I knew him. He was one of a group of my friends in Scotland."

"I didn't know you'd been to Scotland."

"There is much you don't know about me," she reminded me. Meera loved being mysterious, which was why I didn't buy her vampire story; it was all part of her act.

"I didn't stay long," she said, "much too cold up there. I like California better. I think if Carlyle could have come, he wouldn't have suffered so much from his ailments and wouldn't have been so cranky."

"I suppose you knew the people who used to live here too," I said, meaning the house.

"No, I didn't," she said. "I thought I might get some familiar vibrations from the walls, but I felt nothing. So I would have to say I've never been here before. But I am looking forward to visiting the other houses. Perhaps they will have some stories to tell."

I hoped that Meera hadn't heard about the incident at Diana's house. In any case, she bustled off a few minutes later, much to my relief.

I watched her flounce away, and then I went to look for Dolce.

"Who was that strange woman in the Victorian dress?" Dolce asked. "Is she one of the docents in her period costume?"

"No docent. No costume. That was my friend Meera. You remember her."

"The one who thinks she's a vampire," Dolce said, rolling her eyes.

The less said about Meera, the better. Dolce and I took the winding staircase down to the first floor, stopping to look into the bedrooms, the study, the library and the large projection room along the way. We walked out through the salon past a small group of women. We knew them all and stopped to say hello before we continued down the street to the house that belonged to the Van Sloats. I was curious to see how the kitchen looked in the light of day after all the blood had been cleaned up. Had there really been an incident? Or was it just a rumor? After the confirmation story from Jonathan, how could I doubt it?

I wanted to see the rest of the house today, and of course, so did Dolce. I took her around the back to see the sparkling turquoise pool and the gardens, and she was just as impressed as Patti, Maxine and I had been. In fact, Patti was there at the pool house with some friends who were also house-tour hostess volunteers. Dolce went to the bar they'd set up to get us some drinks from a punch bowl. I hoped the punch contained some alcohol, because I always needed a drink after a tête-à-tête with Meera. That was the effect she had on me. Patti left her friends and came up to speak to me at the edge of the pool.

"Rita," she said, "did you hear about Armando?"

"No, I mean, I don't think so." I had a nervous feeling in the pit of my stomach. "Why, what happened?"

"There was an accident," she said. "And a dispute. Someone got hurt."

I felt the color drain from my face. I didn't want to hear about this. Not again. I wanted to pretend nothing happened.

"Who was it—Diana?"

I thought I knew who'd gotten hurt, but I had to be sure. Why would Armando and Diana get into a dispute? I mean, she was crazy about him. Couldn't say enough good things about him. She'd acted as his assistant for our entire lesson. I couldn't see her starting a knife fight. The very idea was ridiculous. In fact, I started to smile nervously.

"Not Diana," she said.

My smile faded. "Then who?"

"Who do you think?" she asked.

I was drawing a blank. No time to think or answer her, because the patio was filling up with people we knew from the shop I had to say hello to. We all oohed and ahhed about the house even though we hadn't seen much yet. Still, just the patio with the pool and the gardens and the view were enough to impress even the most jaded socialite. And I was neither jaded nor a socialite.

"I want to show you the kitchen and the craft room," I said to Dolce, who'd handed me a glass of punch. I was trying to forget what Patti had said and even more, what she hadn't said. "It's where we had our class." Before I had even a sip of the punch, a waiter came out with a tray of champagne. "Compliments of the host and hostess," he said.

"How nice," Dolce murmured. We set our glasses on a table and took the champagne instead. "Have you met her husband?" she asked me.

"Yes, we met him the night of the class. He's a venture capitalist, and he seemed very busy but also very involved with Diana's life at the same time."

"Sounds like the ideal husband. Good-looking too?"

"Not exactly. Oh, there he is now." Weldon Van Sloat was strolling across the patio greeting the voyeurs and neighbors like the lord of the manor he was. I was glad Dolce got a glimpse of him so she could make up her own mind. Was he good-looking enough to be married to Diana, who was not only lovely but smart too? Was he a doting husband or an over-the-top controller?

I said hello to him, but he didn't give me a second glance. Probably didn't remember me, and I couldn't blame him. I was a nobody. I had no capital to invest in any ventures, and he probably knew that by looking at me.

We went inside then and straight to the kitchen. Dolce loved it, as I knew she would. She admired all the period touches as well as the updates, like the Sub-Zero double-doored stainless refrigerator, while I looked for signs of anything out of the ordinary, like bloodstains. But everything was perfect. Not a smudge on the marble counters or the tiles on the floor. Not that I expected there to be.

A woman in a white apron came in, said hello and transferred a baking sheet of canapés onto a decorative wooden tray. Then she took our empty champagne glasses, whisked them away and offered us crisp crackers covered with blue cheese, pecans and a half of a grape. It was a delicious combination.

"Did Mrs. Van Sloat make these?" I asked the woman. I could just imagine Diana knocking herself out preparing for today's open house. What I really wanted to ask was, where is Mrs. Van Sloat?

"No, they're all from Kate's Catering on Fillmore," she said. Then she went out to the living room before I could question her further. I couldn't help wondering why Diana wasn't here. She loved her kitchen, and she loved playing the hostess. Maybe she was in the craft room or one of the many other gorgeous rooms I hadn't seen yet, showing off her house and giving information about its history.

Dolce was equally impressed when I took her to the craft room with its bins of supplies and the spacious counters and work surfaces.

"What luxury to have so much space for your hobbies," Dolce remarked, and I agreed. She didn't ask what I'd made there, and I modestly didn't say anything.

Dolce and I proceeded to take the elevator up to the third floor. No stairs for us. The elevator was vintage and tiny, room for two, with glass walls and a small velvet bench. I loved the idea of it, but even with the glass walls I felt claustrophobic and was glad to get out. I mean, what if it stalled between floors? But it didn't.

We'd only just exited the elevator and taken one step

toward a wood-paneled room with a pool table in the center when I saw Detective Wall standing by the window talking to a tall woman in a chic maxi dress by Marc Jacobs and very high-heeled sandals in the color I call cinder.

Dolce recognized her immediately, or at least she recognized the dress.

"That's the Italian woman from the funeral."

"Guido's ex-wife?" I asked. "Who bought some clothes from you? I thought she'd gone back to Italy." Yet there she was at the Van Sloat open house with San Francisco's best detective. What was that all about? Was she still in town because Jack had ordered her not to leave? Was she staying in town until the murder was solved? Was she a suspect? If I thought I had a chance of getting the answers to these questions, I knew better. Jack would never tell me anything. So I was on my own. If I wanted to know anything, I'd have to do the footwork myself. So I left Dolce admiring some museum-quality landscapes hanging on the wall and walked up to the two of them. They stopped talking immediately, and neither looked pleased to see me. In fact, she actually glared at me. Not that I let that discourage me. Not even when Jack looked at me like I was on the Most Wanted List. But not his list. Someone else's.

I still didn't take these slights personally. It just proved there was something going on. Either Jack was hitting on her or she was hitting on him or they were talking about Guido, her ex-husband. Did Jack think she had something to do with his murder?

Eleven

"Hello," I said brightly. "What a surprise to see you," I added, to Guido's ex-wife. "I thought you'd be on your way back to Italy."

"I was going to leave," she said, "but your town is so charming, I could not bear to go so soon."

The way she said it made me think she was lying through her teeth. But why? Because she didn't want to say she was a suspect in Guido's murder and was required by the law to stick around? I could understand how that might be embarrassing.

"I love your dress. I hear you went on a shopping spree at our store. I hope you are pleased with your purchases," I said.

She smiled briefly but didn't answer. She said she was going to visit the rest of the house. Maybe she was glad to escape the evil eye of Jack Wall, or maybe she was mad at me for interrupting an intimate conversation that had nothing to do with murder. I couldn't imagine Jack forgetting his job for even a minute, but then I couldn't imagine him hooking up with a stylish Italian either, but there they'd been together, having an intimate conversation. It could have been an interrogation; I wouldn't put it past Jack. Or it could have been some romantic small talk, the kind I never had with the detective.

I watched her walk to the door, wondering if I'd ever be able to achieve the effortless European flair she had whether wearing American-designed clothes, like today, or the Italian couture she was used to. She was an even better advertisement for our shop than we were. Too bad she wasn't wearing a sign around her neck telling everyone where she'd bought that dress.

It occurred to me that Jack, being a very hot, rugged American type, might be looking for a fling with an attractive Italian tourist and looking for a murderer at the same time.

"I'm surprised to see you here too," I said. Though I wasn't really. After all we'd been through, I expected him everywhere and anywhere. The surprise was when I *didn't* run into him. "Can I assume you're at work even though it's Sunday?"

"Assume whatever you want. What about you?"

"This is part of my job. Definitely. We're schmoozing with our customers, checking out what everyone's wearing."

"Even me?" he asked. I thought this was a bit disingenuous. He knew perfectly well he was one of the best-dressed men in town. And in this crowd of mostly women, he easily took the prize.

"Especially you. You put the other men to shame in your

two-button wool tweed blazer. No golf or bomber jacket for you."

He merely shrugged, so I continued.

"You're not messing around, and you're not off duty, I assume. I hope you're enough of a metrosexual to enjoy a good house and garden tour. While you're still here on business, or are you?" I asked wide-eyed, as if I thought he'd tell me. He said nothing. Of course he wouldn't talk. I should have known. "You seem to be well acquainted with Guido's wife already."

"I'm investigating her ex-husband's murder, so the answer is yes, we have quite a lot to talk about."

I bet you do, I thought. "I imagine she's almost as eager as you are to find out who killed her husband. By the way, wouldn't it be interesting to know if she's the beneficiary of his property like the school and the chateau?"

Jack gave me a look that said he knew exactly what I was up to and he was having no part of it.

"No idea," he said. "That's not my job."

"Come on. Isn't it your job to establish a motive?" I asked. "Such as money? And what about this girlfriend he was supposed to have? Have you located her yet?"

I looked at him expectantly, although what were the chances he'd tell me if he had? I just had to show him I had some information up my sleeve, like the girlfriend thing. What I didn't say was that I'd heard Guido was trying to get rid of her. What if she'd gotten rid of him first.

"I have some leads," he said.

"Which you got from his ex-wife, I suppose. She'd be the perfect person to talk to about any women in Guido's life who'd want to kill him. That way she could get back at the girlfriend and solve this crime and absolve herself from any guilt."

Jack smiled and I wanted to think he was blown away by my astute observations, but the smile could have just meant he considered my opinions to be absurd. Maybe they were. Maybe they weren't. Maybe Guido's supposed girlfriend was the subject of the conversation I'd interrupted, but maybe it was just an international flirtation between an American cop and an Italian Carla Bruni lookalike.

"Let's talk about your job and your customers. It seems every woman here is connected to Dolce's. Coincidence? Or is something going on there I should know about?" he asked.

"This neighborhood, with its views, elite private schools and mansions, is our demographic. Maybe we don't live here, but our customers do. That's why we're here. We support the charities that the house tour benefits."

"So what did your jewelry class have to do with your shop?" he asked.

"The customers were also the students, that's it. Diana Van Sloat, whose house this is, is one of our best customers and an avid hobbyist. She invited me to join the class, which was excellent, by the way. I can't wait to show you the brace-lets I made. Now I've told you everything I know. Which is more than you've done for me." I should have known by now this relationship of ours was totally one-sided. I talked. He listened.

"I haven't seen the craft room yet," he said. "Where, I assume, these lessons take place. Want to show it to me?"

I couldn't believe he hadn't seen the room. If he really suspected something was going on there. He knew about Armando and the accident and where it had taken place, so why hadn't he headed straight for his target? Waiting for me to show it to him? I didn't think so.

"So what made you decide to take lessons from an Italian artisan?" Jack asked as we wended our way through the spacious hallway lined with portraits.

"Just my never-ending goal of self-improvement," I said lightly. "And I thought that one day I might be good enough to actually sell some of my jewelry."

I paused in front of a portrait on the wall of a man with a dog, and gazed at it. "Looks like Weldon, don't you think? Must be one of his ancestors. I assume you've met him."

"I've met Weldon but not his ancestors," Jack said. "He was at the door when I came in. Very friendly guy."

"I assume he didn't know you were a cop," I said dryly.

"I'm not wearing a uniform, but if anyone asks—"

"Has anyone asked?" I couldn't picture one of these well-dressed, well-coiffed, well-connected women or men asking Jack if he was in law enforcement and if so, was this a social call or . . .

"No, and I'd appreciate your keeping quiet."

"You want me to lie?" I exclaimed with mock horror.

"Of course not. I just don't want you to blow my cover if you don't have to."

"So you admit you're here undercover. But why?"

"It's my day off, and I'm here as an admirer of classic architecture and as a San Francisco history buff. That's all. No one else has put his or her profession on a name tag, have they? Why should I?" He glanced at my breast as if he was checking. He was checking all right, but not for a name tag.

"Nice necklace," he said. "Brass tubes. If there's a plumbing problem, we know who to call."

I fingered my necklace. I knew it was unusual. I'd seen

other people look at it. I assumed they were admiring my taste. Or rather Dolce's taste, which was impeccable.

"I know you only call me when you need help," I said.

"And you only call me when you want some inside information."

"If it's your day off, why aren't you out on the Bay in your sailboat?"

"No one to go with me. It gets lonely out there."

I shook my head. That lonely millionaire act wasn't going to work on me.

"Maybe you should branch out, meet some new people, and I don't mean suspects." I turned and headed for the craft room.

"How would I do that?" he asked a few steps behind me. Even though I couldn't see his face, I knew he'd be wearing a sardonic smile that went with everything he wore.

"I could introduce you to some nice women who are all right here today," I offered.

"I saw them. Just assumed they were married."

"Don't let that stop you," I said. "It doesn't stop them, according to our customers. Not that I ever listen to gossip."

We were in the hallway when he put his hand on my shoulder and turned me toward him. "What's that supposed to mean? Is someone you know cheating on her spouse? Like one of those women who hung around Guido after class? I think you know something you're not telling me."

"Gossip, that's all it is. You don't want me to repeat gossip, do you?"

I flashed on the sight of Guido's nervous face as he stood at the door the night he was killed. Because he had someone with him? Someone's wife? Is that why he was so anxious to get rid of me . . . and of her?

"I don't know anything," I said. "Really I don't."

"Then why do you have that look on your face?"

"I was thinking, that's all. Don't tell me that's a crime. You know I'm just as anxious as you are to find out who killed the chef. Maybe more anxious, since you didn't even know him when he was alive. Or did you?"

We walked to the kitchen before he had a chance to answer my question, although Jack would have found a way to avoid it as he always did no matter where we were.

The kitchen was filled with guests admiring the mural on the wall, the new built-in pizza oven and the custom cabinets. Not only was the catering crew there, but a bona fide pizza chef with a tall toque and a huge white apron was tossing a crust in the air and catching it behind his back. When the tossing was done, he put the crust on the counter, then reached into the oven and took out a pizza Magherita with tomatoes and fresh basil. It looked and smelled delicious with its blistered crust. After he cut it into slices and slid them onto small paper plates, I snagged one.

"Delicious," I murmured.

"As good as Guido's?" Jack asked.

"I don't know. He didn't make pizza in the class I took. Why?"

"Just wondered."

No way Jack just wondered. There was always a method to his questions. If only I knew what it was.

"Diana has gone all out," I said. "Last time I looked, there was just a caterer with canapés. Now this."

"So this is where you had your jewelry class?" he asked.

"No, it was in the craft room. I'll show you." We walked past the other visitors to the room where I'd made my bracelets.

I don't think Jack fully appreciated the room the way a dedicated artisan would have, but he looked into the drawers and studied the floor for some reason that I didn't quite understand. He asked me where each person had sat during the class, and I told him that Armando had circulated as he helped us.

"Have you seen Diana today?" Jack asked when he'd presumably finished his inspection.

"No, I wonder where she is. She should be here. She loves showing off her house. Who wouldn't?"

"You really want a house like this?" Jack asked as women came in, ooohed and ahhed, and went out.

"I'd love it, but I'm afraid it's not going to happen unless I find Mr. Millionaire. Or Billionaire. These days a million isn't really enough."

He leaned back against the wall.

"Your place looks fine to me. Why would you want a big house?"

"Just to show off, I guess. To have big dinner parties, professional guest classes, hire a gardener, throw tennis tournaments."

"Really?"

"No. I don't think I'm the socialite big-party type. But I would like a butler's pantry. But then I'd have to get a butler too."

"Some of my parolees are looking for jobs."

"As butlers?"

"As anything. No reason not to give them a chance. They've paid their debt to society."

"I like your attitude. How's your driver working out, speaking of your protégés."

"He's outside waiting for me."

"Solves the parking problem and keeps him off the mean streets," I noted. "I don't drive either. But I don't need a chauffeur. I have Muni to take me wherever I go. Or Dolce. She drove today."

"So she's around somewhere talking fashion, as usual. You two hustling customers even on your day off?"

"Of course. That's our job. Just like looking for murder suspects is yours. We may look like we're just supporters of good causes and patrons of the arts or whatever, but we're always checking out what designers people are wearing. How long their skirts are, how high their heels and how we can help them look better. Nothing wrong with that," I said, hoping he wouldn't contradict me. "Admit you're not here only to look at the hand-painted tile in the bathroom or the antique chandelier over the dining room table. You're looking for something like evidence or someone who looks suspicious, aren't you?" I didn't wait for him to answer. "Or are you looking at the architecture and getting ideas for home improvement? Though maybe your home doesn't need any improvement." I was hoping he'd invite me to see his home and judge for myself. What could Jack's house look like?

"I don't think you need any improvement," he said with a sweeping glance at my necklace, which rested on my sweater just above my breasts. The temperature in the room seemed to rise, and I suddenly felt like *I* was in the wood-burning pizza oven.

I waved my hand in front of my face in an attempt to cool off. By now I ought to know it's best not to take anything Jack says personally. So I didn't.

"So what do you think?" he asked.

"Of the house? I like this room, and next, I like the kitchen best. I don't like the elevator. It freaks me out. I

would love an extra room for my hobbies like this," I said.
"In the space I have I can barely turn around." I didn't have
to tell him; he'd seen my kitchen and my bedroom. "I haven't
had another dinner since that night you were there, and most
times I don't even cook for myself. If I'm hungry, I hit the
carryout button on my phone or that Vietnamese restaurant
in your old neighborhood."

"*If* you're hungry," he said, stifling a smile.

"Okay, so I ate a piece of pizza. I didn't want to hurt the
guy's feelings. And it was delicious. Now I know what I
want, a pizza oven. Then I could stop ordering out.

"Although sometimes cooking can be intimidating.
Guido was a fabulous cook. So good I was afraid to try to
make anything Italian, even pasta with tomato sauce."

"What about Armando?"

"What about him? He's not a cook." There's always a
reason why Jack asks these questions. And it's never a simple one. I'm always afraid to answer for fear he'll suspect
me of something.

"Did he intimidate you?" he asked.

"No, not at all. He was supportive and encouraging. Just
what you'd want in a teacher."

"Better than Guido?"

"No, not better. Just different. It's like comparing apples
and oranges. Yes, they both start with raw materials, then
make something fabulous out of it. The other night, it was
a small setting, only four of us, and more hands-on than at
Guido's cooking class. Why, are you thinking of taking a
jewelry-making class? I'll tell Diana, and I know she'd be
glad to invite you. She thinks men aren't interested in jewelry design except for the professionals like Pavé in the
East Bay."

"I was just curious," he said.

I didn't believe that for a minute. Jack was curious, but there was something going on in his clever, devious mind.

"Any chance you'd like to come to my house for dinner sometime?" he asked.

My mouth fell open in surprise. "Did you just ask me to dinner at your house?"

"Yeah. If that works for you."

"But you just took me to dinner at that whoop-de-doo restaurant."

"That was business," he said.

"I see," I said. Like all our encounters aren't business. "Will I be the only guest?"

Somehow I knew this invitation was a trick. I was being used as some kind of decoy. I couldn't believe Jack would invite me to dinner at his house without an underlying purpose that had something to do with his investigation.

"I might invite a few other people."

"Are any of them murder suspects?"

"Besides you? No."

"Come on, why would I kill Guido? I adored him."

"I hear you," he said.

"But you don't believe me. I'm surprised you have time to socialize."

"I don't. I mean, after the case is closed."

I knew he'd postpone it. Maybe forever. "You must be working round the clock on the Guido case. Or do you have it solved already?" Of course he knew what I was getting at. I just didn't want him to think I was in the dark any more than I was.

Instead of commenting or answering my question, he looked at his watch and went into the kitchen. The room was full of guests munching on wood-fired pizza. I took a deep breath. Once again I'd escaped from an encounter with Jack without giving away too much. Or learning much either.

"Where is our hostess?" he asked. "Your friend Diana."

"I don't know. I expected her to be here in the kitchen. But it's a big house. She could be anywhere. The tennis court, the movie theatre, the rooftop terrace . . . I'd better go find Dolce."

I left him in the kitchen. I figured Diana would show up at some point. Had he met her? Did he want me to introduce him as just a friend of mine? And why did he invite me to dinner? He said it wasn't business, but that couldn't be true. And who would the other guests be? *If* this dinner ever took place.

I wandered through the house and walked upstairs to the third floor looking for Dolce, looking for Diana, but finding only our customers admiring the billiard room with its dark wood paneling on the walls.

For some reason, talking to Jack wears me out. Partly because I'm always on my guard, afraid I'll say something I shouldn't say. Afraid I'll implicate someone who's totally innocent like myself. I talk a lot when he's around, and I don't know why that is. Why can't I just let him do the talking, and answer in monosyllables like "yes" or "no" or "maybe"?

On the second floor I walked by a room that was not open to the public according to the brochure; I assumed it was Weldon's office. As I passed, a man walked out and I quickly peeked in. It was just what you'd imagine a man's study to be like. The dark walls, the books, the gun case. What? Did all these rich guys have a gun collection? But maybe I was mistaken, since I'd gotten only a glance inside. The man, dressed in a dark suit, closed the door behind him and shot me a stern look, as if he knew I was a busybody. After he left, I tried the doorknob, but it didn't turn.

"Hi, Rita."

I whirled around to see Maxine standing in the hall. "Maxine, good to see you. Isn't this an amazing house?" Of course, it was quite possible her house was even more amazing. But she agreed.

"Did you see the master bathroom? Was that really a fourteen-carat bidet?"

"I don't know, I didn't see it," I said. "That doesn't sound like something Diana would put in." Diana wasn't the ostentatious type at all. "Probably came with the house."

"Have you seen her?" Maxine asked. "I wanted to say hello and thank her again for the class."

"Me too. I hate to leave without see her," I said. "I thought for sure she'd be out greeting everyone." I wanted so badly to ask if Maxine knew anything more about Armando's so-called accident, but there are times when even I know to keep my mouth shut.

"Have you had a chance to make any jewelry at home?" she asked.

Now was the perfect time to say "No, but did you hear Armando cut himself after we left?" But I didn't. I just said I didn't have enough confidence to try them by myself. "I need more lessons," I said. "I hope there will be some."

"So do I," she said. Then she hesitated as if she was going to say something else. I waited, hoping she'd open up the subject we were both avoiding, but she didn't. Instead, she went to see the solarium and I went to find Dolce. She was

standing in the high-ceilinged, arched entryway. She said
she was ready to visit the other houses on the tour, and so
was I, though I hated to leave without finding out what really
happened the night of our jewelry class.

I had hoped Diana would take this occasion to tell Jack
and me what we wanted to know. How the accident had happened, and when our next class was going to be. But that
was wishful thinking. I didn't even catch a glimpse of our
hostess and that was too bad. Even a little strange. Where
was she? Dolce and I followed a small group who were
headed down the street to the next house, just as we were.

Twelve

The next house was smaller and more livable, with a small craft room and an herb garden. I could almost imagine living in it the way I couldn't imagine living in Diana's. I wondered what the other visitors thought. That it wasn't upscale enough to be on the tour? That they wanted their money back? As we toured the second floor of the house, which included a children's playroom and a sunny office, I overheard a woman say this house didn't belong on the tour because it just wasn't posh enough.

Just what I thought might happen. I hated to hear snobby remarks like that. This house might not be posh, but it had a certain charm that was lacking in such houses as Diana's. Don't get me wrong. I loved Diana's house, especially her kitchen, but this place said "Welcome, come in and don't worry about spilling anything or leaving footprints on the carpet." Which reminded me of the blood on the floor. I hadn't seen any. Of course I hadn't. I hadn't seen any blood, and I hadn't seen Diana. Where was she?

When we went downstairs, I noticed the kitchen didn't have a pizza oven or acres of granite counters. It didn't have Diana's lofty taste stamped on it either, but was that such a bad thing? Shouldn't a house reflect its owners' taste and income? Mine did. It was small and compact, and the kitchen looked unused, which it was. Whereas the closet and my bedroom were overflowing with racks and boxes of clothes and shoes, not to mention my jewelry collection, including my new bracelet, which I was currently storing in my refrigerator. Plenty of room there, since I had no groceries on hand or any leftovers at present.

I didn't know the owners of this house. I wanted to peek into their closets when we were upstairs, but even I didn't have the nerve to do that. The woman of the house, whose name was Sheila Hill, wasn't our customer, but she should have been, I thought when I met her on the brick patio where she was talking to a group of visitors like us.

Not that Sheila's clothes looked shabby. Her long skirt and cable-knit sweater and sturdy shoes just looked like something she might have made herself or ordered from the Lands' End catalog. Good-quality materials but not exactly cutting-edge style. I had to admit it wasn't easy being a fashion guru. I spent a lot of my work time and my free time studying the fashion magazines and the women who came into the shop and who I knew wore the latest thing whether they were shopping in a boutique or volunteering, like Diana, as a docent at the zoo or the museums. This woman just needed a Dolce boost. Really, didn't everyone? She said hello and added that she admired my pants.

"Wide-legged print pants. So unusual. Sophisticated yet relaxed," she said a trifle wistfully.

"Comfortable too," I said. When I told her where they came from, she said she'd never been to our shop.

"You should really come and check us out," I told her. "In my opinion everyone should shop at Dolce's at least once a week. I say that not just because I work there. I'd shop there even if I had no connection to the shop. If I could afford it." Which I couldn't. Not at this moment. Of course, if I married a billionaire. Or even a simple millionaire . . .

"Really," she said.

"We bend over backward to serve our customers, getting to know their taste and their style so we can customize our service. Take this necklace," I said, fingering the tubes hanging around my neck. "Who would have thought it would go with this sweater? I should have known the sweater called out for some smashing jewelry. I just didn't hear the call. But Dolce did. She's my boss. That's how good she is," I said.

"You're quite the saleswoman," the woman said with a smile. "I hope your boss appreciates you. Because if not—"

"Oh, she does. That's her over there," I said, pointing to Dolce, who was taking a cracker spread with cream cheese, salmon and capers from a sturdy table on the patio. "That's Dolce."

"Because if not," the woman continued, "I have a job to offer you. I could use someone with your style." She gave me and my whole outfit an appreciative glance. Finally someone noticed. And commented.

What did she say? Was some stranger offering me a job? Doing what?

"Thank you," I said, "but it's my boss who has the style.

Besides, I already have the world's best job and the world's best boss." Only a few weeks ago I didn't appreciate either the way I did now. That's what a murder in your midst will do for you. I glanced at Dolce, who must have heard this conversation because she looked wide-eyed and startled. I hoped she didn't think I was job hunting. Especially when she'd bought the tickets that got us into this house tour. I switched the subject to the house and told the owner it was charming. "Especially your herb garden," I said, inhaling the scent of fresh basil and cilantro planted in pots on the patio.

"Compared to the mansions on this tour, our home is what I like to call cozy," she said.

"Compared to my house, it's a mansion," I said.

"Then maybe you'd be interested in supplementing your income. You do have weekends and evenings free, don't you?"

"Yes, but I'm taking some classes after work," I said. Now that I'd started, I wanted to take more.

"I see," she said as if she really did see that I was not exactly overwhelmed by my hobby. "The job I'm thinking of is one most women enjoy. I think you'd be good at it. It involves shopping." She lowered her voice, put her hand on my shoulder and led me to the far corner of the patio. Out of the corner of my eye I saw Dolce looking at us. No doubt wondering what in the hell I was doing. I wondered too.

"Have you ever heard of mystery shoppers?" she asked.

"Yes, but I'm not sure what their job is." Actually I appreciated having a good mystery to solve even when it involved someone I knew. And God knew I loved to shop. Maybe I ought to pay attention and not be so quick to brush off this offer, whatever it was.

"The job is to evaluate certain stores and their services. Maybe you've even had one of them in your store—what is its name?"

"Dolce's," I said, "in Hayes Valley." Had a mystery shopper come in and I hadn't noticed? "Who hires the mystery shopper, and what's the point?"

"The store hires them to be sure the clerks are doing a good job and that they aren't stealing from the till."

I smiled. "Well, I would have known if my boss had hired a mystery shopper. It's a small shop. I don't need to steal because my boss is incredibly generous. Take this outfit. She insisted I wear it today even though I can't afford anything like it. My whole closet is full of clothes she gave me or sold to me at a discount. I'm the only employee since the other sales assistant was murdered. Dolce and I don't have any secrets from each other." As soon as I said this, I knew I had talked too much, and what I'd said about the secrets wasn't true. Maybe Dolce had kept no secrets from me, but I hadn't told her everything I knew or thought I knew about the chef's murder or the alleged incident at Diana's house.

"I only mention this job opportunity because you look the part of an upscale shopper," she said. "And as a sales assistant who lives in a small apartment, as you mentioned, I thought you might be interested in earning some more money to augment your current salary, as generous as it may be. The hours are your own. Nights and weekends or whenever you're free and the stores are open."

Across the patio a few women stopped for a glass of wine and a canapé and turned to wave at Sheila, the hostess. She reached into her pocket for her card and told me to call her. On the card it said she ran an employment service in the city. No wonder she wanted me to take this job. She must get a commission on everyone she placed.

"Naturally this job is completely undercover. You have to keep it to yourself; otherwise, your cover would be blown and you couldn't do the job."

I nodded, thinking I could never do that. I should have confessed right then and there that I was a blabbermouth and I couldn't keep a secret if I tried, but I didn't. Let's face it: I was intrigued, and I was flattered to be selected out of the crowd for my looks and my clothes. Then I joined Dolce, who I could tell was dying of curiosity.

"Was that woman trying to steal you away from me?" she asked, one hand on her hip.

"Oh, no, that would be ridiculous. I told her I had the best job in the world and you were the best boss."

Dolce sighed with relief and squeezed my arm. "But what did she say?"

"She runs an employment agency." I lowered my voice and looked over my shoulder to make sure no one could hear us. "She wants me to be a mystery shopper."

"A mystery shopper. What's that?" Dolce whispered.

"I'll tell you when we get out of here," I said.

When I explained it to her after we'd visited all the houses and eaten and drunk whatever they'd offered, she was dubious.

"But, Rita, what about your other interests? How will you have time for your classes?"

"I can't give those up, that's for sure," I said. "But she said I could work whatever hours I'm free, which means Sundays, Mondays and nights. Since I love to shop anyway . . . Oh, I don't know," I said. "I'll have to think it over."

"It might be good to have another interest besides the

murder of your culinary teacher," Dolce said thoughtfully as she drove to California Street.

"Do you think I've been obsessive about it?" I asked anxiously. "If I have, I was only trying to help." After all, I might have been the last person to see the chef alive—except for the killer, of course. That made me feel responsible for doing what I could to find out who'd killed Guido. I thought I'd actually uncovered some good leads, which I intended to follow up on. Although, if you asked the police, they would say I was not helpful, that, in fact, I was intrusive. So maybe I should take a part-time job to keep me from getting bored.

"I wouldn't say obsessive," Dolce said as we stopped at a red light. "Maybe 'preoccupied' is a better word."

I pressed my lips together. Did she think I wasn't doing a good job at work because I was preoccupied with Guido's murder?

"Then I think I'll follow up on it and see what the job entails," I said.

She nodded. I don't think she even knew she'd hurt my feelings. Maybe it was time I took a look at myself and tried to branch out. Yes, I'd tried taking classes, but both of them had been followed by some kind of violence; whether it was an accident or not, it was still disturbing.

Dolce had decided we should close the shop on Monday, so there I was, faced with a free day. In the morning I first called Diana to touch bases with her and see how the open house had gone. I couldn't help wondering why I hadn't seen her during the tour, but it was a big house, so maybe I'd been downstairs when she was upstairs, or vice versa. But she didn't answer, so I left a message.

Determined to make the most of my day off, and still stinging from what I interpreted as Dolce's criticism of my "obsessive" interest in the Guido murder, I called my new friend Sheila who wanted me to be a mystery shopper, and she asked me to come to her office downtown when I had time. I said I could come in that morning, so I dressed quickly in business casual before I lost my nerve and asked myself what I was doing applying for another job when I barely had time for work and my hobbies. I hadn't even been to my gym for weeks.

To impress my future employer with my fashion sense, I paired a vintage Emanuel Ungaro jacket from the eighties with a belted, knee-length Lauren denim skirt and some strappy Ivanka Trump sandals. I took the bus to the financial district and filled out an application. Sheila, my new employer, said I already looked the part of the mystery shopper, which was the whole idea of my outfit. After I filled out the form, she said she had no doubt I'd be terrific at the job. She said she had a sixth sense about people, which was why she was in the employment field.

In all modesty I thought I would be terrific at it too. How hard could shopping and filling out an evaluation of the clerk be? It was a dream job, wasn't it? I thought so. She said she'd call and let me know what my first assignment would be. Feeling proud of myself for taking charge of my life and sending myself in a new direction, I walked out of her office with a light step and almost ran into the bartender at Eduardo's.

"Hello," I said. From the blank look on his face, I assumed he didn't know who I was. "I'm Rita," I said. "I saw you at your restaurant."

He forced a smile, then brushed by me on his way into Sheila's office. What was he doing here? Surely he didn't need a job, did he? I thought he had one. Of course, he might be there to help Eduardo find new employees—cooks, waiters, whatever. But why was he so brusque? Probably was in a hurry, I told myself. And he just didn't recognize me. Why should he? I was just another customer. Just in case he said something interesting, I paused outside the office and pressed my ear to the door. I heard him say something like, "I have to get away. Find someone else. It's not working. I told you . . . As far away as I can. Now."

I would have stayed longer to hear this fascinating conversation because this man was still on my list of possible suspects, but a woman in a tailored three-piece microfiber DVC suit and a pair of Rachel Roy platform pumps came and knocked at the door. I moved on, wondering if she was applying for the mystery shopper job too. I thought I had a lock on that job, but maybe not. It wasn't surprising that others would want this cushy job as much as I did.

I took the bus home and changed into tie-dyed Stella McCartney skinny jeans and a ruffled Tommy Hilfiger blouse, with dangly silver ShalinIndia earrings. I looked at myself in my full-length bedroom mirror and asked myself, "Now what?"

The answer of course was I should go to the zoo to look for Diana. If she wouldn't answer my calls, I'd go find her. And if she wasn't doing her docent thing today, I could still have a good time watching my favorite animals, the cute koala bears and the penguins, who looked like they were on their way to work in formal wear.

It would be more fun to go with someone, I thought. I crossed Jonathan off my list; since he worked at night, he was probably asleep. And of course Detective Wall wouldn't be free to simply enjoy the day if it didn't have something to do with crime.

I took a chance and called Nick.

He answered the phone and said he didn't have a tumbling class until tonight and he would like to go to the zoo with me very much. It's nice to encounter someone with manners who acts happy to hear from you whether or not he actually is.

"We should meet at the cage of the hippo at two. And afterward, when they close, we will go to the Cliff House for the atmosphere and for something to eat. The crème brûlée is excellent."

The Cliff House? That called for something a little more upscale than my jeans and ruffles. So I packed my L.L.Bean leather tote bag with a new outfit for the après-zoo activities. In it I put my favorite dress-vest combo. The navy vest was by DKNY, the print dress and the bag were Proenza Schouler. I threw in a pair of high-topped Alexander Wang high heels. That ought to do it for the legendary restaurant that was voted "best restaurant with a view" in San Francisco. Before we left the zoo, I would slip into a restroom and discretely change my outfit. Thank God for Nick, who always came through for me when I needed him.

In my skinny jeans I stopped for lunch at a Mexican fusion food truck where I downed a delicious spicy chipotle shrimp taco smothered with onions, cilantro and a squeeze of lime. Then I jumped back on the Taraval bus, which let me off at the zoo. Fortunately it was a free day, so before I breezed in without paying I asked at the information booth if Mrs. Van Sloat was working today. After consulting a volunteer list, the girl said she should be with the gorillas. Of course. That's what she'd said. Finally I'd get a chance to touch base with her. There was so much I wanted to ask her.

First I made my way to where the new hippo I'd heard about was swimming in his pool with his enormous head out of the water. He seemed to be looking straight at me. But maybe that was just me wanting to be the center of the universe even though I knew I wasn't. Even though the hippo might not appreciate my appearance today, I was feeling good about myself. I liked what I was wearing, and I was proud of myself for branching out job-wise. The bonus would be if I found Diana and had a word with her.

I found Nick leaning over the fence gazing at the hippo too. He was dressed as usual in European casual: tight pants, a Zegna Sport leather jacket with the collar turned up and a form-fitting T-shirt underneath. On his feet he wore a pair of Bacco Bucci crocodile-skin loafers. I wondered what the crocodiles would think of those shoes. Maybe we ought to avoid their area. When Nick turned and smiled at me, I felt a jolt of excitement. Yes, it was time for me to branch out and see some more of the other men in my life. Nick was generous, athletic and had a certain European flair that other men didn't. So take that, Detective Wall and Dr. Jonathan.

"It is good to see you and this hippo," he said. "You look quite stylish and beautiful, as always," he said.

I wasn't sure if he really meant it or if it was Romanian custom to always pay a compliment to a woman. I also didn't know who was highest on his list, me or the animal they called the king of the river.

"Thank you," I said, thinking that he'd be equally impressed with the outfit in my tote bag.

After a close-up look at the three-thousand-seven-hundred-pound land mammal submerged in the pool, I realized how much of him there was to admire.

"I love this hippo," Nick said. "I had read about him, and then you call and tell me to go to the zoo. It is as if it is destiny. Do you know his story?" He nodded toward the hippo.

"I don't remember the details," I said. Even if I did, I knew he wanted to tell me. And who else would know the hippo's story but Nick?

"He came here from Kansas," Nick said.

"Really? They have hippos in Kansas?" I didn't ask how he knew this. I knew he was proud of his ability to read English, which was better than his ability to speak it.

"They had too many there, so they sent this one here. First they had to make for him a larger pool and more land."

"There seems to be room for more hippos," I suggested, looking at the large, fenced-in field. "So he can have company."

"Hippos don't like to share, so all this is for him. They have very thick skin," he added. His smile faded. "Sometimes can come in handy."

"You mean he can shrug off criticism or rejection more easily?" I asked with a sidelong glance at Nick. I didn't know if he knew the double meaning of "thick-skinned." He didn't like to complain about anything, so if something was wrong, I had to pry it out of him. A moment later he suggested we move on to see the gorillas.

I told him I had a friend who was a docent who might give us a tour or at least tell us more about the gorillas. When we got to the Gorilla Preserve, I saw Diana in a forest green jacket and a matching hat that said "Ask Me" on it. She was surrounded by a crowd of visitors to whom she was explaining that the gorillas' natural habitat was lowland tropical forest.

I wondered if I "asked her," if she'd tell me what happened after we left her house the night of our class. But I suspected today her answers would be confined to gorilla behavior, their habitat and their diet. Which was why we were there, after all. I told myself the only thing I could learn today concerned wild animals. I should try to forget about Guido's murder and learn more about the inhabitants of the zoo instead of the inhabitants of San Francisco's Pacific Heights mansions.

When Diana caught sight of us, she looked startled and stumbled over her explanation of the gorilla's natural diet of leaves, stems and insects. I guess I should have phoned and told her I was coming today.

"At the zoo," she said to the group clustered around her, "the gorillas are fed fruit, vegetables, cottage cheese, whole wheat bread and cooked rice."

"Sounds boring," I muttered to Nick, who nodded in agreement.

"Is that your friend?" he asked.

"Yes, I wonder if she gets to feed them their cottage cheese."

"I would prefer to feed the small animals," Nick said. "Like penguins or baby koalas."

That's what I liked about Nick. He was secure enough in his masculinity that he didn't have to act all macho. Another man might have insisted his favorite animals were the lions and tigers. Not Nick.

When most of the crowd had disbursed after Diana finished her talk, I rushed up to her, with Nick following close behind me.

"Diana," I said. "So good to see you."

She nodded, but she didn't seem that happy to see me. Was it because she was in her docent mode and wasn't supposed to fraternize with the customers? But then why would she have invited me for a VIP tour? Or had I done something wrong at her house, either at the jewelry workshop or at the open house?

"This is my friend Nick Petrescu," I said.

She glanced in his direction but ignored the hand he held out.

"I missed you at the house and garden tour," I said. "What a wonderful day." The more she didn't respond, the more I continued to talk, hoping to reach her. "And your house looked beautiful."

"Thanks," she said.

"And the pizza was fabulous. Do you use the oven often?"

"Not really," she said. "Although . . ." She looked over my head and waved her hand at someone. "Sorry, I have to go. I have another primate tour waiting for me. And there's a cobra missing. The world's longest venomous snake. You might want to leave now to be absolutely safe. Good to see you again."

Nick and I looked at each other in alarm. A cobra missing? Why didn't a siren go off? Why didn't they close the zoo? I had to admire Diana for being cool in the face of an emergency like a missing cobra. That was probably part of the docent training. Don't alarm the visitors. But she was so casual about it. Why suggest *we* leave now but let everyone else stay? What was wrong? Had something I said caused her to invent a crisis?

"Are you afraid of snakes?" I asked Nick.

"Only the ones which are poisonous," he said. "I wonder if it's an Egyptian cobra, the kind that killed Cleopatra."

"I believe that was a suicide," I murmured. I looked around at the ground and up in the trees above us in case the cobra was going to drop down on me, bite me and leave me to die an agonizing death while waiting for the ambulance to come with the antivenom. I hoped no one would say it was a suicide. I didn't want to die. I had my whole life ahead of me. Men I hadn't met yet. Racks of clothes to wear. Styles I hadn't tried yet.

"They're not what you call slimy, you know," Nick said. "They have smooth, dry skin."

"I'm sure they do. It isn't their sliminess that worries me. It's the venom. You know, the poison. Do you think we should leave?"

"I'm not afraid," he said. "Why would a cobra attack us when we are harmless visitors?"

I figured if he wasn't afraid of a snake on the loose, then I shouldn't be either. If we saw the snake, Nick would bravely grab it by its smooth, dry body and take it back to its cage, holding it tightly around the neck so it couldn't strike with its poisonous fangs.

To my relief, there were no snakes in sight anywhere and no signs of panic. Quite a few people were strolling around looking at a male gorilla who was beating his chest. I didn't know whether he was warning us or just exhibiting typical male gorilla behavior. I decided it was Diana's job to alert the authorities or the visitors about this snake. Not just us. Instead of leaving now and missing the other exhibits on a day when the entrance was free, I planned to forget about the snake and move on to the penguins.

And so we headed toward Penguin Island. I figured if no one else was running for the exits, then Diana must have been mistaken. But where was she? I'd pictured her giving us a special behind-the-scenes tour. Instead, she'd given us a special brush-off.

"The woman, she is your friend, yes?" Nick asked me. Probably wondering what kind of friend would ignore me like that. I was wondering too.

"Not really a friend," I said. "She's a customer at the

shop. And I have been to her house a few times. I think she takes her job as docent seriously and probably didn't want to be interrupted while she was working. I understand that."

Actually I didn't understand it at all. I had a job, but I always had time to socialize with the customers. Just a "Hello, how are you?" would have been nice. Especially after I'd missed her at her open house. Where had she been that day? I was starting to get worried. Had I said something wrong? Done something out of line? The last time I'd seen her, she was standing at her front door waving a cheery good-bye to me, Maxine and Patti. Then Armando had his so-called "accident." Next Diana was a no-show at her own open house.

I was determined to face off with Diana and ask her what was wrong, because clearly something was. But when I suggested we follow Diana and even join her next tour, Nick said we should first see the penguins. He'd read a lot about them and wanted to observe their behavior and their habitat as close up as we could get.

I felt that way about Diana and her husband. I'd observed their behavior and their luxury habitat up close, and I had more questions. It seemed obvious that Diana was avoiding me as if she thought I was going to butt into her life. But I wouldn't. Not really. I just wanted to know if I'd done something to offend her or her husband. And of course I wanted to know about Armando's "accident." But I would never come right out and ask. Not me. I'd try to find out in some subtle way. Of course I would.

Thirteen

The penguins were fun to watch as they waddled on the walkways and paddled in the man-made pool around the man-made gunite rocks. I leaned over the fence to admire them. "No poison, nothing dangerous here," I remarked to Nick. "No way for them to escape if they wanted to, which I don't think they do. They look happy."

"But all is not calm as what you see on the surface," Nick said. "I read about the problems in the newspaper. So not so happy for every penguin. Didn't you read this story?"

I shook my head.

"Some penguins are homosexuals. Not surprising, since they all look the same to me. Male and female. Maybe they can't tell either."

"They look the same to you and me, but I suppose the penguins know which is which and who's who," I said.

"See the two penguins over there?" He pointed to a couple of identical penguins on a rock by the water. "Many
couples are here like those over there."

"You mean that's a gay couple?" I asked. "Oh. How can
you tell?"

"I can't, but as you said it, the penguins can. I just think
that they might be gay or not. Anyway, they look like they
belong together."

"I don't know how you can tell they're a couple," I said.
"They're just standing there together."

At that moment a man in khaki shorts with an "Ask Me"
button on his shirt came up to the exhibit with a crowd of
visitors.

"Our penguins have a good life here at the zoo," he said.
As usual I was eager to learn more about animals and people too, so I took Nick's arm and we stepped up and got in
with the group. I loved hearing the scoop from well-
informed volunteers like Diana. Only this guy, because of
his uniform, seemed to be a regular zoo employee and not
a volunteer. Even better.

"They've got the water at the right temperature for swimming, fish to eat that they don't have to catch themselves.
What's not to like?" he asked with a smile.

"Is it true some of the penguins are gay?" an older man
asked, looking like he wanted to hear it was just a rumor.
"I read about this gay penguin couple in the paper."

"You may be referring to Harry and Pepper," the guide
said. "They aren't the only gay couple. Many penguin couples, gay or straight, will raise their adopted children
together like humans do. I think I know which story you're
talking about, the one that made the newspapers. Probably
because of the female penguin we call Linda. She had a

reputation for being a home wrecker. Sure enough, she came in and broke up Harry and Pepper's marriage, or rather, their same-sex union."

"Where is she now?" I asked, wondering if he would point her out or if she'd changed her cheating ways.

"She left the zoo some time ago," the guide said. Then he went on to describe other fascinating penguin behavior traits.

"I wonder," I whispered to Nick, "if she's breaking up some other couple's life somewhere."

He shrugged and I glanced around, startled to see Diana at the edge of the crowd, listening and looking upset. Her face was pale, and her brow was creased. Hadn't she heard this story of the penguin Linda before? It was a disturbing story, but I would have thought that working at the zoo, she'd have gotten used to these kinds of things. I was surprised to see her there with the other visitors like us; I'd assumed she was off leading another tour, but maybe she was on her break. I couldn't deny that she'd hurt my feelings when she brushed us off the way she had.

It was not only Diana who was interested in the flight-less birds; Nick was also staring at the penguins with an intensity that worried me. I thought he was over his breakup with his so-called fiancée, but maybe not. Maybe he was hurting but pretending to be fine.

"Nick, are you all right?" I asked. "You can't say your life is like that of a penguin, can you?"

"Of course not. I am not a penguin. I know that. I can find a new girlfriend. Maybe I have found her already." He gave me a sideways look and a half smile that made me think he meant me. What if he did? Could I handle a Romanian boyfriend, or was I jumping to conclusions a little too soon?

I wasn't ready to settle on one man. I wanted a choice, and I wanted Nick to be in my life as someone I cared about. Who else would go to the zoo with me and take me to the Cliff House afterward?

But what about Diana? As if I didn't have enough to worry about. The story of the homosexual penguin couples and the female who broke them up had clearly affected her. Why? Had she broken up some gay couple's affair? Was her husband gay? I couldn't ask her, but at least I could try again to talk to her. As a friend who wanted to help. But when I glanced up, she was gone. Never mind. The zoo was not the place to talk over personal matters unless they pertained to the animal kingdom.

"What about you, Rita?" Nick said. "Any plans for getting married?"

"Married? No." Me, married, when I didn't even have a steady boyfriend? I was glad I didn't live in Romania where I might be forced into an arranged marriage. "I'm not ready to get married at this moment. In America women don't need to marry young anymore. We can wait until our thirties or later and no one says a thing about it. You're the first person in ages who's asked me if I have any plans. Maybe others have thought about it, but never said anything." If anyone would bring it up, you'd think Dolce would, but being single herself, she hadn't said a word.

"I have heard this custom of older people marrying late in your country," he said. "But in my country marriage is very important for happiness and prosperity. We must ask three times of the girl, and she doesn't accept until the third time. Then is the discussion of the dowry. But this is not interesting to you," he said. "Let us move ahead to see some more monkeys. They are always amusing and will make us smile."

"Maybe we should move on," I said.

The next exhibit we came to was the chimpanzees.

"These chimps are our closest living relatives," I read aloud from the sign on the fence.

We watched the playful chimps climb the fence, eat bananas, toss the skins aside and chase each other around the cage.

"I understand they are very intelligent animals," Nick said, leaning forward to watch their antics. "See the one in the back of the cage throwing something at the other one, who is perhaps his rival."

I leaned forward for a better look just as the chimp came racing toward the moat and threw something smelly and rotten right at me.

I stumbled backward. "Ow, oh no," I shouted as I was sprayed with smelly monkey poop from head to toe.

Other visitors jumped back, shocked and astounded. I couldn't believe it. My outfit was ruined.

Nick stood and stared. If I didn't know better, I might have thought he was going to laugh. But this was no laughing matter. I sputtered, I choked and I gagged.

"Chimps are the only species besides humans who throw things at a target. That is what I have read," Nick said with a shrug, as if it was no surprise to have a chimp toss his feces at a visitor. "Now what will you do?" he asked, shaking his head "We must go home."

What, and miss dinner at the Cliff House? No way! I shook my head. "I will just change in the restroom," I said, thankful I'd brought a new outfit. It was a good reminder never to leave home without a change of clothes, even if you aren't going to the zoo.

"But you must have a bathe," Nick said.

I grabbed my tote bag, which he'd been toting around for me, and headed for the ladies' room in the green building. There I stripped off my smelly outfit and wrapped it all, including the shoes, in a plastic bag I kept in my tote. Ignoring the curious looks from women who came and went, I focused on washing my hands, arms and even my legs with the dispenser soap and drying off with wads of paper towels. Then I slipped into my new dress, my vest and my shoes. I ran a comb through my hair, reapplied my makeup and gave myself a pep talk.

"Look at you. You're fine. No one would ever know you'd been attacked by a primate."

A woman came out of the stall behind me and gave me a funny look.

"I'm not crazy," I said.

"Of course not," she said, then she hurried outside.

Nick gave me a thumbs-up when he saw me, and I felt much better. We walked past the anteaters, who, according to the sign outside their area, were solitary animals except for the mothers and babies. They were usually eating or relaxing. It seemed that the relaxing part took up about fifteen hours a day. What a life, I thought. And no predatory females to steal your mate, I hoped. Some people found them to be very cute with their three-foot-long tongue, but I didn't, so we didn't spend much time with them. I was ready to leave the zoo, and Nick was looking forward to eating at the Cliff House. I kept my eyes open for a glimpse of Diana, hoping we might catch her on the way out, but I didn't see her.

I wondered if Nick was aware that the Cliff House was an expensive, upscale restaurant. I'd been there with Jonathan, but he was a well-paid doctor. Nick was a gymnastics teacher. How much money did he have? I decided to relax and enjoy it.

I realized Nick was happiest when he was playing the role of tour guide for his adopted city. Maybe he was that way in Romania too. Some day I'd go there and see. First he'd explained about the penguins at the zoo, then he'd explained primate behavior, now at the Cliff House he was anxious to tell me the history of the place, which had been a San Francisco landmark since the Civil War.

The restaurant was quiet at this time of night. Too early for dinner for most people, but the bar was already crowded. We got a table at the window where we could watch the waves crashing against the rocks below and see the sleek shiny seals swimming and cavorting in the sea.

"The first Cliff House was built in 1863," Nick said, putting the menu aside while he filled me in. "Naturally, since this is such a place for a beautiful scene. But perhaps you already know its story."

I shook my head. I would have said no anyway because he took such pleasure in telling stories about the past. That's where he resembled his aunt. Only he didn't claim to have lived through the times he was describing.

"Well, if we could look at the guest list, we would see three U.S. presidents who came here to the Cliff House, but sadly guest book was destroyed in a dynamite explosion. But many big names of San Francisco, like Crocker, Stanford and Hearst, would drive out in their carriages on Sunday to watch horse races and have recreation."

Nick waved to the waiter, and since we weren't driving,

he ordered a bottle of a certain California white wine I hadn't heard of. The waiter complimented him on his good taste, then he continued.

"I will skip forward past other happenings to the time of the Sutro Baths," he said.

"I've heard of them," I said. "And seen the pictures of the men in one-piece bathing suits and women in bloomers and long black stockings."

"Six large swimming pools," Nick said, seeming almost as proud of this accomplishment as if he'd built them himself. "Plus a museum and skating rink. Not only the rich ones but also so many ordinary San Franciscans came out on steam trains or bicycles to enjoy a day at the beach. Then came the earthquake of 1906, which you know about."

I nodded. I was no history buff, but that date stuck in the mind of everyone who'd ever lived in the city.

"But you know, by some miracle the Cliff House didn't get any damage then, until one year later when it burned to the ground. Sad, yes?"

I agreed. I was wondering how much of the story was left for Nick to tell when he suddenly glanced over at the wall behind us. He said he'd continue the fascinating history later.

"Notice the photographs," Nick said. "I like that one of Judy Garland, famous movie star."

Judy seemed to be watching us from the wall. The autograph under her picture said she was sending her best wishes.

After studying the menu, we ordered crab and shrimp salad with Louis dressing. Served with warm sourdough bread, it was delicious. We followed that with clam chowder rich with cream and huge chunks of clams.

"Nick, this is wonderful. You are so kind to take me to dinner. I must make dinner for you some time soon."

"You told me you studied Italian cooking."

"Oh, I did. But then the chef died."

"Before the class was over?"

"No, much later. It was mysterious. The police think it was murder.

"As for cooking," I added, "you're not bad yourself." He'd supplied me with a few choice dishes when I was recuperating from my sprained ankle.

For dessert we had roasted banana bread pudding instead of the crème caramel. I sighed contentedly. Nick seemed as happy as I was. Even though I had a tote bag full of smelly, dirty clothes and I had a mystery to solve and a new job to contemplate, I was able to put myself in the moment and savor the experience of dining in a famous San Francisco landmark with an attractive Romanian gymnast.

I knew I wasn't supposed to tell anyone, but I couldn't resist talking about my possible part-time job as a mystery shopper to such a sympathetic listener. His eyes lit up.

"This is very exciting," he said. "You are good at this. Catching criminals. Like the woman who killed your worker. That was you who found out the murderer."

"I won't be looking for criminals," I explained, always glad to hear a compliment. "I'm only interested in clerks who are not doing their jobs, that's all. But I appreciate your confidence in me."

"Will you get a discounted price on merchandise?" he asked, looking more enthusiastic than he had all day.

"I think so. If I do, I can buy anything you want. Just tell me."

He took out a notepad from his shoulder bag and jotted

down a few items, like Italian men's boots and Zanella slacks, a Prada belt and some Gucci sunglasses. Yes, Nick had good taste all right. But where did he, a gymnastics coach, get the money for high-ticket items like these? How could he afford to take me to this restaurant? Did he have a secret source of money? Maybe his family was secretly rich and he received an allowance.

"How will you have time for this new job?" he asked as he handed me his shopping list. "You work many hours."

"Yes, but I have two whole days off a week and evenings too. I think it will be useful for me to see how the other half lives. The women who shop at Dolce's are not average citizens. Maybe that's why I need to get out of my comfortable rut and do something different."

"Then you won't be able to join me for trips such as this?" he asked.

I looked around the posh setting and wondered if I was doing the right thing. "I'd hate to miss our outings," I said. He'd taken me on a vampire tour of the city once and I owed him. Was I plunging into yet another venture I couldn't follow up on?

On the way out of the restaurant we walked through the bar, and who did I see sitting by himself but Diana's husband Weldon. Being the friendly person I am, I automatically opened my mouth to say hello, then I realized he probably wouldn't recognize me and even if he did, I was a nobody and not worth acknowledging. I wondered if he was expecting his wife to join him after her tour at the zoo. Maybe that's why he was here on the outskirts of the city.

I looked around outside before we walked to a nearby bus stop, but I didn't see Diana. It occurred to me I could stop by her house and see her, since I now knew her husband wasn't home and there'd be no danger of any conflict. Maybe she'd be more able to speak freely without him around. Although she hadn't seemed willing to talk to me at the zoo today. Still, she'd been on duty and I hadn't been alone. I should give her another chance because I was worried about her.

Nick and I took the bus from the Cliff House back to town. He apologized for not seeing me to my door, but I told him I wasn't going home. I had an errand to do in Pacific Heights. Which was, of course, to stop off at Diana's house to see if she was there. I had a feeling she wouldn't answer the phone if I called her, but if I was actually on her front steps, she couldn't turn me away, could she?

When I arrived, there were no lights on in any windows though it was dusk. I knocked on her massive front door and rang the bell. When a woman came to the door, I thought I recognized her from the night we had our class as someone who had slipped in for a moment to speak to Diana.

"Hello," I said brightly. "I'm Rita, Diana's friend. I don't know if I met you the night of the jewelry design class . . ." I knew I hadn't met her, but I'd seen her just for a moment. I'd said to myself, That's what I need, someone to help me around the house.

"I'm sorry," she said curtly. "Mrs. Van Sloat isn't home."

"That's okay," I said. "I just wanted to see if I left my scarf here yesterday during the house and garden tour."

"I don't think so," she said. "If you did, all lost items were collected after the tour was over. But I don't know where they were taken. You'll have to ask Mrs. Van Sloat."

"I will. I definitely will. The thing is, I checked with the tour people. They didn't have it, so I thought—"

"Then it isn't here."

"But it might be. Behind something perhaps," I said, knowing I sounded lame. "Maybe in the craft room. I was there yesterday."

"I don't think you'll find it there," she said. "I didn't see anything like a scarf."

"Were you here when the jewelry designer cut himself the night of our get-together?" I asked. Not that I expected her to give any secrets away. And I was sure whatever happened after our class was supposed to be kept quiet.

"I don't know," she said, glancing around as if she was afraid someone might overhear her. Of course she'd been there that night. I'd seen her cleaning the kitchen before we left. "I mean, I didn't see anything."

What about now? Was she really alone? Was Diana really not there? Or did she just not want to see me or anyone?

"Could I check and see if I left my scarf maybe in the kitchen or the craft room or in the front closet?"

"Well . . ."

It was clear she didn't want me to come in, but unless she slammed the door in my face I wasn't going to leave without at least taking a peek inside. I didn't know what I was looking for. I knew what I'd love to see and that was the inside of that study with the gun cabinet, but that wasn't going to happen. Even if I got to the second floor, the door to that room would be locked as it had been the day of the house and garden tour.

"I'll just be a minute," I said as I breezed by the poor woman, hoping she wouldn't lose her job over this. "I really need to find my scarf. It's a Hermes, you know." I didn't have a Hermes scarf, but I hoped I looked like the type who'd wear one. It was on my list of must-haves.

She frowned but she didn't try to stop me; she just followed me, clumping all the way through to the kitchen, past the softly lighted rooms with all the strikingly modern furniture I hadn't noticed the first time I came here. But which I'd read about in the brochure they'd handed out at the open house. Everything was perfect today, just as it had been during the house and garden tour. I made a mental note to hire someone to clean up my place just as soon as I could afford it.

When we got to the kitchen, there was nothing out of place, no stains on the floor. Not a speck of dirt or dust. Not with a staff to mop up after spills. Over the massive chopping block in the center of the room hung a rack of knives, a collection a professional chef would be proud to use. Not at all like the ones we used to cut the leather that night. Those were just as sharp, but much smaller. Was that a blank space at the end? Was one missing? Or was I seeing things like missing guns and knives because I wanted to? I so wished that maid would go away so I could browse around, but that was not the way things were going. I was lucky to be in this room at all. I was thinking that the Van Sloats would be less than happy if they knew I or any other snoop was here.

"I guess it's not here," I said. Then I took a chance she wouldn't stop me, and opened the pantry door. "Unless I left it in there."

A phone rang somewhere. The maid looked startled. Why, didn't they get many calls? She reached into her pocket and pulled out her phone. She said something, then she backed away and left the pantry. I heard her speaking softly. I was alone in the pantry. The door was open but I couldn't see her, so she couldn't see me, right?

I reached behind the jars of imported Italian products,

pushing aside basil pesto, marinated mushrooms, artichoke hearts in vinaigrette and organic Tuscan white beans. All because of Guido's influence?

I was looking for something. Anything. My fingers touched on a sharp edge, so sharp I felt a prick. I yanked my hand back, wiped a drop of blood from my finger and then reached in again for a small jewelry knife, which I recognized and quickly stuffed into my purse. I didn't need a detective to tell me I had no right to lift anything from this house that wasn't mine, but I couldn't resist. In a way it was mine if it was the one I'd used to make my bracelet, and I thought it was. But why was it in the kitchen? Why hadn't Armando taken it with him? I was elated.

When I stepped back into the kitchen, the maid was still on the phone, protesting that she was busy tonight and couldn't help whoever needed her. I sidled up to the back door and with my hands behind my back, I flipped a metal knob that might be the lock. I hoped that I'd unlocked the door and that no one would notice.

Then I stood there trying to look innocent. She hung up and glared at me. I had the distinct impression that either she'd seen me take the knife or unlock the door, or she just wanted me out of there for general purposes. Yes, yes, I'm going, I thought but didn't say.

I glanced at the door to the small walk-in freezer that Diana was so proud of, and I shivered. I'd seen too many movies where someone is locked inside. I couldn't leave until I made sure that Diana wasn't in there. Before the maid could stop me, I grabbed the handle and jerked it open. There were shelves full of labeled packages, but no Diana. No body. Suddenly the door closed behind me. Had that sullen, resentful maid pushed it shut? Was she going to leave me here and go home simply because I'd annoyed her?

I gasped and turned the lever on the door. It spun around in my hand and nothing happened. I pounded on the door. The icy air sucked all the breath out of my lungs. I tried to call out, but my throat was too dry. Who would hear me anyway but the woman who'd locked me in here?

Fourteen

A few moments later, though it felt like hours, the woman opened the door and stared at me as if I were an alien who'd suddenly materialized.

"What happened?" she asked.

"I don't know," I said, taking great gulps of warm air. "I couldn't get out. Did you lock the door?"

"Of course not," she said with a look that said I must be paranoid. The woman pointed at the hallway toward the living room. It was time to go.

I hated to leave, but what could I do? Ask to see the rest of the house, which was what I really wanted to do? She coughed nervously, and I finally, reluctantly, left the kitchen with her on my heels. Passing the circular staircase, I had a mad desire to run up to the locked study, but I restrained myself. The elevator, too, beckoned me, but I gave it only a passing glance.

"Please tell Mrs. Van Sloat that Rita came by to see her," I said loudly just in case Diana was there and could hear me. If she did and all was well, surely she'd come running down the stairs calling, "Rita, I'm so glad to see you. Sorry I didn't have time to talk at the zoo, but I was on duty with the primates. Let me make you an espresso in my state-of-the-art, restaurant-quality coffee machine." But the house was eerily quiet.

The woman quickly and firmly closed the heavy front door the moment I stepped outside. If I'd hesitated, I might have lost a foot or had my hand crushed in the massive door frame. I was glad to have found the knife, even though I had no idea what to do with it. It looked like the one I'd used, but was it? And why was it in the pantry? I knew I was missing something else. Something important. And it wasn't an arm or a leg.

It was some big clue to what had happened here. Maybe it was the knife. I hoped so. But if not, it was the gun. I just knew it. But how to put my hands on it? Was Diana really at home and just didn't want to see me? Didn't want to see anyone? Why? She'd been fine during our jewelry lesson. Then Armando had gotten hurt and Diana had disappeared from her usual shopping venue. If I hadn't gone to the zoo, I wouldn't have seen her because she didn't answer my calls. If only I'd had a minute to check out that room with the guns. Though it was probably locked and I didn't know how to pick locks even if I'd had time.

If she wasn't on the premises, then where was Diana now? Having drinks and dinner with her husband? What was wrong with that? Nothing. Just because he gave me the creeps didn't mean he wasn't a decent person underneath. What I knew for sure was that Diana was at the zoo today and she was not in the freezer. Other than that, her where-abouts was anybody's guess.

It wasn't like she was a missing person. I'd just seen her. She was fine. Well, not really fine. She'd looked nervous to say the least. Right now she could be anywhere. She wasn't my problem. I felt stupid for worrying.

I walked slowly down the front walk past the lighted, well-tended gardens. I should have been bounding along, excited about what I'd found, but somehow I could hear Jack's voice in my ear throwing cold water on my enthusiasm.

"You did what?" he'd say. "You stole a knife? I ought to arrest you. You've done some crazy things, Rita, but this is beyond the pale."

I was mulling over what I'd say in my defense besides, "I just had a funny feeling it would be important." That kind of remark has Jack seeing red. Not just seeing red but turning red and warning me to cool it.

Then he'd tell me what he always tells me. "Stop playing detective, Rita, and stick to accessories. Something you're good at."

I could remind him that I'd helped solve two previous mysteries, but he wouldn't want to be reminded. But what if I showed him the knife and he sent it to the lab and we found out something important? Like blood on the blade and fingerprints on the handle. Yeah, like he was going to do that because I suggested it.

As I reached the end of the walkway, I turned and looked back at the house. I couldn't leave yet. I just couldn't. I circled back toward the four-car, ivy-covered brick garage. I'd peek in the window and see if Diana's car was there. Of course, its absence or presence wouldn't prove anything.

But when I looked in the window, the garage was so dark I could see only the outline of several cars. I didn't even know what kind of car Diana drove.

Out on the street they called Billionaire's Row, I felt nervous. Not that there were criminals lurking behind the stately houses or the carefully tended hedges. The only people out this evening were rich residents walking their pampered pets. But the stillness on the ground and the sound of the wind in the leafy acacias and the needled redwoods bothered me. I kept looking behind me to see if someone was following me.

My legs felt rubbery as I turned and walked as fast as I could down the hill to Cow Hollow where I knew I'd find bars and restaurants full of young professionals like me as well as a bus to take me home. I couldn't go home yet. I needed a shot of normalcy among people like me. Not rich. Not poor. Working people. People out having a good time. People who weren't worried about a murderer in their midst.

I decided I needed a drink to calm my nerves even though I'd already had dinner with wine. Even more, I needed to mingle with warm bodies. I didn't want to be alone. I walked into a bar after checking it out from the outside to make sure Meera wasn't lurking there at a table. As much as I needed company, I couldn't deal with her now.

I squeezed between several men in casual designer jeans and button-down shirts who were with women in tight pencil skirts or voluminous pants and clingy tops, until I reached the bar where I ordered the special, a tequila cocktail advertised on a blackboard. It was a tasty blend of grapefruit juice, amaro, vermouth and maraschino. I helped myself to some local, organic bar finger food. I wasn't hungry, but I needed to eat something anyway to calm my nervous stomach. It was good to be in this convivial atmosphere, alone but not alone at the same time.

Proving once and for all that San Francisco is a small town, the next time I looked around I saw Jonathan in the back with a drink in his hand surrounded by a crowd of friends. All this time I thought the reason I hadn't heard from him was because he had to work nights. But here he was. Out on the town. Now I felt worse than I had when I first walked into the bar.

A moment later, as if he'd felt my eyes on him, he turned and saw me. His eyes widened, he waved and started across the room toward me.

"Rita," he said. "I can't believe this. I'm here with my medical team. It's somebody's birthday. Do you come here often?"

I didn't want him to think I was some kind of barfly who hung out by myself picking up men at bars.

"First time," I said. "How are you?

"I'm feeling good," he said. He saw me looking at his drink. "Don't worry, this isn't alcohol. I'm back on the wagon. I'm drinking some fruit juices mixed together like they serve to Mormons and gallbladder sufferers like me."

"But I thought you were cured," I said. "You seemed fine the last time I saw you."

"I am fine, but I'm not really completely cured. The stones are still there. My doctor is watching them so I don't have to." He grinned and he looked so healthy and gorgeous I couldn't believe he was interested in little old me. I knew by his flirtatious manner that he was his same normal self, stones or not. I instantly forgave him for hanging out and socializing without me. "Come on back and meet everyone," he said.

I didn't feel like talking to strangers, but what could I say? "I have to go home now even though it's not even nine o'clock, because I have a knife in my purse that may have been used to attack someone"?

What I did say was, "Can I show you something?"

He said, "Sure."

I beckoned him to follow me out to the sidewalk where I asked him to hold my drink while I pulled the knife out of my purse, holding the handle with a tissue.

"You know the Italian guy with knife wounds who you treated in the ER? Could this be the knife?"

He studied it carefully, then he looked at me. "Where did you get this?"

"You don't want to know," I said.

"It could be the knife. But I see knife wounds and other wounds every day. I can't remember your friend's case very well. Sorry."

"That's okay. I just wondered."

"I do remember that he wasn't badly hurt, if that helps. He said it was an accident. It was, wasn't it?"

I felt foolish. But foolish was better than scared. Now that I was with Jonathan, I didn't feel so scared anymore. He was so big, so smart and so reassuring. Unless someone like the maid or one of the Van Sloats reported the knife they'd hidden in the pantry missing. That's what would send those shivers up my spine. I wanted to leave, but Jonathan insisted I meet his colleagues, since I was a previous visitor to the ER. I followed him to his group, my drink back in my hand, my purse over my shoulder.

I searched the faces of his colleagues and was glad to see the snippy nurses and the admissions clerk who didn't like me weren't there. After Jonathan introduced me around, one of his friends said, "You're the one who makes house calls. Jonathan told us how you brought him some terrible green stuff to eat."

"I do my best," I said modestly. "He got better, didn't he?"

They laughed. I stayed awhile longer, feeling warm and accepted even though I wasn't part of their group. I wasn't even in the medical field. When I said I had to leave, Jonathan looked disappointed, but he walked me out to the bus stop.

"It was good to see you," he said. "I'd take you home, but I feel obligated to stay awhile longer." From the way he said it, I could tell he wasn't just being polite. He seemed to mean it. He wasn't one to hide his feelings. I knew that when he was sick, he didn't even try to act well. I liked that about him. With Jonathan, what you saw was what you got. If he had problems, he kept them to himself, which I appreciated. He promised to call me and waited with me until my bus came, then he headed back to the bar.

The next day I dressed in one of my favorite outfits—it was completely local, organic, green, artisanal and ethically produced. A pair of organic cotton pants in celery green topped by a bamboo sweater in black. On my feet I wore a pair of vegan sandals made of faux leather. Not that I'm a vegan. Far from it. I just felt like going eco-organic today. Did it have something to do with my trip to the zoo and my new-found respect for the animal kingdom? Maybe.

I got to work early so I would have time to tell Dolce what I'd done. I couldn't continue to keep it all to myself. Who better to tell than my boss, my substitute mom and big sister all rolled into one. I started with the trip to the zoo, the run-in with Diana and dinner with Nick. I continued by telling her how I'd gone to the Van Sloats' house and stolen the knife.

She sat behind her desk in her small office staring at me with her mouth hanging open. Clearly she wasn't ready for this massive confession, and I hadn't even told her that I'd applied for another part-time job yet.

"You don't suspect Diana would ever do anything wrong, do you?" she asked. "Maybe the reason she seemed upset at the zoo was because of something that happened there."

"But why would she ignore me?" I said. "Like she didn't know me or want to know me. What had I done to upset her? I couldn't help feeling it had something to do with our guru."

"Which one?" Dolce asked.

"Either Armando or Guido or both. I don't know," I confessed.

"Maybe I was wrong when I suggested socializing with our customers," Dolce said, her forehead creased in a frown.

"You mean I shouldn't have taken that class at her house?" I said. "None of this would have happened if I'd just stayed home or . . ." I sighed loudly. "I've learned my lesson," I said. "No more meddling or socializing. But first I have to do everything I can to find out who killed Guido. I owe it to him. I have the feeling it has something to do with Diana. I have to go back to her house and try again. Either talk to her or her husband." Talking to her husband would be a challenge. I would definitely try to go when he wasn't home.

"Please, Rita," Dolce said. "Don't do that. You just said no more meddling. I don't want you to get involved. The police don't want you to either. Why do you want to? Why do you have to?"

"Because I'm to blame. Don't you see? I was the last person to see Guido alive except for his killer. At least it seems that way. I could have prevented his murder."

"How?" she said, looking perplexed and worried at the same time. "I know how determined you are, and I admire your tenacity, but I can't stand by and let you risk your life. Yes," she said, seeing I was about to protest, "this is serious business. There's a murderer out there, and if he thinks you're on to him—"

"Or her," I said. "It could be a woman, couldn't it?"

"You don't mean Diana, do you?" Dolce asked.

"Or his ex-wife or another woman in his class. Or his girlfriend, whoever she is. Don't you see, I have an obligation to do whatever I can to find out who killed Guido."

"No," she said, "I don't see. I mean, I see where you're coming from, but I don't see that it's your responsibility to find the killer. The police are on this case, aren't they?"

"Yes, of course," I said. I didn't want to say what I thought of their efforts. Jack was a smart cop. He was good at his job. But he didn't want to find the murderer as much as I did. No one did. Not Guido's friends or relatives. It was up to me.

"If you insist on this, Rita, and I can't discourage you, then let me help you."

"It could be dangerous work," I said.

"What do you mean? Do you have a plan?" she asked, tapping her fingers nervously on her desk. I realized she'd made the offer of help impulsively, and I had to let her off the hook.

"I don't really need any help," I said. "It's better if I do this by myself."

Dolce bit her lip. "No," she said, "I can't let you. Whatever you do, I want to be part of it."

"It could involve breaking the law," I said, knowing I would have to go back to the Van Sloat house sooner or later.

"Then we'll go to prison together. Maybe we can share a cell or volunteer together in the cafeteria." Dolce almost looked eager to embark on this illegal venture. Maybe sometimes owning an upscale boutique wasn't exciting enough. Or maybe she didn't want to be left out. Or she hoped to save me from blundering into danger. Whatever her reason, I reached across the desk and shook her hand. I may have had a tear in my eye when I said, "Thank you."

I spent some time in Dolce's office that morning torn between feeling grateful she hadn't told me I was crazy and worrying that I *was* certifiably crazy and had some kind of sick lust for excitement that made me look for murder and mystery under every stone. Or was I just bored with my job again and desperately looking for something to do, such as sneaking around in other people's houses.

I looked up the docent schedule of the zoo online, and then I called the zoo to see when the next primate tour was. They told me to check the schedule online, which I'd already done. My plan was not to take Diana's primate tour, though I assumed it was fascinating. Instead, I planned to tour her house by myself when I knew Diana wasn't home while Dolce stood out front as a lookout. I'd enter from the kitchen, where I hoped the door was still unlocked. And then what? How would I get into the locked study?

I went online again and searched on "lock picking." I

studied the site "Lock Picking for Idiots" for about an hour.
Dolce came in a few times to see if I was okay. I said I was
and asked her if she needed help out there. She shook her
head, but she seemed worried. Maybe I shouldn't have
included her in this scheme. What was wrong with me? Once
I knew how to pick basic locks, I'd be good to go.

I finally took the lock-picking test and I passed! All I
needed now was a few simple tools. I went out and waited
on a few customers, helping them find transitional clothing
for fall, but my mind wasn't on the job. I finally told Dolce
I had to go to the hardware store for an Allen wrench and a
screwdriver.

The other items I'd need, like paper clips, a straight pin
and a safety pin, we already had on hand. When I came
back, I practiced on Dolce's office door. I'd lock it and then
pick the lock. It was harder than it looked on the web site.
Much harder.

After a juicy hamburger with pesto sauce and grated
cheese, onions and tomatoes at the local take-out place down
the street, I stayed late in the office trying to pick the lock
on any and every door in the house while Dolce retreated
to her apartment. How could I be having such a hard time
when I'd passed the written test so easily?

Before I left at ten o'clock, I had successfully picked one
lock once and only once. My head was throbbing, and my
fingers were cold and numb. I asked myself if it was worth
all this trouble. I couldn't answer. Dolce came downstairs
in her tailored robe and insisted I take a cab home.

When I got home, I checked my answering machine.
There was a message from Jack.

"You'll be happy to know we have arrested the murderer

of your cooking teacher, so you can stop your relentless pursuit of justice. Okay, Rita? Did you get the message? Stop, cease and desist."

What? How could he leave a message like that? Who had he arrested? I pressed redial and got Jack on the line.

"Congratulations," I said brightly. "I knew you could do it."

"Thanks," he said. "I wanted to tell you before you read it in the papers tomorrow, since you've been involved, shall we say, in a major way."

I knew what he meant by "major." He meant "inappropriate."

"Well, who did it?"

"I can't tell you that, Rita. Not until the report is public."

"Then why did you call me?"

He sighed loudly. "I thought you'd want to know."

"I do want to know. I want to know who did it. I know, you can't tell me. How about I mention a name and you say no unless you say nothing, then I'll know."

"I can't do that," he said.

I knew he'd say that, so I just started naming names.

"Guido's ex-wife." I paused.

He said, "No."

"Guido's best friend—"

He said, "No!"

"Guido's girlfriend."

He said, "Rita!"

"His brother or his cousin who we saw at the restaurant the night I caught on fire."

"No. You can stop now."

I said, "I only want to help you."

"That's what you always say."

"I mean it."

"Please don't."

"All right," I said. "I won't. I can hardly wait until the report is public. Congratulations on cracking the case. That's what you policemen say, isn't it?"

"No, we don't," he said.

When he hung up, I was sure he didn't have the right person. But I thought I did. At least I'd narrowed it down to two people. If only I was a better lock picker, I could get the murder weapon and have it tested.

The next day I wore a vintage seventies' long animal-print skirt in honor of my zoo friends and a white Anthropologie peasant blouse with a pair of Kork-Ease leather sandals. I tucked my hair up under a big hat that shaded my face. I wanted to look like I belonged in Pacific Heights so if all else failed no one would remember me as the woman who broke into the Van Sloat house. And if the maid saw me she wouldn't recognize me. But I couldn't stand to look like a Pacific Heights wannabe copycat. No matter how much I needed to be in disguise.

I told Dolce as casually as I could that Jack had arrested the wrong person. I wanted her to know we needed to move fast. *If* she was still in. I didn't want to push her, but I really wanted some company in this effort. I assured her she'd be in no danger and wouldn't be breaking any laws by standing outside the house while I "entered."

"I'm with you, Rita," she said. Though she didn't look happy about it or convinced it would work. The only other choice was that I'd have to do it myself, and she wouldn't hear of that. So at noon we put up a "Closed for Lunch" sign on the door and I took my extra large Gucci leather tote and filled it with my tools. I would have liked to have practiced with the tools again, but I had to find the real killer before it was too late.

First I checked with the zoo, and a nice woman told me that Mrs. Van Sloat was scheduled to take tours of the big cats today from ten o'clock until one and would I like to reserve a space. I thanked her and said I'd come next week. Then I called Diana's house and no one answered. I could only hope and suppose that Mr. Van Sloat wasn't there. Dolce said she'd drive in case we needed a quick getaway. I didn't know what to think about her talking like a criminal, but since I was actually going to break in to someone's house, which was a criminal act, it was probably appropriate. Still, I didn't want to think about it. I kept seeing the look on Jack's disapproving face when he hauled me in for breaking and entering.

I was grateful to Dolce that I didn't have to stand on the corner waiting for the bus while my nerves went into overdrive, or worry about being let off by a taxi driver who might later testify in court that he'd dropped me off in front of the house that was broken into. I was fighting off waves of fear and terror at getting caught taking an antique gun from the Van Sloat house or even worse, being caught without the gun by that maid who would recognize me and might call the police this time.

As she drove, Dolce ate an apricot cardamom donut from Dynamo Donuts because she always ate when she was nervous, but my stomach was twisted in knots and I had to refuse the chocolate rose geranium hazelnut pastry she'd brought for me.

She parked about a half block from the historic house where the Van Sloats lived. While Dolce stayed in the car, I walked casually up to the front door and rang the bell. No one answered. Not Diana or Weldon or that maid. I breathed a sigh of relief. I phoned Dolce and muttered, "No one at home."

Then I went around the back of the house to the kitchen entrance where I'd stealthily unlatched the door. But would it still be unlatched? My palm was so sweaty it stuck to the doorknob. I turned it a few times and it opened. I couldn't believe my luck. I was almost giddy with relief. As if that solved all my problems. Probably not, but I was on a high and didn't want to think about what would happen next. Maybe all housebreakers think that way.

The plan was that after I let Dolce know I was inside, she'd stroll down the street keeping an eye on the house with her phone in her pocket in case she had to call me or I had to call her. But she wouldn't linger for fear a neighbor would call the police and report a suspicious character casing the place.

Inside the kitchen there was total silence except for the very quiet whirring of some major appliance, maybe the refrigerator. I tiptoed across the floor, scarcely daring to breathe. In a few seconds I'd left the kitchen and walked through the dining room with the long dark walnut table permanently set for twelve, a huge bouquet of fresh flowers in the center. Did they ever entertain twelve guests? I didn't get the feeling that Weldon would be a gracious host, but what did I know? Just because he didn't welcome me to his house didn't mean he didn't invite his own friends or business associates. He had to be proud of Diana's culinary efforts.

I warned myself to concentrate and not analyze the Van Sloats' social situation. I was there for only one purpose, as my heavy handbag reminded me. It gave me a bit

of confidence having the tools, though I was hoping against
hope that the door to that study would be unlocked. But two
lucky breaks in one day? Was it possible? I dared not count
on it. I figured time was on my side. I could fiddle around
with my tools until I got the door unlocked. Then I'd go in
and take the gun from the case, using a handkerchief in my
pocket so as not to disturb the fingerprints that would lead
to the arrest of . . . Who? Weldon, of course. But why? The
usual. Jealousy, of course.

Fifteen

••

I figured it was Diana who'd stayed after class that night of Guido's murder. Not to have an affair with Guido, but just to get some clarification on a recipe or something. She wouldn't have had an affair with the chef. But Weldon, being the jealous type, had found her there after class, flew into a jealous rage and shot Guido with his pistol. I had no proof yet, but today I was going to get it.

All I needed was the pistol with its missing bullet. I'd present it to Jack. He'd have it tested. He'd find the fingerprints and arrest Weldon and give me a citizen's award. The one I'd never gotten before but so richly deserved.

From the living room I walked quickly and quietly up the stairs to the second floor, my heart pounding so loudly I was sure the neighbors could hear it.

The door to that study wasn't even locked. I almost

laughed with relief. I didn't need my tools or my newfound ability to pick locks. I walked in and there it was, the gun in the glass case. I opened the door to the case, pulled out my handkerchief and removed the gun from its oak display stand. My hands were shaking, but I wrapped the gun in a clean towel I'd brought and placed it into my bag.

I felt like patting myself on the back or at least jumping for joy, but I would restrain myself until I was out of the house. I closed the door to the study behind me, and then I heard the footsteps downstairs. I stopped and backed down the hall toward the tiny elevator. If it was the maid again, I'd think up something, anything. What was she going to do if she didn't believe me? I was a friend of Diana's. She wouldn't call the cops on a family friend, would she?

The footsteps got louder. The elevator door was open. I stepped in. The footsteps got louder. Someone was coming up the stairs. It was Weldon wearing a business suit and carrying a briefcase under his arm. I gasped, leaned back and accidentally pressed against the control panel, which closed the door of the ancient elevator with a loud clank.

He stopped and looked around. I sucked in a breath and tried to make myself invisible, hard to do in a glassed-in elevator. Then he stopped on the stairs and stared at me. I leaned back as if I could hide. I couldn't. His face turned red, then almost purple. He pointed a finger at me and shouted, "Stop!"

I was wedged into the elevator and had inadvertently pressed all the buttons. With the door now closed, the elevator creaked and started to descend.

I pushed a button labeled "Stop," and the elevator stopped between the floors.

"No," I muttered, "that's not what I meant." Now I was

stuck between floors with a mad killer outside waiting for me. I tried to move the lever on the door, but it didn't budge. Even if it did and the door opened, what would I do, jump out?

"Come out of there. Now," he shouted.

I yelled that I was stuck, but I don't think he heard me. He ran back up the stairs and returned to the stairway holding a rifle. I knew where he'd gotten it. From the same place I'd gotten the pistol.

"Don't move," he shouted, pointing the gun at me. "I've called the police."

I couldn't decide if that was a bad thing or a good thing. If he'd called the police, did that mean he wasn't guilty but I was? I was definitely guilty of housebreaking. What about him? I dreaded seeing the look on Jack's face when I turned up at his police station. He'd tell me he'd found the killer, gotten a confession and the case was closed. He'd never believe I had found Guido's killer, and I was beginning to have doubts myself. If only the gun in my bag had Weldon's fingerprints on it. But what if it did? It was his gun. If only the bullet matched the one that wasn't in his heart after all, that would help, wouldn't it?

I didn't hear sirens. I didn't hear anything. I wanted to call Dolce. She'd be frantic with worry by now, but I was afraid to make a move.

Just then I heard the front door open. When I turned my head, which was hard to do in the stalled elevator, I looked down and heard Diana's voice, but I didn't understand what she said.

"Stay where you are," Weldon yelled at her. "There's an intruder in the elevator. I've got my gun, and I've called the police."

Her voice rose. "The police? Why did you do that? I told you—"

"Not about you. I saw her on the surveillance camera. She stole my gun, and I caught her. I told you no one needs to know about you and that chef."

My knees gave way then, from fear and from shock. I sank to the old worn boards of the elevator floor, still clutching my bag. What did he mean, "you and that chef"?

"You know . . . I didn't mean . . ." she said.

"You didn't do anything," he said. "That's all you have to say."

I knew what I was hearing was important, but I didn't know what it meant or how to put it together.

It seemed like an eternity that I was stuck in that elevator. Diana and Weldon stayed downstairs while we all waited for the police. I think I dreaded their arrival more than anyone. Unless either Weldon or Diana was guilty. If they were, they didn't act scared, they acted annoyed. And where was Dolce?

When the police arrived, I was glad to see the cops were no one I knew. Not yet. They worked on the old elevator while I cowered inside until finally they got a ladder and I crawled out and down the ladder.

When Diana saw it was me, she stared at me in disbelief.

"Rita, what are you doing here?" she said. "Did you really take Weldon's pistol?"

"I can explain everything," I said.

"If you'll give it back, we won't press any charges," she said.

I said I had to go to the police station.

I hated to do it. Not only did I face charges of breaking and entering, but I also faced the ire of the police chief. Nevertheless, I quickly gave my handbag to one of the officers, who drove me down to the station after taking a report from Weldon Van Sloat about how he'd surprised a robber in his house. He pointed at me. I didn't say anything. What could I say? I had broken into their house. I had taken a pistol. I thought that one of them was involved in Guido's murder, but I didn't know which one and I couldn't prove it. I sank down in the backseat of the patrol car feeling despondent.

When I saw Jack, I didn't even try to protest or excuse myself.

"I'm guilty," I said morosely. "Arrest me. Lock me up."

He raised his eyebrows. "Where's the Rita I used to know? The one who wouldn't go quietly? The girl who was going to solve my murders for me?"

I was just about to tell him that girl was gone forever when my phone rang. I looked at Jack. He shrugged.

"Go ahead. Answer it."

"Rita, where are you?"

"I'm at the police station," I said to Dolce. "Where are you?"

"I'm at the Van Sloats' house. They just left for the airport. Rita, I heard everything. You won't believe it."

I turned to Jack. "It's Dolce. She heard everything." I handed the phone to him.

I heard him say, "Yes . . . yes . . . I see . . . I will. Thank you."

Then he picked up another phone and had someone stop the Van Sloats at the airport. "Pull them off the plane if you have to," he said.

"So you were wrong," Jack said to me. "Looks like you're not guilty after all. Your boss heard everything. She's on her way here."

"But I thought you caught the killer."

"It was a ruse to stop you from interfering. I see now it didn't work. You caught the killer yourself," he said.

"But how can we prove it?" I said. "I know how you operate. It's her word against theirs. They'll say they didn't do it." I stopped and looked at Jack. "Wait. Who did it? Not both of them?"

"From what Dolce said, it was Diana, but her husband wants to take the blame."

"I don't believe it," I said. "Why? She adored Guido. Thought he was wonderful."

"Maybe Guido didn't adore her. Not enough," Jack said.

When Dolce got to the station, her hair was standing on end from the wind and the fright she'd had. I'd never seen her when she wasn't perfectly dressed and coiffed. Her face was red, and she couldn't stop shaking. She said Jack was right. She explained that seeing I didn't return from the Van Sloats', she got worried. She went into the house from the kitchen door, as I'd done. She heard the police arrive, and instead of coming out she hid in the pantry where I'd found the knife. She wasn't sure what to do. And she didn't want to be arrested like I was. From there she heard Diana confessing tearfully to Weldon that she'd had an affair with the chef, but after he told her he'd tell her husband, she shot him the night I went to see him.

"Mr. Van Sloat was shocked, but he said he still loved her. I must say that was unexpected," Dolce said in a small voice.

"You mean she just happened to have the gun in her purse?" I asked. "That sounds like manslaughter, right, Detective?"

"We'll see," he said. Never one to tip his hat, although he never wore a hat to tip.

I wanted to stick around until the Van Sloats were appre-
hended and brought in, but Dolce wanted to go home. She
was keyed up and exhausted at the same time. Jack complimented her on her courage, and she smiled tearfully. I realized Jack didn't want us there once he'd gotten our statements
and I'd turned over the gun. He had one of his underlings
drive me home, and Dolce got into her car and went home.

Later that evening after I'd had a soothing hot bath and
wrapped myself in a huge terry-cloth robe, I ordered a large
pizza with homemade fennel sausage, tomato, bell peppers
and mozzarella cheese from Azerbyjohnnie's to be delivered
to my house along with a grilled asparagus appetizer and
chocolate biscotti for dessert. After what I'd been through,
I deserved it. I realized only then just how big a chance I'd
taken on one of the Van Sloats being guilty. I wanted to
believe it was because I was brave and smart and intuitive,
but I also felt lucky that the elevator failed and that Dolce
was my backup. Before the pizza arrived, Jack called me.

"You'll be glad to know that Diana confessed and so did
her husband."

"That's love," I said. "I guess it is anyway. Who do you
believe?"

"Who do you believe?" he asked me.

"I don't want to think Diana did it. I'm betting on her
husband. I never liked him."

"That's not the way it works, Rita."

"Well, it should," I said. "I'll bet you he's the one who
attacked Armando. He's the possessive jealous type." Jack
didn't confirm or deny my statement. "And he hid the knife
in the pantry, didn't he?" Still no confirmation from Jack.
But sometimes silence is an affirmation. So I changed the
subject and I asked, "Have you had dinner?"

"Not yet."

"If you leave now, you might get here before the pizza guy arrives."

"I'll bring some wine," he said. "We'll celebrate."

I changed into loungewear with a pair of plaid flannel Juicy Couture drawstring pants and a long, striped, hip-hugging, super-soft cashmere autumn sweater. I was dressed for celebrating my innocence and Jack's success in apprehending not one but two confessed killers for the same crime. He had to be pleased, he had to be hungry and he had to be grateful to both Dolce and me. He was.

Dolce's Fashion Advice for the Summer–Fall Transition

1. Keep your legs tan year-round, especially if you live in California. Use a full-strength sunless tanner, but first exfoliate and moisturize your legs. Apply the tanner using a washcloth but not a loofah or a pouf because they cause streaks. Don't shower for six to eight hours after application. The color needs time to rest, and so do you. Or, try a body bronzer for instant temporary results. Much easier and faster.

2. Don't go too matchy-matchy with your accessories, as my good friend Sandra would say. As I tell my customers, mix and match. Wear bold dangly earrings and carry a satin clutch. Add some classy pumps and a hoodie. Have fun!

3. Bodysuits are making a big comeback. Who knew? At Dolce's we're ready to update your wardrobe. How about a bodysuit paired with a waist-defining full skirt or a form-fitting tank top with a pair of wide-legged pants. Also check out the below-the-knee skirts you can wear in the warm months with sandals and into winter with boots.

4. Play with patterns. Mix stripes with prints. Tie the look together with color, maybe a white background. Maybe red, white and blue.

5. Go for the boho look. Start with jeans, either skinny or relaxed. It's your choice. Add a vintage element, whether it's worn-out cowboy boots or some old jewelry.

6. Play with texture. Try a faux-fur jacket over a girly dress or a jacket made of feathers over your T-shirt and jeans.

7. Have an urban uniform ready to go, like skinny jeans with a long-sleeved black T-shirt and your ballet flats, or for those cool fall days, your knee-high boots, of course!

8. It's all about the prints! Check out the batiks—the skirts, shirts and dresses. Add a pair of beaded earrings and sandals to complete the hippie look.

9. Florals aren't done with just because summer's over. Take a blazer to wear over your flowery frock.

10. Scarves are more important than ever. As a beach wrap, a halter dress, a sarong or a turban. For so long, fashion was about the "it" bag or the "it" shoe. Today it's the "it" scarf. The scarf is the ultimate multitasker. Tweak it, twist it, loop it, tie it, knot it. Your scarf is your best friend, and you can't have too many of them. You can get great mileage from your scarves. Drape them over a tunic. Or sash them at your hips in the shape of a skirt. Don't let scarves intimidate you ever again.

11. Update your wardrobe by taking a long look in your closet. See if some of your cardigans or dresses would look cute worn backward. Yes, I said backward. A zipper in front instead of in back gives an old dress a new, and maybe even better, look. What about that old chain necklace in your drawer? Wrap it around your wrist a few times and voilà! It's a new multichain bracelet.

12. Combine big bold stripes with ruffles. Stripes are everywhere these days. They toughen up a flirty dress or add pizzazz to a polka-dot top.
13. Go glam. Keep a red lipstick with you at all times for a touch-up. Wear skirts and heels instead of pants for a change.

Recipes

Since Rita is a noncook, she strongly advises you to sample Indian food in a reputable restaurant instead of cooking at home, but it if you must, then follow these recipes and invite friends in for some authentic dishes and prepare to be the talk of the town. Also all those people you've invited will then owe you a dinner. What could be better?

Indian food, courtesy of Jonathan's favorite restaurant.

Vegetable Samosas

FOR THE DOUGH

1 cup all-purpose flour
2 tablespoons oil
A pinch salt
Water

FOR THE FILLING

3–4 potatoes, boiled, peeled and mashed
½ teaspoon garam masala
Salt to taste
Red chili powder to taste
1–2 green chilies, finely chopped
½ teaspoon crushed ginger
½ cup cooked green peas
A few chopped cashews (optional)
A few raisins (optional)
1 tablespoon finely chopped coriander leaves

FOR THE DOUGH

Mix together the flour, oil and salt.

Add a little water at a time, stirring after each addition, to create a kneadable dough.

Pat the dough and knead it several times until it is soft and pliable.

Cover the dough with a moist muslin cloth and set aside for 15 minutes.

FOR THE FILLING

In a large bowl, combine the mashed potatoes, garam masala, salt, chili powder, green chilies, and ginger. Mix well.

Add the green peas, cashews and raisins, and mix well.

Add the coriander and set aside.

FOR THE SAMOSAS

Roll the dough into small balls, and then flatten each ball into a 4- to 5-inch circle.

Cut each dough circle in half to create two semicircles.

For each samosa, take one semicircle and fold it like a cone, using water to seal the side. Place a spoonful of filling in the cone, then pinch the top of the cone to close it, again using a drop of water to seal the dough.

Heat enough oil of your choice in a deep pot and deep-fry the samosas, a few at a time, until golden brown. If you're afraid of deep-frying or prefer a less-fattening version, sauté the samosas, a few at a time, in a small amount of oil in a frying pan.

Serve the samosas hot and crisp with chutney

Navratan Korma

3 tomatoes

1 tablespoon vegetable oil

¼ cup dried fruit (such as raisins mixed with cashew nuts)

2 onions, grated

1 ½ teaspoons ginger paste

1 ½ teaspoons garlic paste

Salt to taste

1 teaspoon turmeric

1 ½ teaspoons red chili powder

1 teaspoon ground coriander

> 2 teaspoons garam masala
> 1 tablespoon ghee or butter
> 1 cup milk or water
> 3 cups boiled vegetables of your choice, such as a combina-
>   tion of potatoes, carrots, green peas, French beans, cau-
>   liflower, cabbage and green beans
> 2 tablespoons cream
> Coriander leaves for garnish

Boil whole tomatoes until tender in a pot of water, then allow to cool. Puree the cooled, drained tomatoes in a blender, or use canned tomato puree.

Heat 1 tablespoon of vegetable oil on medium heat and lightly sauté the dried fruit for about 1 minute.

Add the onions and the ginger and garlic pastes and sauté until golden brown.

Stir in the salt, turmeric, red chili powder, ground corian-der, and garam masala and continue sautéing for 2–3 minutes more.

Add the tomato puree, stirring well, and cook the mixture for 4 minutes. Make sure the mixture doesn't stick to the bot-tom of the pan.

Add the milk or water. Bring the mixture to a boil and reduce the heat, cooking until the sauce becomes thick.

Finally, add in the vegetables and cook for 5–7 minutes until heated through.

Serve the navratan korma hot. Sprinkle cream and chopped coriander leaves on the navratan korma before serving with long-grain rice.